examine those perfect dimples—

"Holy shit!" Snake exclaimed under his breath.

Howard snapped his head up. Both of his brothers stared over his shoulders, their mouths agape, and their eyes as round as biscuits.

"What?" he asked, twisting his neck to follow the trail of their gazes. His jaw went lax, the bottom of his chin all but slapped against his chest. The sight he stared at knocked the air out of him harder than being thrown off a wild bucking bronc.

Inside the canvas, the flickering light of the lantern made his tent glow brighter than the moon. The white, heavy tarp had become pale yellow, and a dark silhouette moved about inside the gently billowing sides. It was a moment before his eyes locked on the shadow and registered what he saw, sending the impulse to his brain.

Randi was undressing, and the light projected each movement against the canvas screen more clearly than the finest painter could create. Her graceful, womanly profile moved with perfection as she drew her gown over her head. The contours of her breasts, flat stomach, the inward arch of her lower back, and her long, slender legs became clearly visible to onlookers.

"Shit!" Howard leaped to his feet. Almost as an afterthought, he grabbed the hat off his head and swiped it at both of his brothers, knocking theirs askew. "Turn around!" he demanded before storming off toward his tent.

Jogging across the grass, he shouted, "Randi! Randi! Dowse the light!"

The silhouette inside stalled.

"Dowse the light!" he repeated.

Praise for Lauri Robinson

SHOTGUN BRIDE, The Quinter Brides, Book One:
"This firecracker of a story should not to be missed."
    ~Coffee Time Romance

BADLAND BRIDE, The Quinter Brides, Book Two:
"An amazingly well-woven story. Lauri Robinson has
created not only a wonderful couple, but also a
believable family. Skeeter is a charismatic, charming
hero, and Lila is a great match for him. These
characters are colorful, vibrant, and full of life. They
surround you with their wit and realism."
    ~Romance author Mallary Mitchell

"I love the McBride series, these books are
wonderfully written and they all connect together
but have a story all their own to tell."
    ~Tonya, You Gotta Read Reviews

"*LAWMEN AND OUTLAWS ANTHOLOGY* is a
thoroughly enjoyable set of stories. Each story had
its own cadence and feel to it and I enjoyed them all
very much. My favorite was *SHERIFF MCBRIDE* by
Lauri Robinson."
    ~You Gotta Read Reviews

"*AN APRIL TO REMEMBER* is a wonderful story, a
must read for someone who loves a bit of everything,
heartache, catastrophe, romance, and passion."
    ~WRDF Reviews

"*AN APRIL TO REMEMBER* will touch your heart
and make you weep with gratification that we have
authors such as Robinson. This was a wonderful
read and I wish it could go on forever. It's a keeper
for any bookshelf!"
    ~ Long and Short of It Reviews

Boot Hill Bride

The Quinter Brides, Book Three

by

Lauri Robinson

This is a work of fiction. Names, characters, places, and incidents either are the product of the author's imagination or are used fictitiously, and any resemblance to actual persons living or dead, business establishments, events, or locales, is entirely coincidental.

Boot Hill Bride: The Quinter Brides, Book Three

COPYRIGHT © 2009 by Lauri Robinson

All rights reserved. No part of this book may be used or reproduced in any manner whatsoever without written permission of the author or The Wild Rose Press except in the case of brief quotations embodied in critical articles or reviews.
Contact Information: info@thewildrosepress.com

Cover Art by *Nicola Martinez*

The Wild Rose Press
PO Box 708
Adams Basin, NY 14410-0706
Visit us at www.thewildrosepress.com

Publishing History
First Cactus Rose Edition, 2010
Print ISBN 1-60154-738-2

Published in the United States of America

Dedication

To Liz, Connie, and Jackie.
The best daughters on earth.

Chapter One

Southwestern Kansas
1885

Another scream split the air. Louder, longer.

Oh, dear Lord, it's all my fault. Randilynn
Fulton huddled as close to the back wall of the
outdoor privy as humanly possible and rubbed cold
fingers against the chills racing up and down her
arms. *Please don't let him hurt Aunt Corrine.*

Her thoughts, or perhaps fears, tumbling
together made her glance down. Running through
the streets of Dodge wearing nothing more than a
nightgown would be extremely foolish, but she had
to do something.

Seems she had a calling for foolishness. Slipping
out of the house, while it was full of customers, had
been extremely foolish as well. Had someone seen
her? Had Danny J learned Aunt Corrine had been
hiding her in the little alcove above the kitchen? Her
heart pounded, echoed in her head and amplified the
sounds swirling about. She'd never met Danny J, the
man who ran the woman's boarding house, but had
heard enough to be duly afraid.

The trembles in her knees increased, snuck over
her body from head to toe. With pin-pricking stings,
the frost-covered grass penetrated the thin layers of
her nightgown and pantaloons. The coldness, along
with the darkness of the late night hour made every
limb shake. She tucked her chin to her chest and
tightened every muscle to gain control of the
trembles. It was to no avail, even her teeth chattered

together.

"Think, Randi, think. There has to be something you can do," she whispered.

Abruptly, the screams of the woman stopped. Randi snapped her head up. Deep rough shouts followed by more crashing hung in the air for long minutes before everything went deathly quiet.

Randi covered her mouth with a trembling hand and peered about. Searing cold, pitch-black air surrounded her. Danny J's elaborate house sat on the edge of Dodge City. She didn't know the layout of the town, but there, too, she'd heard enough to be duly afraid. Squinting, she struggled to see the light-colored sand of the well-used dusty road near the gate of the whitewashed fence surrounding the property. The thought of the lonely dead-end road intensified her lack of options. She didn't have a clue as to where the sheriff's office was located.

She lifted her rump and scooted along the back side of the outhouse to peer around the other corner. Though she couldn't see it from here, a short distance up the road between Danny J's and Dodge, a new building was being erected. The rafters and support beams were up, she'd watched them rise from the ground almost a week ago, but since then the site had been quiet.

Slowly, focused on not making a sound, she rose and eased her way around the privy. The silence of the night rang in her ears. If she left there wouldn't be any proof, and Danny couldn't blame Corrine for hiding her. Were they looking for her right now?

At the front corner of the outhouse, she peered toward the big house, searching the windows for movement. Lanterns lit the glass, but no shadows flickered beyond. She swallowed against the frantic beat of her heart and flipped around. After sucking in a deep breath, she balled handfuls of her nightgown with both hands, hitched the hem high above her knees, and sprinted across the yard toward the fence.

The chest-high boards glimmered in the moonlight, highlighting the painted vertical planks fit too tightly together for her to squeeze between. Increasing her speed as she drew closer, she thrust her hands forward and grabbed the top. A smothered grunt slipped between her clenched teeth as she thrust her body over.

While she soared through the air an ear piercing rip sounded and the material of her nightgown tightened around her neck. The unexpected tug brought her sailing body to an abrupt halt. A shocking sensation of weightlessness vibrated her body. Then the tight hold let loose and gravity pulled her down as if she was a heavy solid rock.

Air gushed from her lungs as she hit the ground. Fire exploded in her chest, but fear gave her no time to dwell on it, nor check for additional injuries. She rolled onto her hands and knees, forced her lungs to accept new air, and leaped to her feet again.

Twigs, pebbles, and stiff grass tore at the bottoms of her icy feet as she ran, pumping her arms to gain as much speed as possible. By the time she slowed her pace near the building site a sharp pain bit at her side like a hornet's sting, and her lungs flamed. With a final burst of energy, she raced forward, scanning the security of the area as she ran. Not a single flicker or flutter made itself known. Seconds later, breathless, she wrapped her arms around one of the tall support beams and clung to it, gasping. The cold air burnt as hard going in as it did coming out.

Still huffing, but half expecting to see someone bounding after her, she flipped her head up, looking back toward Danny J's. Through the blackness of the distance she watched lights in two upstairs bedrooms go out. She locked her flaming lungs and waited. Then she heard it—a far off sound—the clip-clop of horse hooves. Shivers began to ripple over her body again.

She pulled her gaze from the house and flipped around. Moonlight highlighted the glossiness of new wood. The smell of fresh cut boards filled her nose. Whatever the structure would become, it would be huge. The frame work was twice the size of Danny's place, and though she hadn't seen much of the cow town, she assumed his had to be one of the largest in Dodge.

Surely there had to be a place she could hide. Stiff and tingly, her toes curled against the cold ground beneath her feet. She rubbed them together, hoping the friction would help, and slipped her fingers from the beam to slowly ease her way around the frame of the building. Ears perked to the growing speed of the clip-clops.

Piles of lumber and large bricks of sandstone were neatly stacked in rows around the foundation. She huddled behind one stack, fighting encroaching fear and praying the clopping sound would pass the building site and fade into the night air.

It did, and that along with the chills settling into her bones, made her shake and tremble. She eased from her crouched position. The rider must have been a customer leaving, she rationalized. Rubbing some warmth into her arms, Randi also concluded she couldn't return to Danny J's and had to find some kind of protection from the frigid air—soon.

Behind the largest pile of timber a square tent stood. Her sigh of relief left a ghostly, steamy swirl in the air. She twisted her neck and listened. The quiet screamed in her ears.

Not a single sign of life appeared anywhere in the darkness. It was as if even the ever present Kansas wind had halted its relentless pursuit to cross the prairie at breath-taking speeds. Silence throbbed all around as she slowly crept closer to the tent. Even though the property appeared to be abandoned, nothing lay around haphazardly. Instead, the stacks of materials and provisions were as organized as a cook's pantry.

Just this afternoon when Aunt Corrine carried her up a bite to eat, she'd commented on the site and about the scarcity and expense of building supplies. Randi shook her head with a wave of sorrow for whoever had purchased all the supplies, imagining it wouldn't be long before scavengers loaded up whatever they wanted.

Creeping closer to the tent, she hoped no one would raid the place before morning, nor before she figured out a plan. The icy chill encompassing her body confirmed she had to warm up before catching her death of cold. Rubbing her arms, she cautiously walked around the structure. Ropes secured the thick canvas flaps, and surmising that meant it was uninhabited, she quickly moved back to the front. With stiff stinging fingers she diligently worked the knots on the front flaps. By the time the last one let loose, her bones ached and every inch of her body, shivering uncontrollably, stung as if covered with ice.

One hand pushed aside the heavy canvas, and she tiptoed in. The faint moonlight couldn't filter through the material. Blinking and squinting, she begged her eyes to adjust and survey the interior.

Damp grass no longer slid beneath her feet, instead the rough fibers of a canvas floor covered the cold ground, and she moved forward. Faint images showed boxes and crates lined both side walls, and a large feather tick mattress stretched out from the back wall to fill the center area. A squeal emitted as she leaped onto the bed and tugged the top folded blanket off a pile of many. After wrapping it around her shoulders, she unfolded two others, flapping and tucking them over her torso and legs. In a matter of minutes, her skin began to tingle as heat flowed through her body.

Warmed enough to investigate the rest of the bedding, she slipped out her hands. On the bottom of the pile she found two fluffy pillows and a set of sheets. Steadfast neatness she'd acquired years ago made her crawl off the mattress and start over, making the bed up properly.

While tucking the bottom of the covers neatly under the mattress, she caught a corner of her gown. She ran a hand over the nightdress and frowned. It hadn't been the back of her gown that had caught on the fence. One entire side was ripped from hem to waist, exposing a large amount of bare flesh. The bottom was streaked with dirt and wet from her hurried dash over the frost-filled ground. She pulled the nightgown over her head and laid it across the foot of the bed before crawling into the promised comfort.

The shivers slowly ebbed as welcome heat cocooned her. Tucking the covers below her chin, Randi settled her head deeper onto the feather pillow. What was she going to do if Danny J had injured Aunt Corrine? This whole escapade hadn't turned out the way she'd planned. If only her father hadn't married Belinda. No, if only Mama hadn't died. Then her father would never have remarried, and she wouldn't have had to come and live with her mother's sister.

She twisted onto her side, blinked at the sting of tears. "I'm sorry, Mama, so sorry. I know it must be a shock for you to learn Aunt Corrine is..." she swallowed the lump in her throat, "one of Danny J's women."

The tears came in earnest. She fought them, but it was no use, especially since she concluded her life

was beyond dismal. Penniless and half-naked, she was completely alone, with no place to go.
****
Howard Quinter felt like an old mare who'd been rode hard and put away wet. If his family wasn't showing up tomorrow to help with the building of his restaurant and hotel he'd pull Ted to a halt and let them both get a bit of rest. The gelding was as tired as he. The trip to Wichita had taken longer than expected but, wanting the furnishings to arrive as soon as possible, he'd had to make the trip. The opportunity to visit the city's opera house in order to have a firsthand idea as to how he wanted to decorate his place had arrived unexpectedly, and it had taken a full three days to place the order with the warehouse there.

The swell of pride expanded his chest. His hotel promised to be the finest around, and the meals he'd prepare for his guests would be talked about from the Mississippi to the Rockies, at least that's what both of his sisters-in-law encouraged him to believe.

Cooking had been his mistress for years, all he ever wanted to do. He'd been antsy to start building since last fall, only Ma's constant urging to wait for spring had held him at bay. Two weeks ago, when February had given way to March, he'd traveled the eighty miles from Ma's place to Dodge and set about finding workers to construct the building.

Tomorrow two of his brothers, Snake and Bug, would arrive to help as well, and if he wasn't there when they arrived they'd start building without him—which wouldn't be good. They were fine men, hard workers, but neither of them knew the layout of the design he and his oldest brother, Kid, had created, nor did they know what needed to be done first. He had to be there to supervise.

The heels of his boots touched Ted's sides, encouraging the horse to pick up his sluggish steps.

Hopefully, he'd make it to Dodge in time to get a few hours sleep before the morning light arrived.

Fighting to keep his eyes open, he and Ted ambled into the cow town an hour or more later. At three in the morning, few people mingled about, even most of the dance halls and saloons were closed. He glanced about as his lethargic mount meandered to the far side of town. Howard's tired mind took in the names painted across the buildings. The Lone Star, The Long Branch, The Alamo, The Buffalo House.

He rubbed a hand against scratchy, heavy eyelids. Concentrating was impossible. It didn't matter. By the time he had his building built the name he'd call his establishment would settle in his mind.

The rafters of his place, shooting high above the other buildings, came into sight. Minutes later his body drooped a bit more with thankfulness of arrival as he brought his horse to a stop near the tent.

Ted stomped his hooves and gave a long shake as soon as the saddle left his back. After settling his riding tack on a stack of wood, Howard released the gelding into the nearby paddock he'd built and gratefully stumbled to his temporary shelter.

He entered, listlessly pulling the boots from his feet as he walked across the canvas floor. After setting his gun belt on the floor near the edge of his mattress, he stripped down to his birthday suit, let the clothes lie where they fell, and crawled onto his bed.

Half a thought wondered why the tent flaps had been untied and why the blankets were already stretched over the feather tick, but his mind was too tired to worry about it for more than a split second.

****

The morning sun worked hard to penetrate the thick canvas of his tent and the thin skin of his eyelids. Like a mule hitched to a plow, the light pulled his sleep-encrusted mind from much needed slumber. Howard rolled onto his side, tugging the covers over his face to block the intrusion.

The blanket tugged back. Irritated, he pulled harder. The cover wouldn't budge, held tight by some unknown force.

An eerie feeling crept over his skin. He scowled, now fully recognizing the warmth of something pressed against his back. Whatever or whoever lay next to him stiffened the same moment he did.

He reached down, grabbed his six-shooter, and flipped over, simultaneously bringing the barrel of the gun to point at whoever else lay upon his bed.

Air locked in his lungs.

The biggest brownest eyes he'd ever seen stared back at him. A mass of tousled and disheveled chestnut-colored hair swirled around the head of a breathtakingly beautiful woman. Her round eyes were framed with long thick lashes and seemed to be glued to the end of his pistol, which almost touched the tip of the little nose in the middle of her face.

He swallowed, blinked, and swallowed again.

The gaze from those brown eyes followed the barrel of his gun, and then crept along the length of his arm before settling on his face. Both of her cheeks grew scarlet, and her pert lips formed a perfect *O*.

He lowered the gun. The handle slipped from his fingers. With a thud the weapon landed on the floor and skidded several feet away.

"Who? How?" Having no idea where to start questioning, he shook his head.

"I—uh—" she started.

Before either of them could say another word, bright white light filled the area.

He swung his head about, squinted at the brilliance and watched his brothers, Snake and Bug, enter the tent. They stalled mid-step, their eyes growing wide, and their mouths dropping open.

He glanced to the girl beside him and then back to the doorway, his mind too overwhelmed to form a solid thought.

Snake's face formed an odd frown. With a sorry-looking one-shoulder shrug, his brother slowly took a step sideways.

The next instant, Howard's entire body broke out in a cold sweat. His mother, all five feet of her, stepped into the tent.

The wide skirt of her red gingham dress floated to a halt when her gaze settled on the bed. Her hands slapped onto her hips, and a scowl covered her face, which was turning redder than her dress. Ma Quinter, even though she was a foot shorter than all five of her sons, never failed to put the fear of God into each and every Quinter brother, Howard included.

His mouth became dryer than Kansas in August.

Ma lifted one hand, thumped his youngest brother on the back of the head. "Bug, go find us a preacher."

Chapter Two

Randi thought she might wet the bed. She'd never been this scared. Tightening every muscle, she wished she could make her body shrivel up and disappear. Her groggy mind still tried to decipher the man lying next to her, let alone the two tall men and one very angry-looking woman staring down at them.

"Maybe we should let Hog explain the situation," one of the men said with a worried frown pulling on his face.

Quick as a wink, the woman shot a little foot out and kicked the man in the leg. "There's nothin' to explain." She gave the man on her other side another whack on the back of his head, hard enough to send his hat askew. "Bug, I told ya to go find a preacher. Now get to it."

The one called Bug held up his hands to protect his head and looked at the man in the bed next to her for a silent split-second before he turned around. The other man shook his head as he too swiveled about to follow the first one out the flap of the tent.

"Ma, we don't need a preacher," the man on the bed beside her said. His voice was deep, sounded almost like a growl. Randi shivered harder.

"I say we do." The woman took a step closer to the bed, peered at them with eyes filled with fire.

Randi pulled the covers tighter beneath her chin.

The man beside her started to say something, but stopped when jumbled voices sounded outside the door. She didn't have time to swallow the lump

11

forming in her throat before someone else flew into the tent.

"Randi?" Aunt Corrine, dressed in her customary bloomer costume, slid to a halt near the foot of the mattress. The dark blue lace-fringed trousers were drawn in at the ankles with silk ribbons, and as usual, her matching dressing sacque wasn't tied shut. The open front flaps exposed a low-cut lace-covered silk camisole.

The pounding in Randi's chest overrode any initial embarrassment. Her aunt was alive, but why would Corrine leave Danny J's before dressing? Had he kicked her out?

Aunt Corrine's startled eyes fell on the torn and stained nightgown lying across the bed. "Oh, Randi!" she exclaimed, slapping a hand to her exposed cleavage.

Randi pressed a hand to her breastbone, and then stifled a groan. Just when she thought things couldn't get any worse, she realized she had on less than Aunt Corrine. Her cheeks burned. Why couldn't the ground just open up and swallow her whole?

"Is she here?" a familiar voice asked from outside the opening.

The air she gulped in was hotter than a full-stoked oven. Her head snapped up, and her chin fell down. "Daddy?" Her voice sounded like a screeching kitten.

The man beside her shuddered, and his head whipped around to gape at her. He eyed her with a startled, questioning gaze. "Daddy?"

The flap flew open.

"What the hell is going on here?" Her father flew through the opening, slowing only because his feet stumbled upon something. His arms flayed as he skated through a pile of clothes before he caught his balance near the foot of the bed.

Men's britches, shirt, and unmentionables flew

about as her father kicked them from beneath his polished boots. She glanced to the man beside her and froze at the sight of a massive bare chest. Lord, was he as naked as she? Her face blazed. Unable to think of anything she could possibly do, she pulled the blanket up and ducked her head beneath the heavy wool.

"Who are you?" The voice of the short woman demanded with all the fury of a ten-foot giant.

"Who are you?" her father questioned in reply, just as heated.

"Stephanie Quinter, that there's my son, Hog."

A groan, sounding much like a rusty hinge, rumbled in Randi's throat.

"I'm Thurston Fulton. The girl is my daughter, Randilynn."

"I done sent my other boys to get the preacher."

"Thurston! Thurston! Did you find her?" another female voice, high-pitched and irritated, rang out.

Randi slipped farther beneath the covers, tried with all her might to disappear into the mattress. *Not Belinda too.* Had the doors to hell just opened and were calling her to enter? Confusion made her brows tug. What were they doing here? How'd they know where to find her? Better yet, how had she ended up in bed with a man?

"Yes, my dear. I've found her," her father answered.

She didn't peek over the covers, didn't dare. Her body trembled uncontrollably. An arm encircled her back, and a hand settled on her shoulder, giving a gentle consoling pat. She glanced out of the corner of her eye and caught the man gazing her way over the edge of the blanket.

The eyes were a soft gray-green and filled with worry. She tilted her head a touch to get a better look. His face, round and friendly-looking, was suntanned and made the short blond hair on his head look gold. The yellow waves were disheveled, sticking out here and there, and did little more than make him look all the more likeable.

Likeable! What was she thinking? Did she know him? No, she hadn't met anyone since arriving in Dodge. Was he one of the customers from Danny J's? Had he followed her last night?

All of a sudden the blanket was snatched from her face. She caught the edges before they fell below her chin and exposed her lack of clothing.

"Randilynn, how dare you!" Belinda screeched, reaching for another handful of the covers.

Mid-air, the man caught Belinda's hand, kept it from yanking the blanket away. His eyes narrowed as he gave her step-mother a menacing stare while his other hand tugged the wool from Belinda's fingers.

Startled, Belinda took a step back and twisted her neck about. "Thurston!"

The man resettled the covers below Randi's chin, and his arm, still looped around her shoulders, tightened a touch. The friendly gesture made her want to fold into his shelter. Randi fought the urge and glanced to her father. His angry frown made tears well in her eyes. She hung her head, wished again she could just disappear.

"Thurston, this is terrible. Absolutely the worst thing possible," Belinda said. "It's all your fault."

"My fault?" Aunt Corrine questioned with disbelief.

Randi glanced up to see the two women furiously flaying their index fingers at each other.

"I'd say it's all your fault. You're the reason she has no home." Corrine took a step closer, poked Belinda in the chest with her finger.

Belinda thrust her finger below Corrine's nose. "We've given her everything! Everything!" Belinda screeched, as she twisted her long neck. "Thurston!"

Corrine didn't miss a beat. She turned her gaze and finger to her father. "And you! You know what I think of you. You slimy—"

Her father's voice mingled with Corrine's and Belinda's and soon shouts filled the tent. The man's hold on her shoulder tightened. No longer able to control her urge, and as if it was the most natural thing in the world, she turned and buried her face in his shoulder. His cool flesh felt heavenly to her burning skin.

The yelling increased, and she quit listening, stopped trying to decipher who said what to whom, until, above the rest, a deep rumbling voice growled, "Get out! All of you get the hell out of here."

An invisible board jutted up her spine, made her head snap up when she realized it had been the man who shouted.

The tent went silent for a moment before her father said, "I will not get out! That's my daughter in bed beside you."

"We need to get the sheriff, Thurston," Belinda said.

"No need for the sheriff, I got the preacher coming," the woman named Stephanie Quinter insisted.

"The preacher?" Aunt Corrine twisted about to stare at the bed.

Shocked? Embarrassed? Randi had no idea what she felt and gave up trying to decipher it. Bowing her head, she moaned.

"This is my tent, and I'm telling you all to get the hell out of here," the man insisted.

She tugged up the blankets, used them to cover both ears as the shouts renewed. They came from all directions. Male, female, screeches, sobs. Her mind swirled. There were so many topics, not one settled long enough to form a solid thought. The bellowing and bawling was enough to wake the dead. She squeezed her lids shut again, blocked out red faces and crying eyes, and wished she could do the same with her ears.

A loud blast ripped through the chaos.

Instinctually trying to hide from the gunshot, her body jolted, and her fingers searched to grab something solid. They latched onto warm muscled flesh, and she twisted, burrowing into the body beside her.

Silence hung in the air. After a few quiet seconds, Randi realized the bare flesh of her breasts was pressed against something warm and solid. She lifted her head from the crook of the man's neck and peeked down.

Lord! She was sitting on his lap, well almost on his lap, and her hands were wrapped around his bare torso. One of his hands held the blanket snugly across her shoulders, the other rested on the back of her head, holding it in place. She lifted her eyes, slowly raising her gaze to meet his.

"Are you all right?" he half mouthed, half whispered.

Blood rushed up her neck, into her cheeks. It burned the flesh from the inside out.

His eyes asked the question again.

She had no idea if she was all right or not, but nodded nonetheless before she eased her hands off his balmy skin. Her palms burned as hot as her cheeks.

His hand slipped from her hair, held the blanket taut as she twisted back around and scooted an inch or two away from him. She clutched onto the edge of the cover and tucked the wool below her chin again. The sulfuric smell of gunpowder clung in her nostrils.

The woman who'd introduced herself as Stephanie Quinter held a gun almost as long as she was tall. The long double barrels pointed toward the roof of the tent. Randi's gaze followed the barrel, up and up, tipping her head toward the tattered edges of a large hole flapping in the wind. Sunlight shone through the opening and blazed a stream down on the short, little woman.

"Now that I got your attention..." The woman flipped the gun about and stuck the stock against her shoulder. Randi cringed as the round ends of the barrels pointed toward her father and Belinda. "No one's gonna get the sheriff. The preacher'll be here any minute." The end didn't wobble as the weapon shifted, came to point at Aunt Corrine. "All that snifflin's irritatin' me."

Aunt Corrine squeaked as she gave a compliant nod.

"Ma, there's no need for a preacher. It's a simple misunderstanding," the man said.

The gun once again moved, stopped to point straight at the bed. "I think we all understand everythin' just fine," Stephanie Quinter said, her brows arched in a distinct, knowing way.

"She..." the man started. His gaze shifted, landed on Randi.

Unable to mutter a word, she grimaced cowardly and gave a slight shrug.

He started again, "I—"

"Will marry my daughter or you'll find yourself planted in Boot Hill!" Her father pointed a finger at the two of them.

The gun swung a bit more. "We ain't gonna start shoutin' at one another again."

"Yes, ma'am," her father said and lowered his hand. His feet shuffled a touch.

Shocked, Randi glanced back at the gun-wielding woman.

The wide brim of her gingham bonnet flapped as she nodded, and frizzy gray hair peeked out around her serious face. The gun lowered a mite. "These two'll be gettin' hitched as soon as the preacher shows up."

Belinda opened her mouth, but the other woman was quicker. The gun barrel snapped up again, level with Belinda's nose. "I don't want ta hear no more of your caterwaulin' either."

Her stepmother huffed and puckered her lips. The slow, meaningful shake of her father's head made Randi gasp. She'd never seen him reprimand Belinda for anything. The sight almost made her smile before she remembered the serious nature shrouding them. Surely her father wouldn't make her marry the man next to her. She didn't even know his name, for heaven's sake. Dread crept up her spine. *Yes, he would.*

Her gaze shifted and she swallowed. Hog. At one time during the past few minutes someone had called him Hog. That was an unusual name. She gave her head a quick, clearing shake, trying to scold her mind for wandering again. No wait, Howard. He'd said his name was Howard.

He stared at her. It was a thoughtful and not necessarily unpleasant look. Calming warmth wrapped around her spine, floated all the way up her back before rippling over her shoulders. All of a sudden it was as if they were the only two people in the tent—in the world.

Howard tried to pull his gaze off the girl, but it was impossible. An indescribable flush had rushed from his toes to his ears and paralyzed him as if he were drowning in those big brown eyes and could do little more than sink lower. He blinked and dug deep in his reserve to find the strength to tug away from the invisible force, then turned to glance around the tent.

This couldn't possibly be happening. Not to him. His mother had used her shotgun to marry off two of his older brothers, but both of those situations had been different. Kid had to marry Jessie to keep Russell from hanging, and Skeeter had to marry Lila 'cause she'd been pregnant. This was a simple misunderstanding. Somehow this Randilynn girl...she certainly had a pretty name. It matched her pretty face.

He clamped his teeth together, forced his mind to stay focused. For some reason Randilynn had been sleeping in his bed. Due to the fact he hadn't slept in two days, he'd been too tired to notice. That was it, nothing had happened. End of story. There was no need to contact the sheriff. No need for a wedding. He opened his mouth, ready to explain.

The tent flap opened again.

"Ma, this is the best we could find," Bug said. He and Snake struggled to lead a stumbling man into the tent. They each held an arm of a tattered, stained suit coat as the bone-thin man wearing it tried somewhat unsuccessfully to find his balance.

Ma spun around. "What the...That man's drunk."

"It's Dodge City, Ma," Snake said with a shrug.

Howard took a deep breath. "Ma, I told you there's—"

She stomped her foot and sent an angry gaze to the bed. "And I told you there is." Tucking the gun against one hip, she used the other hand to grab the preacher's arm. The man swayed, then stumbled as she dragged him to the foot of the bed. "Get ta preachin'!"

The preacher hiccupped. His head weaved as his bulging red eyes settled on the bed. Both hands fumbled to pull a tattered book from his breast pocket. "Beerly belobubbed," he mumbled between little wet-sounding belches.

"Oh, for Christ's sake!" Howard started to flip the covers off, but as cool air blasted his skin, he remembered his lack of clothing. Stark naked, he tucked the edge of the blanket back in place. "Ma!"

She lifted her gun. "Hush up, now." Glancing back to the preacher, she said, "Keep preachin'."

Howard waved a hand in the air. "Put that damn thing down. You ain't gonna shoot me."

Faster than a bullwhip, Randilynn's father snatched the gun from Ma's hands. The man reminded him of a snake oil salesman, fancy duds, oiled hair, and not an ounce of honesty in his short squat frame. Howard steeled his eyes and met the man's gaze. A frog croaked in his throat. The man's beady dark eyes held more raw hatred than a member of the Dalton Gang.

"Maybe she won't, but I will." Pointing the barrels of the gun directly at Howard's chest, where his heart beat against his rib cage with enough ferocity to cause a heart attack, Thurston Fulton growled, "Don't say another word." The man's angry gaze went to the wobbling preacher. "You heard the woman. Hurry up!"

Howard knew when he saw a man who meant business, and at that moment he'd swear he was inches away from the small cemetery on the outskirts of town which got its name from the number of men who'd died with their boots on. Boot Hill. The thought made him shiver from head to toe. He didn't have any boots on but highly doubted that was a requirement to be planted there nonetheless.

He glanced at Randilynn. She trembled just as hard. Having no idea what else to do, he settled his arm around her shoulders and patted her arm as the drunken preacher stumbled through the reading of their nuptials.

The preacher hiccupped again, and let out a slushy burp before he proclaimed, "I preenunce youz huzbund 'n waf."

Chapter Three

Tears the size of raindrops trickled down Randilynn's face, and Howard swore he had the fixin's for the worst headache imaginable. It felt as if his brain was being squeezed and would soon ooze out his ears. He patted her shoulder and pinched at the bridge of his nose with his other hand.

The preacher, still swaying as if a stiff wind was whipping him about, started mumbling something about getting paid, which made everyone else in the room start talking at once.

His head was going to explode. The pressure had become more than he could take. "Get out! All of you get the hell out of here!" Securing the end of the blanket across his hips with one hand, Howard reached over with the other and grabbed the end of the shotgun. A hard yank forced it to slip out of Thurston Fulton's hands. Flipping it around, he tucked it in the curve of his elbow and waved it at the crowd. "Get out! Now!"

Everyone froze, their stares glued on the double barrels of Ma's prized gun.

He cocked a finger, pressed it against the second trigger hard enough to make a soft click emit and let everyone know the slightest move would send the shell exploding out the end.

They scrambled. The preacher was the fastest. He'd gained his balance, and as if the devil himself nipped at his heels he ran for the doorway closely followed by the half-dozen others.

The tent flap fluttered, snapping in the wind, and then slapped shut.

Howard stared at the canvas doorway for several minutes. Watched how the wind tried to flip it open. Maybe if he sat here long enough he'd awaken and praise the Lord it had all been a bad dream.

The silence became thicker than bread pudding. He could easily cut it up and serve it with raisins and whipped cream. A hiccup, moan, or some other such noise beside him made him realize there was no waking up from this dream. He laid Ma's gun on the floor and twisted to gaze at the woman next to him.

Once again her tousled hair and rosy cheeks made the breath in his chest stall. If he didn't know better, he'd think just what everyone else had been thinking. After all, what man on earth would be able to control himself waking up next to her? Disheveled or not, he'd never seen a more stunning woman, not even in a dream or two.

She blinked, look at him expectantly.

His befuddled mind couldn't think of a thing to say, well nothing appropriate, anyway. Shrugging his shoulders, he held out his right hand. "Howard Quinter." He almost groaned aloud.

Still clinging to the edge of the blanket tucked beneath her chin with one hand, she grasped his big hand with her other, tiny, trembling one. "Randilynn Fulton."

Now what, he thought, but instead said, "Nice to make your acquaintance," and gave her icy little hand a gentle pump.

"Likewise, I'm sure," she murmured.

He pulled his hand from hers, used it to scratch his head and brush the hair that should have been cut a month ago away from his face. "Well, I—I reckon we ought to get dressed."

Her face became even redder, but at least big tears no longer trickled down her face. "Yes, yes, I suppose we should," she said, nodding her head like a little bird searching for a flight path.

His cheeks had grown extremely warm. *Damn.* He hadn't blushed since he was a schoolboy. He scratched his head again. "Well, uh, you want to turn around?"

"Oh." She whipped her face toward the wall faster than an escaping wren. "Yes, yes, of course."

He rubbed both hands over his face, took a moment to massage at his pounding temples, before he flipped his legs over the edge of the mattress. With a corner of the blanket, he kept his hips covered and tried to reach his clothes with his feet. The ensemble of unwanted guests had scattered every article. He couldn't even reach a sock. With a backwards glance, he checked to make sure she wasn't looking.

At that moment, he forgot how to breathe. Simply, utterly, forgot. The wool blanket still covered her front, but her twisted position revealed her bare back, left it open to his gaze. Creamy-white skin flowed from her shoulders to her hips. It curved here and there, forming a sight not unlike what he'd expect to see near a European fountain—a statue made of the finest marble, chiseled into the essence of beauty. The blanket pooled across the mattress just below the top of her pantaloons, the waistline highlighted by two remarkable dimples in the lowest curve of her back. Majestic Virgin is what the artist would title the creation.

His body jolted, then grew tight as his blood heated close to boiling temperature. He shot off the bed, grabbed his pants, and tugged them on in record speed. His heart beat so hard it made his breath catch and throbbed strong enough to make his veins bulge under his skin. Once his pants were secure, he eased his speed, taking time to gain a reasonable amount of control over his shaking limbs.

He pulled on his shirt and turned back to the

bed. A tattered and torn gown hung off the foot. He walked over and picked it up. Examining the cotton, he asked, "Is this all you have to wear?"

She scooted about, faced him. Big glistening eyes stared at him. Her weary gaze met his, and she gave a slight acknowledging nod.

The gray blanket was now tucked beneath her armpits. She lifted one hand and plucked at her hair. The mass of tousled auburn waves fell to cover her shoulders, yet left enough creamy skin peeking out to prick at his already heightened senses. But it was the cleavage above the edge of the blanket that made him ogle for a moment before twisting about.

He walked over to his storage chest, pulled out a pair of britches and shirt. Moving back to the bed, he laid them near her feet. "Here."

"Thank you," she murmured and pulled the clothes closer.

"I'll, uh..." He glanced about the small space. "I'll go wait outside."

"No!" She reached out, grabbing his arm. "Please don't go out there without me." She struggled to keep the blanket held tight with one hand while the fingernails on her other hand dug into his arm. "Just turn around, it'll only take me a second to get dressed."

There was no way on earth he could deny her pleading look. He closed his eyes. Sighed. "All right."

She eased her hold, and he pivoted and stared unseeingly straight ahead. The shuffle of material behind him echoed in his ears, sounding much louder than possible. He squeezed his eyes shut and tried to ignore the teasing visions playing behind his eyelids.

"Done!"

He shook the quivers from his body and turned about to gather his socks and boots. A low groan rumbled in his throat. He should never have looked.

His white shirt, though buttoned all the way, left a large amount of glossy skin exposed below her neck. She'd tucked the shirttails into the brown britches he'd given her and tiny hands held the much too large waistband in a bunched knot. She looked adorable.

His eyes strained to blink as they floated back to the shirt. Damn! He could see right through the thin material. Leaping back to the trunk, he pulled things out right and left, letting them flutter to the floor. Finally, snatching what he looked for, he held up a piece of rope and sliced it in two with the knife from his boot.

"Here, tie the pants up with this." He kept his eyes averted, handed the rope to her, and then started to dig in the trunk again. This time he pulled out a red-and-black plaid wool shirt. "And put this one over the other one."

"Oh, thank you. It might be a bit chilly out yet."

The air huffed out of his lungs. He rubbed at his now pounding temple. Chilly? Not even a blast of arctic air could relieve the heat racing through his body.

"There all set," she said. "What do you think?"

He turned around and swallowed, forcing his gaze to wander from her head to her toes.

"Oh." She sat down on the bed. "I guess I should roll up the pant legs a bit."

A small sense of relief allowed a morsel of tension to ease from his tight body. At least most of her flesh was covered. His eyes caught the gown again. "You don't have any clothes?"

"Of course I do." She lifted the other leg to roll up twelve inches or so of extra material. "It's just that they're all at Danny J's."

Slapping the trunk lid shut, he sat down on the top. A knot twisted in his stomach. "You're one of Danny J's girls?"

"No." She shook her head. "I didn't plan on running away last night, so I didn't take the time to get dressed."

He drew his brows together, tried to figure out what she meant. Was she running away before she became one of Danny's girls, or after?

She continued rolling the pant legs. "You see, Aunt Corrine's been hiding me since I arrived. Actually, I got to town the same day you started to build here." She settled her feet on the floor. They looked extremely tiny poking out beneath the thick cuffs she'd created on the bottom of the pant legs.

"No, I don't see. What do you mean, hiding you?"

Her chin dipped. "She didn't know what else to do with me. I didn't either. It wasn't at all what I expected."

"What you expected?"

She gave a negative gesture and grimaced.

Was he truly this dense, or did she really not make any sense? "I think we need to back up a little. Start over."

"Uh? Start over?"

"Yes, start over." Voices from outside mingled in, but he wasn't ready to face the mob again. "Your father..." A foul taste filled his mouth, and his eyes strained as they popped open. "Wait a minute. Thurston Fulton is your father?"

She nodded.

"The Thurston Fulton who's running for governor of Kansas?"

She nodded again.

"The Populist?" Howard cringed at his tone. The newly created political party had been playing havoc on the plains. They were worse than any vigilante gang and, unfortunately, had more power behind them.

She grimaced—an odd little look he didn't know how to interpret.

"Doesn't he live in Topeka?" he asked. That's where most of them did their scheming. Populists felt the government should control all railroads and banks and were making a mess of things for the cattlemen and city folks alike.

"Yes, and so did I, until a few weeks ago." A long sigh left her chest.

He pushed his political views aside, focused on Randi. "Why don't you start right there?" A twitch pulled at his brow. "Tell me what happened a few weeks ago and end your story with how you ended up in my bed last night."

"Well, all right. Let's see…"

He glanced up. *Let's see?* Oh, God, what had he done now? Was he a complete idiot? Was she a politician too? Could talk for hours without saying a darn thing?

She wrung her hands together. "Well, I think I need to start with last summer."

"Huh?" The throbbing in his temples was back.

"You see last summer my mother passed away. She'd been sick for some time, so it was really a blessing. But terribly hard."

"I'm sure it was. I'm sorry."

"Thank you," she acknowledged with a slight head bow. "You see, my father was already signed up for the Governor's race. His party elected him just the day before she died. People don't want to elect an unmarried man, so he had to marry Belinda. She's been involved in politics for years, so she was the best choice. But they had to wait a respectable mourning period before getting married. People wouldn't like if he disrespected Mama by getting married too soon, either."

Howard's mouth had fallen open. He slapped it shut, and holding the back of his head, waited for her to continue. She honestly couldn't believe what she was saying, could she? No one was that naive, were they?

"They decided six months. So in February, he married Belinda. That's when she told me I'm too old to live with them and needed to..." she paused for a few seconds, then said, "move out."

"How old are you?"

"Twenty." She rolled her eyes in an exasperated way. "I know—well on my way to becoming an old maid—Belinda tells me so all the time. But Mama was sick for a long time, and I took care of her. She needed me. I didn't have time for anything else. And I told Belinda I didn't have to live with them. I could live at the farm." Her head lowered until her chin touched her chest. "But it was sold."

He rubbed a hand over his lips, afraid the assumptions jumping into his mind would leap out his lips. Thurston Fulton was not only a Populist, he was a complete ass.

She brushed several strands of hair from her cheeks. "Aunt Corrine was the only one of Mama's family who ever wrote. Mama loved getting her letters. They were full of tales about buffalo hunters, cattle drives, street dances, and all the other fascinating events in Dodge City. So...when Belinda said I had to either get married or leave. I left." Those big doe eyes settled on him. "I mean, I couldn't marry Edward Keyes, he's older than my father." A sigh slipped out. "So, I bought a ticket to Dodge."

He rested his elbows on his knees. His family was a little rough around the edges, but they weren't despicable. Right now his mind was deciphering her father and Belinda to be about as loathsome as they come. "What happened when you got to Dodge?"

"I had written to Aunt Corrine, but she never got the post. When she wasn't at the train station to meet me, I figured the best way to find her was to ask someone. Sure enough, a man at the depot knew where she lived. But I must admit, I was a little shocked when I discovered she was, well, you know." Her cheeks turned a blushing pink.

He nodded. Everyone knew Corrine Martin was one of Danny J's girls. Danny's prized queen, to say the least.

"Aunt Corrine wanted me to leave as soon as I arrived. But I didn't have anywhere to go." Her face scrunched into a dreadful frown. "I suspect she was afraid Danny J would put me to work if he found me at the house. So, she hid me in a little room upstairs—just until we could figure out what I should do."

"What happened last night?"

"The cook Danny J has isn't very good, and whatever was in the soup she made yesterday didn't settle with me." Her cheeks grew pink again. "I woke up in the middle of the night needing to—well, while I was outside a fight started inside the house. I don't know who it was, but there were all kinds of screaming and crashing. I—I—uh, didn't dare go back inside. I remembered this place, so ran down here to hide and—"

"Randilynn! Randilynn, I need to speak to you!" Her father's voice bellowed near the door.

Her eyes grew wide with apprehension, and the color drained from her cheeks. The way she crossed her arms to rub at the shivers encompassing her from head to toe made Howard turn to the door and shout, "She'll be out in a minute."

"I need to speak to her now!"

He rose and stomped across the tent. Tugging the flap aside, he glared at the man. "I said she'll be out in a minute."

"Listen here, young man—"

Ire raced up his spine. "No, you listen here. Randilynn is no longer your daughter. She is now my wife, and I said she'd be out in a minute." He met the man, eye to beady little eye.

Thurston Fulton turned dynamite red, and Howard thought the man might shoot skyward at any moment. He gestured toward Snake and Bug standing a few yards away, silently asking the boys for assistance. His brothers walked over, and stopped, one on each side of Thurston Fulton.

The shorter man glanced at the two much younger, much stronger, men towering over him. His Adam's apple jiggled as he swallowed. "All right, then. I'll, uh, I'll be right out here when she's ready."

Howard didn't respond, just let the flap fall shut and turned back around. He kept his gaze averted, afraid she might see his anger. The nightdress still lay across the foot of the bed, and he used the sight to continue their conversation. "How'd your gown get torn?"

"It snagged on something when I jumped the fence."

"The fence around Danny J's?"

She nodded.

He lifted a brow. "It's close to four feet tall."

Her gaze caught his. A bright twinkle shined in her eyes as she solemnly admitted, "I know."

A chuckled tickled his chest, but before it emitted, the seriousness of the night's events hit him like a tornado. Had he just called her his wife? Shit! She was his wife. All of a sudden his legs had the strength of wet leather. What the hell was he going to do with a wife?

Randi held her breath. The man filled the tent from top to bottom. He had to be six and a half feet tall, if not seven, and she'd never seen someone so broad. The shoulder seams of the shirts she wore hung to her elbows and the bottoms went below her knees.

Yet, she wasn't afraid of him. His face, besides being quite handsome, was kind, and didn't raise any fear. But she was very worried as to what he thought of her. Did he despise her for hiding in his tent? Hate her for the wedding that just took place?

She began to tremble. The silence was more than she could take, and a strange desire washed over her, made her want to know everything about him. Her voice quivered as she asked, "Where were you last night?"

He looked at her. A deep frown pulled on his brows.

She tugged her gaze away, fluttered a trembling hand. "The place looked abandoned," she offered in explanation.

"I'd gone to Wichita to order furniture and fixtures." He stepped away from the door and walked over to sit back down on the large trunk.

"What are you building?"

His face softened. "A restaurant and hotel."

"Really?" Her heart began to beat erratically.

"Yup. I plan on it being the finest establishment around."

"Oh, how exciting! Mama's grandfather owned a hotel and restaurant in New York. She talked of it often." Randi pinched her lips together, tried to stifle the excitement tingling over her skin. A sad thought sent the warmth away like a cold wind. "When the land run started she and her parents came west, and she never got the chance to go back."

He nodded but didn't comment.

She rubbed her feet together, unsure what to say next. Elongated shadows moved about outside the tent, reminding her they couldn't stay in here forever. "Um, Mr. Quinter?"

He lifted his face, looked at her expectantly.

Her heartbeat increased tenfold. "I'm, um, really sorry for what happened. The marriage and all..." She took a deep breath and forced the rest of her confession out, "But I really don't know what to do about it."

31

"Well, Randi, I guess I don't really know what to do about it either."

Deflated, she nodded, having hoped he had a plan.

"But we'd better come up with something." He glanced toward the door. "Before we go out to face the mob."

Her hand flew to her lips. A giggle threatened to erupt. It was stupid, she knew, the colorful group filling the tent earlier was certainly nothing to laugh at.

A gentle smile covered his face, one that said he agreed with her giggle. "Isn't that what they reminded you of? A lynching mob?"

She nodded, let part of the laugh come out. It sounded like a snort. Flames licked at her cheeks.

He laughed aloud. "I guess I should be glad they found a preacher. Beats the hell out of a stiff rope. Or Boot Hill."

She gasped. "Oh, surely they wouldn't have…"

"Guess we'll never know." He shrugged.

Her eyes grew wide.

He let out a low laugh, and one eye winked at her.

The action caused her cheeks to tingle, again, and allowed a small sense of relief to filter over her system, but not for long. "What are we going to do?" she murmured.

His face grew serious. "I have to be honest with you, Randi. A wife really isn't in my plans right now." He shook his head, pointed toward the doorway. "I have a lot to do building this place, getting it started."

"I could help," she blurted.

"No, I don't think so," he said, shaking his head.

"I understand." She didn't, but felt she had to say she did. "I'm sure I can make my father understand the situation. I'm sure I can go back to

Topeka with him and Belinda." She hated the thought, but what else could she say?

A deep scowl covered his face. "No. No, I don't think I like that idea."

She bit her lips together, wished she could think of something to say.

He let out a deep breath. It hung in the air like an ominous buzz. After a few moments, he scratched his head and said, "No, that won't do at all." The next instant, he slapped his hands on his knees and then stood, stretching one of his hands toward her.

She glanced between the large hand and his face.

He wiggled his fingers. "Come on. Whether we like it or not, we're married."

"But what are we going to do?" She laid her hand in his. It was so large, warm, and comforting, she almost wanted to cry. Instead, she stood.

"I guess we'll just have to play it by ear." He tugged her toward the door.

"Play it by ear?" She stumbled and sucked in a gulp of air. The bottoms of her feet hurt from her late night escape, stung as if she'd stepped in a pile of broken glass.

He steadied her by grasping her other elbow. His gaze landed on her toes. "No shoes either?"

She curled her toes, tried to tuck them beneath the hem of the britches. "They're—"

"At Danny J's," he finished.

She nodded, but didn't lift her eyes, kept them locked on the top button of his tan-colored shirt.

The tip of one of his fingers slid beneath her chin and lifted her face. "I'll send one of my brothers down to get your things."

She would have spoken, but for some reason a thick lump had formed in her throat. Tears threatened to spill from her eyes.

His hand moved to pat her back, and his chin

settled on the top her head. "None of that now. There's nothing to be afraid of."

How did he know fear stirred in her stomach?

"Randi?" He leaned back, looking down at her.

"What?" The word barely squeaked out.

"I know you don't know me from Adam, but let me assure you, as long as I'm near, you have nothing to fear. Not from your father, not from Belinda, not from anyone. I won't let anyone hurt you. I promise."

His promise made a wave of something she couldn't quite explain flow over her body. It was warm and soothing, like a warm cup of sweet tea in the depth of winter.

She glanced up, meeting his kind gaze. Quelling an instant river of grief tumbling across her stomach, she nodded, hoping he believed she understood. Problem was *he* didn't understand. Nobody did. Her father and Belinda never hurt her on the outside, never did things people could see. The injuries they inflicted were on the inside, where it really hurt.

Chapter Four

Howard pulled the flap open and held it aside for Randi to step out. The sun, high in the sky, instantly reminded him how much of the day had slipped by. At least his brothers had been busy. Two other tents had been erected and several of the men he'd hired last week were busy sawing lumber into the pre-measured dimensions he'd left for them.

A cold chill raced across his shoulders when he noticed Randi's father, step-mother, and aunt sitting at a table outside the tent set up for Ma. A fire pit, already aflame, hosted a tripod. He couldn't hear the words, but saw his mother's animated body language as she filled large tin cups from her tattered old pot.

"Damn, when it rains it pours," he muttered.

"Excuse me?" Randi asked.

"Nothing. Just thinking aloud, I guess."

"Oh." Randi's gaze followed his and settled on the unusual tea party. He could only imagine what she thought but had to believe it was close to the dread swimming around in his guts.

"Ready?" he asked, looking down and trying to read what was behind her frowning stare.

She swallowed and took a deep breath. "I guess I'm as ready as I'll ever be."

He fell into step beside her, steering her toward the group with the arm settled around her shoulders as if it was born to be there. She certainly was a dainty little thing and so damn pretty. He had to be thankful for that. The women in Dodge weren't always known for their looks. Plenty of the gals in the dancehalls didn't have enough teeth left to shake

35

a stick at. If Ma had to marry him off to one, at least Randi wasn't hard to look at. He frowned, agitated by his own thoughts. A wife was the last thing he needed. Why couldn't he have a normal family? And why did his mother have to marry her sons off like some kind of overzealous father with a parlor full of girls?

Randi's steps faltered, his arm tightened to lead their stroll around a batch of green leaves that were sure to be full of goatheads. Cautious of her bare feet, he picked a trail as safe as possible. When she flinched for about the fourth time, he stopped, scooped her up, and carried her the last few yards. Justifying his actions by telling himself he had to get some work done today and couldn't spend all day tiptoeing through the weeds.

Setting her down on the canvas spread out in front of Ma's tent, he turned to Corrine Martin. "I'm gonna send my brother to get her stuff. Will you go with him to make sure he gets it all? She can't walk around without any shoes."

The woman, whose bloomers were brighter than the western sky, stood. "Oh, of course, Mr. Quinter." She glanced between him and Randi for a moment before she took a step forward and asked her niece, "Are you okay?"

Randi looked at him with big thoughtful eyes for a few seconds before she turned back to her aunt. "Yes, yes, I'm fine. You know where all my things are?"

"Yes," the aunt assured.

Bug and Snake had made their way to the small gathering as soon as he and Randi had started walking that way. Snake stepped forward. "I'll go get her things."

Howard nodded his thanks before turning to Bug. "You got the men started?"

"Yup, all under control."

36

"Good, I'll be over as soon as I can."

Bug glanced at the group, gave a slight nod. "All right." He followed Snake and Corrine away from the campsite.

Howard pulled another chair closer to the one behind Randi, waited for her to sit down before he took a seat. "Are you hungry? Want some coffee?"

Her hands fidgeted in her lap. "No, no I'm fine, thank you."

He took the cup his mother held out. The contents were hot, burned all the way down, but he needed the fortification. He'd never faced off an angry father before and almost wished he didn't hate Thurston Fulton so much already.

After the last swallow went down, he set the cup between his feet and lifted his gaze to the man. "What was it you needed to talk to my wife about?"

The coffee in the man's cup sloshed over the rim as he pulled it from his lips. "Oh, well." He set the cup down on a small table and wiped his hands on a white handkerchief before he thrust one forward. "Mr. Quinter, I must say, it's a pleasure to make your acquaintance."

Anger rolled in Howard's stomach. He leaned back in the chair and crossed his arms over his chest. So Thurston Fulton now knew he was one of the Quinter boys. He could almost see dollar signs in the man's eyes. His gaze went to his mother.

A grin the size of Texas covered her face. She was proud of her boys, had a right to be. His oldest brother, Kid, had one of the most successful cattle ranches in the state, and his brother, Skeeter, had become quite wealthy finding old bones and other artifacts on his property out near the Kansas Badlands. There wasn't a politician in the state who hadn't tried to get their fingers into the Quinter's pocketbooks. Some, Howard had to admit, were good, honest men, who wanted what was best for the country overall, but it seemed—to him anyway—that for the most part a large number of politicians had their own agendas and didn't really care about being a leader for the people they represented. In his mind, Populists were at the top of that list.

"I believe we may have gotten off on the wrong foot," Thurston Fulton said as his hand fell to his side.

"I don't believe I was on my feet," Howard said.

"Uh?"

He stared at the other man. From what he discerned, Populists were little more than crooks who felt they got the raw end of the deal when the North won almost twenty years ago. These southern delinquents were still out for revenge. The party's main plan seemed to be some kind of sub treasury scheme, where the dollar was backed by silver instead of gold. Unfortunately, in some cases, farther east from his understanding, they were collecting support faster than a squirrel gathers acorns, but their followers were mainly poor Missouri dirt farmers looking for aid anyway they could get it.

"Oh, yes, on your feet. Yes, yes, it was a pun. I get it," Thurston Fulton said after several seconds of deep thought.

Howard squinted, forced himself not to rub at the throb forming in his temples again. Damn, he never had headaches. Yet that's what Thurston Fulton was—a God-damned walking headache. And it appeared he was now his father-in-law. Tension tugged at his spine, but he held the want to shake it from his shoulders.

People often told him he was a man of few words. Howard didn't know if he agreed with that or not, he just never found too many people he wanted to talk to. He let the air pushing on his lungs out in a long sigh. The act left him feeling somewhat deflated.

"Well, let me say, my daughter has made an excellent choice for a husband. I must apologize for my earlier behavior. It wasn't until a short time ago when your mother mentioned, well..." he paused briefly, then changed his trail of words, "Well, that I realized how perfect you are for each other." The man gestured across the lot, toward the building site with one hand. "Your hotel—Randilynn will make the perfect hostess. She has hosted many parties for me. During the time her mother was ill, she handled all of the party planning. And did an excellent job of it. Didn't she, Belinda?" Thurston glanced toward his wife.

Howard noticed the black-haired Belinda was several years younger than Fulton. Not that it mattered. Furthermore, the amount of kohl around her eyes and the beet juice on her lips made her look like she should be one of Danny J's girls instead of the wife of a man who hoped to become governor.

"Oh, yes, yes, my dear. Randilynn is the best hostess. You're certainly lucky to have married her, Mr. Quinter." Belinda's eyelids fluttered a mile a minute as she spoke, and she wiggled one finger at him.

He felt like grunting in disgust. His gaze went to Randi. Open mouthed, she stared at her father and step-mother with a look of disbelief. When she noticed he watched, she bowed her head and squirmed. Even her toes fidgeted. He laid a hand over the fingers tugging the tails of his red and black shirt. Her gaze lifted, moisture surrounded her eyes. The sight made his lips tighten in anger. He turned back to her father.

"I'll ask once again. What was it you wanted to talk to my wife about?"

The man looked like a little weasel the way his tongue darted out to wet his lips. His beady eyes danced to and fro while his Adam's apple worked about in his neck.

A politician who didn't have a silver tongue, that had to be a first.

"Mr. Quinter, I mean, Howard, I can call you Howard, can't I?" Belinda leaned forward, placing a hand on his knee.

The touch sent a quiver up his leg. He pulled his leg aside, forcing the hand to fall away. "Mr. Quinter is fine."

Belinda's eyes grew wide, clearly shocked by his rebuff. "Oh, well, Mr. Quinter, perhaps you could show me around your building site. I think Thurston and Randilynn would like some privacy. You know a heart to heart, father-daughter talk."

Randi's hands quaked beneath his. He gave them a reassuring squeeze and replied, "No."

Belinda's eyes bugged. "No? You won't show me around your site?"

"No, I won't show you around the site. If you want to see it, go ahead, just watch for snakes." The woman made his skin crawl. And the way Randi shook like a leaf from head to toe made his ire peak. Leaving her alone with Fulton would be like leaving the hen house door open with a fox sitting nearby.

Belinda sat back in her chair, huffed out what she must have thought was a refined gasp of air. She put him in mind of a washed up stage actress and not a very good one.

Thurston rubbed his palm over his pant leg. "I just wanted to ask my daughter if this was the union she wanted. A father needs to be sure his daughter marries well." Almost as an afterthought he added, "And is happy."

Randi's head snapped up. Her face held a dumbfounded daze.

Howard frowned. Was there a glimmer of hope in her eyes? She couldn't possibly believe her father's line of bullshit. His jaw tightened as he declared,

"You didn't seem too concerned about that when you were pointing a shotgun at my chest."

Everyone's mouth fell open as they stared at him. Howard shrugged. "You didn't." He included his mother in his round-about glance. "None of you were willing to listen to a word either one of us had to say."

Ma plopped the pot in her hand down on the table with a thud. "It was just the shock of it all. Not at all what we expected," she said.

"It wasn't what we expected either," he said.

"Hog—"

"Mr. Quinter—"

His mother and Randi's father started speaking at the same time. Howard held his hand up, stopping them both. Snake appeared, riding into the yard with two carpet bags tied to his saddle.

"Randi's belongings have arrived." Howard turned to her. "Is there anything you want to say to your father?"

Her eyes glistened with unshed tears. After a moment of hesitation, she shook her head.

"All right then. I'm sure you'll all excuse us." He didn't wait for anyone to answer, just scooped her into his arms and carried her to the tent.

She didn't say a word, and he didn't encourage her to speak, for if she had, he wouldn't have known how to answer. His mind was awhirl with the morning's events and with the work that was not getting done. He'd always known a woman could cause more havoc than a hunting party of braves, but he'd never believed he'd experience it firsthand.

He set her inside the flap and handed in the two bags Snake passed to him. "I'll make sure no one comes in."

"Thank you," she whispered as the flap fell back into place behind him.

He stood outside the tent wondering what to do

next.

"You doing all right?" Snake asked.

Howard walked a few feet away from the tent, lowered his voice. "Why the hell did you go find a preacher?" His fingers itched to grab his brother's shirt collar.

Snake held up both hands in defense. "Don't blame this on me." His brother, who was barely a year older, clicked his tongue as he pointed one finger and thumb and made the age-old sign of a pistol and closed one eye as if he were setting the gun's sights. His smile was wide, as if he'd just told a joke everyone enjoyed.

Howard glared.

Snake lowered his hand and shrugged his shoulders. "You were the one who went and got the preacher for Ma when it was Kid and Jessie, and Skeeter and Lila." Shaking his head, he added, "You know what Ma's like."

Howard rubbed both hands over his face. In the twenty-four years he'd been alive he'd rarely seen a time when any of the boys defied their mother. "Yeah, I know." One hand went to massage the tension in his neck. "Hell, a wife's one thing, but one who has a slimy politician as a father—that's a whole different recipe." He glanced toward the group still sitting outside Ma's tent. "I should have let her shoot me."

"Aw, come on, little brother, it can't be that bad." Snake slapped a hand on his shoulder.

Howard let his eyes fire stones at his brother faster than a good sling-shot.

Snake shrugged them off like water rolling off the brim of his floppy leather hat. "Look at Kid and Skeeter, they're happier than catfish in the mud."

"Yeah, and look at all the hell they went through." A tidal wave of anxiety rippled over Howard's body.

Snake opened his mouth, but closed it again and nodded. "You got a point there."

Howard pointed to Thurston Fulton. "That man is going to make our lives a living hell. Count my words."

Snake let his gaze linger on the group engaged in their unorthodox tea party for a silent length before he asked, "What can I do to help?"

"I don't know, yet, but as soon as I do, I'll let you know." Howard looked around the site and could almost see his dream slipping away. "I gotta go talk to Bug, let him know what needs to be done today. Stay here and make sure neither that man nor his wife bother Randi."

"All right."

Howard started to walk away, then stopped and turned back to his brother. "No peeking either. I'll only be gone a few minutes. And I'll be watching."

Snake let out a short laugh before swallowing the rest of it to nod, but the stupid grin on his brother's face made Howard wish he'd been fortunate enough to have been born an only child.

****

Randi had held the tears at bay while her new husband carried her across the field. She'd come to Dodge to escape her father's plan of marrying her off to a stranger, and yet, not only had he found her, but he'd succeeded in his goal. As he always did.

She pinched her lips and closed her eyes. What she wouldn't give for the simple everyday life she'd known before learning Thurston Fulton was her father—taking care of mother, cooking, baking, gardening, not having to face anyone for weeks on end. Later when mother had become an invalid, there was a time or two she'd wished for a visitor, wanted to talk to someone whose deep ragged coughs hadn't made speech too much work to endure. But even on those days, when she wished for company, she'd never wished that company be her father.

She was sure—even though she couldn't recall—there had been a time she wanted to see her father, know the man who sired her. Perhaps when she was little and mama wasn't ill she had wished for a real family. But in those carefree days of her early childhood, mama had been all she had—and needed. They'd had each other and that was enough. Mama never talked of him, never wondered where he was or when he'd return, so neither had Randi.

Yet, a few moments ago, Thurston Fulton sounded proud of her, and said he wanted to know if she was happy. Had he loved her—and mama—all these years and work had simply kept him from being with them? Her swirling mind had wondered why he'd told Howard she used to host his parties. She'd never played hostess in her life—he'd always had Belinda for that, even while mama was alive.

When Howard had released his hold, lowered her feet to the floor of the tent, and said something, she'd murmured her thanks and twisted, afraid he'd see the tears in her eyes. As soon as the tent flap slipped closed, the tears fell in earnest. Brushing them away didn't help, they continued to flow. Now, through the blur, she bent down to pick up the bags Howard shoved through the flap.

She hesitated before lifting the bags. On the other side of the canvas, Howard's brother, Snake, said something. Randi leaned closer to the flap.

Footsteps thudded as the men walked a few steps away. She eased the flap open a touch, held an ear near the opening, and listened. Her body began to tremble from head to toe. She slapped a hand over the gasp emitting from her lips and stepped away from the flap. Eavesdropping only hurt the dropper, the pain ripping at her chest proved it. Her bags felt like thousand-pound feed sacks. She half-carried—half-dragged them to the bed. Howard's anger-filled voice echoed in her ears as she collapsed onto the mattress.

"Why the hell did you go find a preacher?" he'd said.

She shouldn't feel this hurt, he'd already told her he didn't want a wife. But he'd been so nice about it all, so kind to her. To hear his furious tone while talking to his brother shattered the ounce of happiness she'd felt at the way he'd stood up for her.

What had she expected? He was forced to marry her. The question was—what was she going to do? All of a sudden the small alcove at the brothel didn't seem so dismal, almost felt like a safe haven. Dread lowered onto her, even that little hovel was no longer an option. By now everyone at the house knew she'd been living there.

She glanced around the tent. There was no way she could stay here. Not with the way Howard felt. A deep sinking feeling filled her stomach. Perhaps she could go talk to her father and ask him to take her back to Topeka with him. A quiver ripped up her spine. The couple of months she'd lived at her father's house had been awful, to say the least, but what else could she do?

Light filtered through the canvas, and she peered around the space. Even living in a tent with barely enough room to turn around in would be heaven compared to living with Belinda again, but she had to be fair. She was not Howard's problem and couldn't expect him to provide for her—hastily married or not.

Conversation sounded outside the door. The thought of ignoring it did occur, especially since she recognized Belinda's voice, but for some reason she couldn't. Pushing the air from her lungs, she rose and moved to the flap.

"Howard said no one's to disturb her." Snake's wide shoulders blocked the opening.

"But he surely didn't mean me. I'm her step-mother, and she may need assistance fastening her gown," Belinda answered.

Snake didn't answer, and a moment later someone tapped the side of the canvas. The material slapped and rippled all the way to the other end.

"Randi, do you need any help getting fastened?" Howard's voice rang clear.

She stepped back and scurried to the bed. "No, no, I'm fine. I'll be out in a few minutes." Garments flew out of the bag left and right as she ruffled through until finding what she needed. Belinda knew full well her gowns all buttoned up the front, knew she didn't need any help. A new shower of horror descended upon her, returning to Topeka with her father and Belinda was the last thing on earth she wanted. She'd broken free, and never, ever would go back. No matter what.

The voices outside the door continued, but hushed enough she couldn't make out a single word. As fast as possible she pulled off the pants and shirts and put on her own clothing. The pitiful wrinkles of her underclothes were tolerable, but the deep creases marring the pale yellow dress would infuriate her father. She tried to stretch a few of the deeper ones from the material, but it was hopeless.

Unfastening the buttons, she pulled off the yellow dress and grabbed the dusty blue one she'd made last summer. It had tiny white stripes, and seersucker didn't show creases like linen. Pushing the last pearl button through its fastening loop a thread snapped. The tiny button slipped from her fingers and bounced across the floor. She flinched.

Her father would be just as mad if she came out with a button missing, and his ire was nothing to mess with. Now she had no choice but to wear her gray skirt with matching jacket. But the traveling suit was highly unsuitable for a day dress, her father wouldn't approve at all.

Nerves boiled in her stomach. She flopped onto the bed just as Howard's voice sounded again. "Randi, are you all right in there?"

"Yes." She tried to keep the sobs from sounding in her voice.

The flap opened a touch. "Are you dressed?" he asked uncertainly.

"Yes." She wiped at her eyes and nose with both hands.

He walked in, took one look at her, and scurried over to kneel in front of her. "What's wrong?"

It had all become too much. The sobs building in her chest burst. No one had ever been this kind to her. She was a pitiful creature with nothing to offer, dependent on the kindness of strangers. She sobbed again.

He clutched her hands. "Randi?" he asked, softly.

She had to answer, but what could she say? "I—I lost a button," blurted out her mouth.

"A button?" he asked, sounding dumbfounded.

She buried her face in her hands.

"A button ain't nothing to cry over."

"I-I c-can't go out th-there without a b-b-button," she blubbered into her palms.

"Well, then put on that yellow dress."

"I-it's w-w-wrinkled."

"Well—what about this other one?"

She peeked through her fingers. Her gray skirt hung from his hand. "That's a traveling suit," she howled.

"A traveling suit?"

"He'd never approve," she all but wailed.

The bed bounced as Howard sat down beside her. "Is that what's wrong? You're afraid your father won't approve of how you look?"

She squeezed her eyes shut.

"Half an hour ago you were wearing my britches and shirt. You didn't care then what your father thought."

A frown pulled on her brows. Yes, she had cared, she just hadn't cried over it. Besides half an hour ago, she didn't know how upset he was over their wedding. A new sob rolled out of her chest, making her snort and sniffle. The overwhelming emotions encompassing her from head to toe ate the last amount of control she had. Twisting about, she flopped face first onto the bed and smothered her cries into a pillow.

"Aw, hell!" he exclaimed. The bed bounced again and a few seconds later he shouted, "Ma? Ma, come here and bring your sewing kit."

Chapter Five

By the time she exited the tent both her father and Belinda were gone. Randi didn't know if the fact made her happy or sad. While still pondering the thought and gazing at the empty table near the other tents, Snake arrived at her side. He informed her Belinda and her father had gone to town to reserve a hotel room. The news was like a double-edged sword, for it surely meant they planned on staying in Dodge for a least a day or two.

At the same time, the information Ma Quinter had shared in the tent gave her the smallest amount of hope. The woman had talked non-stop while she sewed. Most exciting had been the fact that her two older son's had been forced into marriage. And it appeared all had turned out perfectly. The woman was convinced things would be the same for her and Howard.

Stephanie Quinter, or Ma, as she insisted on being called, sounded rough and gruff, but underneath was kind and had quickly enticed Randi to dry her tears. Having been alone for so long, the friendship Stephanie offered filled a strong craving inside Randi's soul.

"Well, come on now, no dilly-dallyin'. It's been a coon-dog's age since we had breakfast. We gotta get some lunch going for these boys. They're bound to be about starved by now, and there's nothin' worse than a hungry man, he gets grumpier than a snake in a bag." Ma hooked their elbows and tugged her toward the other tents.

"What are we making for lunch?" The thought of

cooking increased her outlook. She'd missed preparing meals and creating new dishes. It had been her job for as long as she could remember, but after Mother died and she'd moved to Topeka with her father, his cook banned her from the kitchen. Belinda had said it was unsightly for someone in her position to be seen in an apron.

"Kid, I told you about him and Jessie," Ma started.

She nodded, remembering Kid as the oldest Quinter son. He and his wife, Jessie, lived near Nixon, and had two children, a boy and a girl, who Ma proclaimed to be the most wonderful younguns on earth, besides the two the next brother, Skeeter, and his wife, Lila, had.

"Well, he's got lots of cattle, so I have enough beef to feed half the state. Thought we'd just fry up some potatoes to go with it."

"Or I could make Beef Wellington." Randi's heart skipped a beat. She hadn't made the dish in so long. It had always been one of Mother's favorites, but they rarely had beef, chickens had been their mainstay. That and whatever game she'd managed to acquire. She pinched her lips together knowing the thought had been unfair. Even after her father had started to visit, their pantry hadn't increased. Belinda said they shouldn't expect it either. She'd said politicians were like preachers; they work for the people and didn't receive an exuberant amount of money to feed their families.

"Uh? Beef what?" Ma stared at her with wide eyes.

Randi let her wandering thoughts float away and returned to the conversation. "We don't have an oven, do we?"

"Nope, not yet. But knowing Hog the first room finished will be the kitchen." Ma Quinter pointed toward the building where men sawed and hammered.

Randi's feet stalled, and she gasped, shocked by the transformation taking place before her eyes. "Oh, my. The sides are almost all up. They certainly work quickly."

"Yup, when my boys set out to do something, they don't waste their time." Ma tugged on her arm.

Randi fell in step beside the other woman, twisting every once in awhile to catch sight of the massive building and the men scrambling about. She tried hard to get a glimpse of Howard, but Ma Quinter stormed forward like she was on her way to a fire. Her quick glances did catch sight of Snake and Bug, but not her husband. She held in the want to sigh loudly and turned to Stephanie.

"Your sons certainly have interesting names."

Ma laughed. "Yup, their daddy did that. Gave them all nick names and they stuck. The boys aren't always too fond of them. Kid is really Kendell. Skeeter is Steven, Snake is Scott, Hog is Howard, and Bug is Brett."

"Oh," Randi let the names sink in. Mother had always called her Kitten. She'd said from the time Randi had been born, she snuggled in like a kitten in her lap.

"So, what's the beef William stuff?"

It took Randi a moment to comprehend what the woman meant. "Beef Wellington. It's beef baked inside a thin pastry. It's quite delicious."

A very thoughtful look covered Ma Quinter's face. "Hmm, I think things are gonna turn out better than I imagined."

Perplexed, Randi asked, "Excuse me?"

The bonnet on the other woman's head fluttered about as she shook her head, and her shoulders hiked up and down a few times before she said, "Nothing. So what else do you know how to cook?"

"Oh, lots of things. My great-grandfather had a

hotel and restaurant in New York years ago, and when my mother was a little girl she stayed with them. When she was ill she would talk about all the fancy dishes they used to serve, so I ordered some cookbooks and learned how to cook many of them for her." The cookbooks were safely tucked inside her carpet bags, the few things Belinda hadn't made her destroy—only because she didn't know about them.

"You don't say?"

"Yes, I love to cook." They stopped outside Ma's tent where a complete camp site had been set up. Tables, chairs, washing station, a fire pit with a wide tri-pod balanced over it, and several other necessities sat about.

"Does Hog know all this?" Ma rubbed her chin.

"No." Worry tugged on Randi's face, and she cringed, not wanting to upset him anymore than he already was. "Will he be mad?"

"Mad?" Ma guffawed. "What man would be mad to know his wife can cook?"

Randi let out a long sigh, almost afraid to admit another one of her many faults. "I'm afraid I don't know much about men."

"Well, honey. The way to a man's heart is through his stomach and for Hog that's double fold." The woman moved toward a wagon with a billowing canvas top.

She followed. "So Hog-oward likes to eat?" It was a stupid question. Howard was the largest man she'd ever seen. He wasn't overweight, she hadn't seen a wrinkle of excess anywhere on his broad chest and flat stomach, but a man his size must need a large amount of food to maintain the breadth of a body so immense.

"You could say that," Ma said. A large smile curled the ends of her thin lips. "You certainly could say that." She climbed into the back of the wagon. "So what do you want to cook?"

A rush of happiness she couldn't control made Randi scamper in behind the other woman. "Well, let's see what you have."

****

Howard lifted his head to wipe away the sweat dripping in his eyes. The workmen he'd hired were outdoing themselves. More had been accomplished this morning than he'd expected in a full day of work. While he'd been getting hitched, the hired hands had assembled the walls. He'd arrived in time to help raise the fourth one.

Through an opening in the wood, he caught sight of his mother and Randi strolling arm in arm toward the other tents. His hand fell to rest on a support beam. Her long hair had been rearranged, neatly pinned to the back of her head, and the sides puffed out like a sun bonnet.

His eyes continued their appraisal. Her straight shoulders and back gave her the ambiance of style and affluence. The soft even sway of her trim hips made her blue skirt swirl about her feet as she walked. Perhaps Thurston Fulton had been right. She would make the perfect hostess for his establishment.

"See something you like there, brother?"

He sucked up, swallowed his outlandish thoughts, and gave Bug an icy stare.

His youngest brother pushed him aside to gaze between the boards. "Hmm, not bad if you ask me."

An irritating pinch stung his stomach. "No one's asking you, and you better keep those eyes in your head if you know what's good for you."

Bug let out a deep laugh that bounced off the walls. "Oh, I know what's good for me, just wondering if you know what's good for you."

He tapped Bug's chest with one finger. "You getting back to work is what's good for you."

"Funny you know?"

"What? What's funny?"

"I just always figured Ma's shotgun would get Snake hitched before you. Good thing I ain't a bettin' man." Bug reached down, took the extra hammer lying by his feet, and chuckling, strolled away.

Howard's gaze went back to the women. They were both in the back of the storage wagon. What was he going to do with her? Whether she'd make a good hostess or not, he really didn't have time for a wife. And most definitely didn't have time to deal with her father. Having an alliance, no matter how strained, with the Populist Party would damage his business before it even opened. He had to get rid of Fulton immediately, the railroad and cattlemen he expected to cater to would be appalled by the politician.

A thought exploded in his head. Snapping his fingers, he turned about. *Skeeter!* Minutes later, he found Snake on the far side of the building. "I gotta go to town."

"What for?" Snake asked, gesturing toward a buckboard piled high with building equipment. "Maybe I have it in the supply wagon."

"I need to send a wire to Skeeter."

"Skeeter? What for?"

Howard raised his eyebrows. "I'm gonna ask him if he'd like a visit from the next governor of Kansas."

Snake started laughing and gave his head a short quick shake. "You really dislike your new father-in-law don't you?"

"Yes, I do," Howard admitted without thought to how it sounded.

"You better make it a long wire. Skeeter'll need to know details."

He laid his hand on Snake's shoulder. "I'm thinking more about Buffalo Killer. The brave might like to meet a politician."

Snake let out a low whistle. "Your new wife

might not like it if her father comes back scalped."

"Naw, Skeeter won't let it go that far," he said, but a slight twinge did tickle his spine.

"You must know a different Skeeter than I do if you believe that."

Howard smirked. "Well, Lila won't let it go that far."

Snake nodded. "That I can agree with."

"I'll be back in an hour or so." A smile tugged at his lips. Buffalo Killer was one of Skeeter and Lila's best friends, and a hell of a guy. But if there was one thing the Sioux hated, it was politicians. Getting Thurston Fulton out of town for a while would give him time to figure out what to do with Randilynn.

He certainly couldn't let her move back to Topeka with the man. Maybe he should send a wire to Kid as well, find out more about that girl's university in Boston he tried to send Jessie to right after they got married.

****

Guilt made Howard's stomach roll. Not over the wire, Thurston Fulton deserved any loathing Buffalo Killer would show him, but wondering if his actions would somehow hurt Randi made bile blister the back of his throat. This overwhelming need to protect someone was new to him, and no matter how he tried, it wouldn't dissolve.

He'd protected his sisters-in-law before. There was that time he and Snake helped Jessie capture the cattle rustlers while Kid was in jail. And he'd watched over Lila while she was morning sick and Skeeter was out searching for the madman who was set on killing her. But those times were different. Neither Jessie nor Lila was his wife.

The word held a lot of weight. What was it about a preacher saying a few words that made a man's life turn upside down and inside out? Hell, he hadn't even known her a full day, and yet, she was all he thought about.

The sun mocked him as it shone glory and joy down upon the earth. He pulled the hat from his head, pushed the sweat-filled hair off his forehead, and resettled the rim above his ears. "Hell, it's only noon. I've only known her half a day." The building site grew before him, and he heeled Ted into a faster canter.

A wondrous aroma filled the air as he brought the horse to a halt beside his tent. The rumbling in his stomach encouraged him to speed up the time it took to care for the animal before moving toward the smell.

A grunt rumbled out his mouth when he noticed Thurston Fulton and Belinda had returned. The woman had cornered Randi near the well he'd dug at the back of the property, and she was waving one finger beneath his wife's nose. Randi's head was bent so low, her dainty chin almost touched her chest.

His feet dug into the ground and ire made his muscles ripple. Throwing the saddle over a large stump without care, he stomped past the tents and toward the well.

"It's disgraceful I tell you. Absolutely disgusting!" Belinda's screeching voice floated to his ears.

"Randi?" he said while still several feet away.

Her face snapped up and relief reflected in her doe eyes as they settled on him. They seemed even larger surrounded by her now ashen skin.

"Howard," she barely squeaked.

The way she said his name made his heart somersault. He reached her side in mere seconds.

"One of the boys can fetch water for you," he said, lifting the wooden bucket out of the weeds surrounding her feet. The action gave him something to do, hitting Belinda wouldn't be polite.

He'd never even thought about hitting a woman before, but seeing how pale Randi looked, he really wanted to knock Belinda into next week.

"Oh, it's no trouble," Randi whispered. "I've always hauled water."

Her voice was shaky, troubled. He crooked a finger beneath her chin, forced her face up to make sure no marks marred the skin. If someone had struck her he would have to retaliate. There were no tell tale signs, and a soft pink blush formed on her cheeks as he stared at the perfection of her face.

He couldn't bring himself to look at the other woman, knew his tongue would slip. He wrapped his fingers around Randi's elbow and steered her away from her stepmother. When they were separated from Belinda by a few yards of spring grass, he asked, "What's going on?"

"N-nothing." She glanced over her shoulder.

He made her keep walking, putting more distance between them and Belinda. "I see your father and Belinda are back." It was a stupid comment, but his mind, full of rage, and his heart, full of something he had yet to define, made comprehensible thoughts impossible.

She nodded. "Yes, they arrived a bit ago." Her footsteps faltered. "Your brother said you went to town. Did you get what you needed?"

"Yes, yes I did." He let go of her elbow and wrapped the arm around her shoulder, looking down at her. "I'm sorry. I should have asked if there was anything you needed before I left."

Her mouth dropped open. "Oh." A smile formed as her lips drew together. Her cheeks grew a healthy, pinkish color. "There's nothing I need, but thank you for asking."

The blood in his head swirled until he grew light headed. Damn, if she wasn't the prettiest thing. Just looking at her had the ability to take his breath away. He coughed, tried to think of something to say.

"I should have asked before I went to town." His feet stalled. Aw, shit, he hadn't meant to say it aloud.

She stopped beside him, giggled. "That's okay. It's the thought that counts."

What happened next was more of a surprise to him than finding her in his bed had been. Of their own accord, his lips lowered to brush over hers. The first touch made his whole body quiver. Her taste was intoxicating, sweeter than honey. He moved his lips over her delicate mouth, searching for a deeper taste. His arm tightened, drew her closer. She didn't resist but did tilt her head a touch higher, giving him more access to her mouth, which he immediately took advantage of.

Someone cleared their throat in a very annoying way and broke the spell surrounding him. He lifted his face to peer over the top of Randi's head.

Belinda glared at them. If her eyes had been a pistol, he'd have been shot dead center. Her hands were braced on her hips, and one toe tapped at the ground. He glared back, until she flipped her head and twisted about to stomp toward the tents.

Randi's cheeks were as rosy as a sunrise when his gaze settled back on her. Her eyes, big and brown, held a sparkle he hadn't seen before. He leaned down, kissed a brow above one of them. "Come on. Let's get this water to Ma before she has a fit."

She didn't move. "Ma—I mean y-your mother invited my father and Belinda to lunch." Her eyes had grown dim again.

He used the arm around her to tug until she started walking. "Yeah, I figured she would." His fingers on her shoulder plucked at the wide strap of the apron she had on over her dress. "I see Ma put you to work, too." He wanted to change the subject, didn't like the sadness floating about her.

"Yes, I'm afraid that's what made Belinda so mad," she said, gazing down at the apron skirt.

"That you're hauling water? I'm sorry—"

"No," she interrupted. "It wasn't the work part. It was the apron. She doesn't approve of them."

"She doesn't approve of aprons?" His impression was right, Belinda Fulton was a dimwit.

"Actually, it's the cooking she doesn't approve of."

"She doesn't approve of cooking?" He'd never heard of such a thing.

Randi shrugged and nodded at the same time, her face twisted into the cutest little grimace he'd ever seen. His heart jumped, skipped around in his chest like a rock over water. He'd never known someone who could make him feel so many things all at the same time.

All together it made him smile, and he let out a laugh. He pulled her a little tighter to his side. "I knew there was a reason I didn't like her, besides the fact she's about as appealing as a rattler in a cave."

Randi didn't have time to suppress the giggle before it leaped out of her mouth. She had no control over it. Had no control over the way his kiss had left her body so giddy she'd probably be floating right now if his hand wasn't on her shoulder, forcing her feet to stay on the ground. She couldn't fathom what it was about him, but the minute she'd heard his voice, the sky around her had brightened. Even the dark cloud from Belinda's badgering had disappeared. There was something about the way he looked at her. It made her feel like...like she was a person. An odd thing, she knew, since she'd always been a person, but this was different—extremely hard to explain—even to herself.

They were still chuckling when they walked around the corner of the tent. The icy stare Belinda sent their way was hard to ignore, but Randi did her best and ultimately refused so much as a glance her stepmother's way. The sun shining upon her and the light carefree feelings dancing inside her body like a jar of fireflies were too enjoyable. She didn't want any of it to end.

"Whatever Ma is cooking sure smells good," Howard said with a touch of bewilderment.

Randi glanced up, took in his somewhat apprehensive look. "You sound surprised."

He set the bucket on a small bench near the tent.

"I am." His lips brushed against her hair as he whispered in her ear, "Ma isn't known for her cooking."

"Oh?" She turned. His face was very close to hers. Less than an inch, and if she stretched just a mite, their lips could meet again. Her heart began to beat unevenly.

"Nope," he said, then as light as a butterfly's wings, his lips brushed over hers before he turned to walk toward the table.

Randi took a moment to catch her breath. Knew if she tried walking she'd look like a one-legged goose. This was certainly a day of firsts. Her first kiss, her second kiss, her wedding…

When her knees no longer threatened to collapse, she let out the air in her lungs and moved to the tripod. Maybe there was hope. Maybe their marriage could work—if only she had something to offer up in the bargain.

The Dutch oven had cooked the meat to perfection. It fell apart in long succulent strips as she stirred, mixing the thick chunks of beef into the gravy surrounding it. Ma's supply wagon was full of spices, some Randi had never even heard of, and every cooking utensil imaginable. The last hour, before her father and Belinda returned, had been marvelous. She'd missed cooking almost as much as she missed Mama these past few months.

Her brows tugged together. Howard had said his mother wasn't known for her cooking. Then why would she have all these supplies? Randi shook off the question. She didn't really have time to contemplate it right now and turned to the other pot to poke the potatoes. They, too, were done. Completely involved in the meal, she scurried about to complete the feast. When the potatoes were whipped to perfection with a touch of sweet cream and butter, she carried the pan to the table and went back to retrieve the meat.

Carrying the other kettle, full of sliced carrots, she found herself wishing she had Mama's china serving dishes instead of the cast iron pots. The gold-rimmed hand-painted china had disappeared a few years ago, and she still wondered what had become of the lovely dishes. The precious china along with the meal would certainly give Howard a reason to think about keeping her as a wife, wouldn't it? That was it. She could offer her cooking skills in exchange for staying here.

Randi bit her lip and glanced across the table to where he stood. A soft ripple of emotions tickled her insides, and she looked away. A moment later, a washing of understanding happened, flowing over her like the warm sun. It said Howard would provide her a safe haven like she'd had with Mama. One that promised she'd never have to live with the fear and uncertainty she'd experienced living with her father.

The side of her face began to tingle, and she turned back to Howard, meeting his thoughtful gaze. He smiled at her. The action made a flush of warmth rise into her face. She gave him a quick grin before lowering her lashes. At that moment her inner-self made a quick vow—no matter what it took, she was staying.

Ma had everything else set out, so Randi laid the cloth she'd used to carry the hot dishes to the table on the end of the bench seat and glanced about, somewhat unsure as to where to sit.

Howard reached for her hand and tugged her forward to sit beside him on the long bench. Belinda's puckered lips and glare sent a shiver rippling over her shoulders. Between Howard's kisses and nearness, and all the cooking, she'd forgotten about Belinda's displeasure. Besides belittling her about cooking, Belinda had made it extremely clear what she thought of Randi's other behavior. She'd claimed if word got out she and Howard had been caught in bed together—before the wedding—her father's chances of becoming governor would be seriously affected. It was all her fault. Randi bowed her head, settled her trembling fingers in her lap.

"Well, it's gonna get cold if you don't dig in," Ma said, breaking the silence around the table.

"Allow me," her father said, taking the lid off the cast iron oven. "Mrs. Quinter, your plate please."

Ma Quinter handed him her plate. "Thank you, Mr. Fulton."

Howard lifted the plate in front of Randi and handed it across the table to her father. "I believe there are two Mrs. Quinters at this table."

Randi held her breath.

"Oh, of course, you're right," her father said as he scooped food onto her plate.

The other dishes were passed around, the potatoes, the carrots she'd glazed with honey, the platter of bread. Randi took a helping of each, but her stomach rolled with each spoonful. It was foolish to be so hopeful, and wrong to think only of herself, her happiness. Belinda had told her more than once she was selfish, and it appeared her stepmother was right. Randi wanted to stay married to Howard because anywhere was better than living with Belinda, but truth be told; she needed to stay married to him to save her father's campaign.

When everyone's blue-speckled plates were full and the others began to eat, Randi twirled her fork around on her plate afraid anything that went down her throat would most likely come right back up. No matter what her reasons were, none of this was fair to Howard. None of it was what he wanted—needed.

As if he heard her rambling thoughts, Howard's gaze burned the side of her face. She peered at him out of the corner of her eye. A fierce frown covered his face, pulled his lips into a straight line.

Inwardly she groaned. A deep disturbing boil grew in her stomach.

"Aren't you hungry," he asked.

She shook her head, "Not really."

"Randilynn, don't be rude, eat your dinner," Belinda snapped, clearly disgusted.

Howard set his glass down with a solid thud. His voice was low and held a warning growl, not unlike what Randi imagined a wolf sounded like.

"Don't speak to my wife with that tone." His eyes glared across the table at Belinda.

Chapter Six

Randi groaned—aloud this time. The air around the table sizzled like a lightning storm was about to erupt. She swallowed the lump in her throat and lifted her fork.

"Sorry, I guess I am hungry." Praying her stomach wouldn't erupt, she wrapped her lips around the forkful of potatoes.

Her father cleared his throat. "Forgive us, Mr. Quinter, it'll take us some time to get used to the idea Randi is no longer our little girl." He patted Belinda's hand.

"Well, get used to it." Howard stared at her father. "Quick."

The false pasted-on smile on her father's face, one she'd seen many times before, made the potatoes become lodged in the back of her throat. Randi gulped, tried to force them down. It didn't work. The air locked in her lungs began to burn. She tried to cough, but the potatoes blocked her airway. Panic filled her mind. Nothing worked. She couldn't swallow, couldn't breathe. The fork fell from her fingers. She pressed her fingers against her throat to push the food down.

"Randi?" Howard glanced at her.

Water filled her eyes. Her lungs had become an oven. She clawed at her throat with both hands. Nothing helped.

"Randi!" He jumped up and pulled her off the bench.

The world swirled. The next thing she knew he'd flipped her over one of his arms and slapped her back.

The potatoes thrust out of her throat, splattered across the ground. She slumped in his hold, gasping for air, needing to refill her burning lungs. After a few seconds, her gasping slowed, and her quaking body calmed.

Howard eased her back up, twisted so he stood in front of her. "Are you all right?"

Her throat was on fire, but she nodded. "Y-yes," nodded again. "Thank you."

His handsome features were twisted with concern. "Are you sure?"

Tears stung her eyes. She tried to hold them at bay, but couldn't. She nodded, and then shook her head. She wasn't okay. She was never okay. A sob tore over her raw throat. Pain made the sound even louder. Lifting both hands, she tried to hide behind her palms.

"Come here," he whispered, pulling her forward.

His wide chest and broad shoulders shrouded her, gave a shelter she'd never known. She dug her face into the soft material and wept.

Big hands rubbed up and down her back. The soothing action penetrated deep into the raw gaping wounds only someone who'd never known real comfort could explain. In one way, it was hard for her to accept, in another, it filled a yearning so deep she wanted to snuggle in and never leave.

"Shh," he whispered in her ear. "It's all right."

She rubbed her cheek against his shirt, nodding, and knew he told the truth. Somehow he understood she wasn't crying because of the choking.

He stepped forward, forced her to move with him. His hold never eased, strong arms kept her secure as they walked. When he stopped, she lifted her face. They stood several yards away from the table near the bucket of water he'd carried for her.

He lifted the dipper, held it up. "Here, take a

drink. It'll help."

She obeyed, let the cool water trickle down her dry throat.

After several soothing sips, he asked, "Had enough?"

She nodded and lifted her hands to wipe the tear residue from her cheeks.

His hands wrapped around her wrists, gently tugging her hands off her face. He winked at her, and a smile turned his face into one of the most glorious sights she'd ever seen.

"Aw, sweetheart," he murmured as he leaned forward. His warm lips pressed against her forehead, stayed there for an extended length of time.

When they slipped away, she felt much better, as if his touch had erased her pain, her worries. How did he do that?

"Feel better?"

She smiled. "Yes, I do. I-I'm sorry about that."

He glanced at the table, then back to her. "Want to try again?"

Did she?

Not really, but knew she had too. A deep sigh blew out her mouth. "Yeah."

"What I said this morning is still true. You have nothing to be afraid of. I won't let anyone hurt you."

As if she had no control over it, her hand rose to his face. The side of his jaw filled her palm. A shadow of whiskers tickled her skin as she caressed the area. She met his gaze, which held a tint of deep concern.

"You are a very, very nice man."

His eyes twinkled like stars at night, and he winked at her. "Well, thank you, ma'am." He nodded his head in a very charming way, and then his gaze grew a touch more serious. "You're a very nice woman."

Her heart flipped in a delightful way, it made a giggle tickle her chest. Before her mind had a chance to stop her mouth from speaking, she admitted, "I'm glad it was your tent I snuck into."

He leaned down, kissed the end of her nose. "Me, too."

****

The evening meal was much less eventful, but just as delicious, a fact that made Howard follow his mother to the well. "When did you learn to cook? I've only been gone two weeks, and you didn't know how to make food taste this good before."

Ma's eyes glistened with merriment as she handed him the bucket of water. "I was wondering when you were gonna ask. I expected it 'afore now."

"I've been a little busy today," he answered, his eyes wandering to where Randi stood near the back of the supply wagon washing supper dishes.

Mixed with a lilting giggle, Ma answered, "I ain't learned. And don't plan on learning, but your new wife," she let out a low whistle, "that little gal can cook up a storm. She's worse than you. That's all she talked about all day—cooking and fancy named dishes. Sheesh, it's enough to make a mind bust from all the twittering."

Water sloshed onto his boots as he skidded to a halt. "Randi cooked supper?"

"Uh-uh, and lunch." Ma patted her stomach. "Mighty fine fixin's if I say so myself."

His gaze bounced between Ma and Randi, wondering what to say. He'd observed her several times during the day working side by side with Ma, but he'd assumed she'd been assisting.

"You best take her that water, she's gonna need it to rinse the dishes," Ma said and started to walk toward the fire. Over her shoulder she asked, "When you gonna get her a real stove? I'm thinking I might like tastin' that beef William she talked about."

He caught up with her. "Do you mean Beef Wellington? She knows how to make Beef Wellington?"

Ma nodded. "Yup, she wanted to make it for lunch, but can't without an oven."

His hand tightened on the bucket handle seconds before it slipped out. "I'll be damned," he muttered.

Ma thumped him on the chest. "See how good I am at finding the right gals for my boys. Don't know why you all try and put up such a fuss." She shook her head and then patted the bun of her gray hair as she strolled toward the tent, shoulders squared with pride.

Howard gathered his shocked mind and carried the bucket of water to the supply wagon. He dumped a good amount into the steaming basin of rinse water and began to dip the dishes stacked near it, rinsing the suds away.

The faint light of the moon highlighted the perfect curl of Randi's smile. "Thank you," she offered, "but I can do this, you must be exhausted from working all day." Her head tilted toward the building site. "I can't believe how much you accomplished today."

He didn't stop rinsing, kept piling clean dishes on the other side of the basin. "Yes, we had a good day, but you accomplished just as much. The meals you prepared were very good. Where did you learn to cook so well?"

Her head bowed, and her gaze settled on the wash water. "My mother."

"She must have been an excellent teacher."

"She didn't actually teach me how. I mentioned this morning that her family had a hotel back in New York…"

When she didn't continue, he encouraged her. "Yes, I remember you said that."

"She missed the foods from home, so when I got old enough, I taught myself to cook some of the dishes so she wouldn't be so lonesome for her family." She set the last clean dish down and picked up a thin towel. Moving around him to start drying the ones he'd rinsed, she added, "I've never cooked over an open fire, so I didn't know how things would turn out."

"They turned out perfectly," he mumbled, more to himself than her. The meals were better than his cooking, which was something to be considered. Since he'd been old enough to stand on a stool and stir a pot, he'd been cooking. It had happened by default, he'd been honest when he said Ma didn't know how to cook, never had. When his brothers had jested him, teasing only girls knew how to cook, he'd taken a back role in the cooking, only did so when the coast was clear. It hadn't been until after Kid married Jessie, and he'd taught her how to cook, he'd stepped forward and admitted he enjoyed the task and wanted to cook in a fancy restaurant some day.

The fact Randi knew how to cook was a surprise. Besides teaching Jessie, he'd also taught Lila, his other sister-in-law, which had caused him to believe most young women didn't know how to do much more than boil water. Randi's knowledge was something to take into consideration. He would need assistance in the kitchen, especially during the first few months when he'd be busy getting the business off the ground. Jessie had offered, so had Lila, but they both had small children to look after, and their husbands wouldn't appreciate their wives being gone for any length of time. The Quinter men were very possessive when it came to their women.

A featherlike touch tickled his mind. Perhaps that's where this overwhelming need to protect Randi came from. It was natural, given the way both

Kid and Skeeter guarded their wives, why would he be any different?

A hard tug on the dish in his hand sent his thoughts to dust, and he released the plate. Randi dried it while he continued to rinse the last of the stack. Whether she could cook or not had never been a problem. The problem was her father—the Populist. That was enough to ruin his business before it ever got off the ground.

"Something troubling you?" Randi asked, her voice quivering.

"Hmm...No, no, just have a lot to contemplate," he admitted. "I've scheduled my grand opening for the first of May and have a lot to get done between now and then."

"May first?" She turned and squinted, as if trying to see the building site through the darkness that had befallen. "That certainly is an ambitious goal."

"Yes, but with all the help, I think it's doable."

Her top lip was caught between her teeth, she nibble on it as she took the last dish from the wagon bed. "I'll—I will help in any way possible."

"Meals like you prepared today are a help. Men are always more productive when well fed." He picked up the water basin. "I'll dump these, and then I need to talk to Bug and Snake about tomorrow's duties," he said, needing the time to sort out a few wandering thoughts.

"Thank you, and thank you for helping with the dishes," she said hesitantly.

He mumbled a response and carried the basin away from the camp site. This whole situation just kept getting deeper and deeper. Randi's cooking skills would make her a real asset while the building happened. The men would be well-fed, and Ma would have time to sew the draperies, linens, and uniforms for the wait staff he soon had to hire. He sloshed the water from the pan and stared unseeingly at the stars above. Married or not, it wouldn't be fair of him to ask her for assistance. The marriage was no more her choice than it had been his.

But her help would certainly make his opening date easier to accomplish, and once the hotel was up and running, he'd have a touch more time to decide what to do about their precarious situation. His steps faltered, she'd offered to help, but did she want to? Did she even want to stay in Dodge? He'd never asked what she wanted, not even when she'd told him the story of how she'd ended up in his bed.

He walked back to get the second basin of dirty water and waited near the front of the wagon until Randi had entered the second tent his brother's had erected, the one now holding the contents of the supply wagon. His forehead tightened with a new problem, one that hadn't occurred to him until this moment. Where was she going to sleep tonight?

He quickly emptied the second tub and set it aside before entering Ma's tent. A pair of wire-framed spectacles sat on the end of his mother's nose as she peered at the pages of a magazine.

She glanced up, looking at him over the top rim of the glasses. "At first I thought Lila was silly when she said your employees should have uniforms, but now I think she's right, and I found the perfect outfits for them. Look at these." She held up the pages for him to view.

With a wave of his hand, he said, "I'll look at those later. Randi needs to sleep in here with you."

She set the book on her lap. "In here? There ain't no room for her in here."

"Sure there is." He pointed to the three small cots set up.

"Nope. One's mine, one's Snake's, and one's Bug's. No room for any others."

"Snake and Bug can sleep in my tent."

"You gone daft?" Ma asked.

"No—"

Ma leaped to her feet. Making her interruption to his explanation more abrupt, she tossed the magazine onto her chair. The pages slapped shut. "This here is Dodge City, Hog. Ain't no way two women are gonna sleep in a tent, alone. Uh-uh, no siree! No telling what kinda hoodlum might come sneakin' along of the night."

"The boys and I will be just across the way."

"Yeah, and won't hear us a hollerin' until the hoodlums done broke in. I can't believe you even thought up this harebrained idea in that noggin of yours. Randi's sleepin' in your tent, and your brothers are beddin' down in mine. End of discussion," she said in her no nonsense way.

He couldn't give up yet, the idea of sleeping with Randi every night wasn't distasteful, which is exactly why he couldn't let it happen. Manly urges took over whenever she was near. Actually, that was a lie. A very strong sex drive had wracked his body all day, and the desire hadn't ebbed even while he'd labored as hard as two men.

His voice was an octave too high when he said, "The boys can sleep next door in the supply tent."

"Nope. It's packed full. And that's where I'll be doin' my stitchin', and don't go thinkin' I'll let my stitchin' machine sit outside just cause you're afraid to sleep with your wife." Ma's voice grew louder with each word.

By the time she finished, flames licked at the tops of his ears. He glanced to the doorway, hoping his brother's hadn't heard, yet knowing they had.

"Ma, hush up!"

"Don't tell me to hush up! You may be bigger-'n me, but I'm still your Ma and will wallop you good if'n you don't watch your mouth." Her well-known, don't defy me gaze shot from her blazing eyes.

Howard cowered as if he were still six years old.

"Now, go on, get outta here! I got things ta do before turnin' in." She shooed him to the door with both hands.

The cold night air slapped his cowardly feelings aside, replaced them with anger as he stomped toward the fire where his brothers sat. Randi had rejoined them, his red plaid shirt tucked tight around her seersucker dress. All of their gazes settling on the blaze of the fire said they'd heard at least some, if not all, of Ma's outburst. He ran a hand through his hair.

"Problems, little brother?" Snake asked with a snigger.

He clinched his teeth so hard pain shot across his jaw. Ignoring the low guffaws coming from both of his brothers, he walked over to Randi. "It's awfully chilly out, you best head on into the tent."

Her gaze flashed between Ma's tent and his.

His body was too tense to speak, so he pointed toward his tent.

She stood, clutching the shirt with both hands. "All right. I'll-uh-I'll see you all in the morning. Good night, Bug. Good night, Snake."

Both boys responded by standing and bid her a good night. Her gaze didn't flutter his way but settled on the ground as she turned to walk toward the tent. A tidal wave of regret washed over his body, and he shrank onto a stump near the fire, his back to her sluggish departure.

The silence popped and snapped with more friction than the fire emitted. He ignored it for as long as he could.

"We-uh-gotta lot done today," he said, hoping his brothers could be drawn into a simple conversation.

"Uh-uh," Snake said, a hint of laughter still tickling his voice.

"The blacksmith said he'd have my pipe driver done day after tomorrow," Bug said, clearly trying to hold the humor out of his tone.

Howard nodded. "That's good." With the toe of his boot he nudged a log deeper into the flames and watched bright yellow sparks rise up and disappear above the swirls of smoke. The boys didn't speak, nor did he. What could he say? They'd heard Ma proclaim he was afraid to sleep with his wife. How on earth was a man supposed to respond to that? It wasn't that he was afraid. It was…He swallowed the log in his throat. Damn, he'd never be able to sleep lying next to her. Even sitting here, stinging from the cold of the night, his fingers tingled, wanting to touch her silky skin, caress the curve of her back and examine those perfect dimples—

"Holy shit!" Snake exclaimed under his breath.

Howard snapped his head up. Both of his brothers stared over his shoulders, their mouths agape, and their eyes as round as biscuits.

"What?" he asked, twisting his neck to follow the trail of their gazes. His jaw went lax, the bottom of his chin all but slapped against his chest. The sight he stared at knocked the air out of him harder than being thrown off a wild bucking-bronc.

Inside the canvas, the flickering light of the lantern made his tent glow brighter than the moon. The white, heavy tarp had become pale yellow, and a dark silhouette moved about inside the gently billowing sides. It was a moment before his eyes locked on the shadow and registered what he saw, sending the impulse to his brain.

Randi was undressing, and the light projected each movement against the canvas screen more clearly than the finest painter could create. Her graceful womanly profile moved with perfection, as she drew her gown over her head. The contours of her breasts, flat stomach, the inward arch of her lower back, and her long slender legs became clearly visible to onlookers.

"Shit!" Howard leaped to his feet. Almost as an afterthought, he grabbed the hat off his head and swiped it at both of his brothers, knocking theirs askew. "Turn around!" he demanded before storming off toward his tent.

Jogging across the grass, he shouted, "Randi! Randi! Dowse the light!"

The silhouette inside stalled.

"Dowse the light!" he repeated.

She moved across the interior, met him at the door. "What?" She poked her head out between the flaps.

"Dowse the light!"

"But I'm not done—"

"Dowse the light!" he shouted loud enough to be heard on the other side of Dodge.

"All right," she said and within seconds the tent went dark.

A heavy sigh oozed out of his lungs. The faint sounds of laughter floated on the air. He didn't bother looking back toward his brothers, knew it was worthless to try and subdue their reactions.

When the hard knots of tension let loose a fraction, enough to where he could breathe, he opened the flap and stepped in the dark tent.

Chapter Seven

Randi tugged the covers up to her chin and stared at the ceiling of the tent. Thick heavy foreboding filled the small space. Howard was clearly upset with her, and the knowledge made her tremble from top to bottom. Soft thuds sounded as he undressed and prepared for bed. She'd half-excepted him to find someplace else to sleep after the altercation with his mother, the one where he'd made it as plain as the nose on her face he didn't want to sleep in the same tent as her.

She drew in a breath and tried to find an ounce of grit. "I-uh-I'm sorry," she squeaked.

"Just...go to sleep," he muttered, not necessarily unkind but with a biting edge. A second later, he tugged the blanket aside and slipped between the sheets to lie beside her.

"But really, I'm sorry—"

"Randi." His voice held a tone of warning.

She gulped and tightened her muscles against the shivers. Shame settled upon her like a thick cloud when his deep sigh mingled with the quiet air.

"I-uh..." She had no idea what she wanted to say, just knew she wanted him to know the last thing she wanted was to cause him trouble, and she was dreadfully sorry for whatever had made him so upset.

"You do know that when you light a lamp inside a tent at night people can see in, don't you?" He sounded incredulous.

Utterly confused and still staring at the nondescript tent ceiling, she asked, "What?"

"At night, when its dark out and you light a lamp inside a tent, people can see right through the canvas."

It took a moment for his statement to weave its way through her dulled mind, but when it did, it was as if he'd thrown a bucket of water on her. Anyone who cared to look would have seen her undressing.

"Oh, no," she muttered. "Did Snake and—"

"Yes," he answered.

"Oh, no," she groaned, completely mortified.

"Don't worry about it now, try to get some sleep," he said, flipping onto his side.

She didn't answer but rolled over so her back faced his. *Don't worry about it? Get some sleep?* Now that would be an impossible task. She'd never been so humiliated in her life, and all he could say was get some sleep?

The space between them was wide enough to allow a draft of cold air to flow beneath the blanket. She squeezed her eyes shut and prayed for her body not to shiver against the chill. It didn't work—she started to shake harder than a scared rabbit, probably more from what had just happened than the chilly air.

The mattress shook, and heat instantly covered her back.

"Come here," Howard whispered in her ear as his arms, one under her neck, the other over her waist, pulled her up against his warmth.

The embrace not only sent away the chill but filled her insides with a tender glow. Her mind began to wonder if he'd seen her undressing. The thought didn't cause embarrassment, but something else, and though she'd never experienced it before the feeling was deep, and womanly. Her body heated up a good ten degrees, like a small fire had been built in the very pit of her being.

He wiggled a bit more, fitting his body around

77

hers like frosting on a cake. All of a sudden she felt extremely satisfied and happy. She bit at the smile forming on her lips, a touch fretful at upsetting him again. "I really am sorry," she whispered.

"Shh." The touch of his breath floated over her neck, and his hand, lightly resting on the nightgown Ma had repaired for her today, softly patted her stomach.

Held as such, in the most comforting cuddle imaginable, there was little she could do except float into a relaxing, dreamlike euphoria that soon led to deep slumber.

Hours later, when a pale pink streamer of early morning sun danced across the patch in the center of the tent ceiling, she opened her eyes and found she was alone, tucked inside the covers like a baby in a bunting. Randi wiggled her arms, loosening the tight covers a bit, and glanced around the empty tent. The faint sounds of hammers filtered into the space. She sat up with a start.

The men were already working and here she was sleeping in like a princess in a palace. Her eyes settled on the lamp on the table before she snatched her dress and underclothes from the chair and tugged them under the covers. The task was difficult and took much longer than she wanted, but not willing to stand beside the bed and dress, she didn't flip the blankets off until her dress was settled over her head.

She quickly pulled the skirt down as she stood and then sat down to tug on her socks and shoes. After making up the bed and putting the tent in order, she retrieved Howard's red plaid shirt and exited the area. Crisp, clean morning air met her, and she buttoned the shirt while making her way to the cook site.

A glance over her shoulder didn't reveal any workmen, mainly due to the high walls that had been lifted the day before. The glistening morning sun, barely peeking over the horizon, shined on the new boards, reflecting off the feather swirls of frost still clinging to the structure. Pounding continued to fill the air, and Randi turned about as Ma Quinter stepped out of her tent.

"Land sakes, what time did that fool get up and start poundin'?" the woman asked.

Randi shrugged, used the motion to pull the thick shirt tighter to her body.

"Well, I'll get the fire goin' if'n you wanna get a pot of coffee started."

"All right," Randi agreed and moved to the storage tent. Yesterday, she'd help Ma arrange all of the supplies, more than she'd ever seen at one place and time, in the extra tent. Due to the large chunks of ice packed in sawdust, surrounding the crates of beef Ma had brought, it was colder inside the tent than outside. Blowing into her hands, she quickly gathered the coffee pot and the small tin of ground coffee beans and went back out to break a thin film of ice off the top of the water in the bucket before filling the pot.

Snake and Bug moved about, one adding sticks to the flames taking life in the fire pit, the other hauling an arm load of larger logs to form a pile near the circle of rocks. Her gaze went to Howard's tent and embarrassment of what the boys may have seen the night before blazed into her cheeks.

"Morning, Randi." Bug tipped his hat, a friendly smile covering his face.

From his crouched position, adding yet another log to the fire, Snake quickly offered, "Hey, Randi. Morning." He, too, acted nonchalant, as if nothing had happened the night before.

"Good morning," she replied with a sigh of relief, extremely thankful for their behavior. Perhaps they hadn't seen anything. Perhaps she had dowsed the light before anyone besides Howard saw her undressing.

"Didn't Hog sleep a'tall?" Bug asked.

"Excuse me?" she asked.

Bug gestured toward the building site with his head, dark brown eyes squinting with what looked like frustration. "Hog, didn't he sleep at all last night?"

"I-uh..." she started, but stopped, wondering if Howard had slept. She had—like a baby. As a matter of fact with the warmth of his arms cradling her like a newborn, she had never slept so well—ever. Her brows pulled taut on her forehead. When had he left the comfort of the bed? She hadn't awakened all night, not until the pounding had filtered into her dreams. Hot blood rushed into her cheeks. The dream had been quite pleasurable and shocking to her now awake virginal mind. She squeezed her eyes shut, forcing the late night visions from her mind.

The blush, as well as the increased beat of her heart, made her gulp for air and rush to the tri-pod to find something to occupy her. Squeezing her shaking fingers, which had nothing to do with the chilly morning air, she tried to make them function enough to spoon coffee grounds into the water and then set the pot atop the small grate.

"I swear I'd just fallen asleep when his blasted pounding started," Bug said, still gazing at the work site.

"You know your brother has had his tail tied in a knot to get this restaurant up and running. Quit belly-aching and get over there to help him," Stephanie Quinter said as she rounded the tent. "We'll have breakfast ready in half an hour." She waved a hand to Snake. "You get, too!"

The boys grumbled under their breaths but sauntered off toward the building, and Stephanie turned to Randi.

"You know how to make sausage gravy?"

"Yes, ma'am."

"Well, get to it. I'll gather the leftover biscuits from last night," Stephanie instructed, pulling the thick shawl around her shoulders tighter. "Ain't none to warm yet in the mornings. I told that boy to wait until April, but, oh no, he wants it up and running by May. No patience, I tell ya, none of my boys ain't got no patience."

It appeared as if the woman was waiting for her to agree, so Randi nodded, but didn't comment as she moved to the supply tent. Her eyes once again wandered to the half-built structure. More men began to arrive, some on foot, some on horseback, and she recognized several as ones who'd helped the day before.

By the time she walked out of the tent, hands full of breakfast supplies, the site looked like an ant hill, workers scurrying every direction and with precise movements completing their specific tasks. She sliced potatoes to fry in one pan, while the sausage began to sizzle in another. The cooking soon consumed her, and thoughts of Howard's short night were sent to the rear crevices of her mind.

When the meal was cooked to perfection, Stephanie lifted the large iron triangle out of the back of the supply wagon and split the air by banging against it with a short rod. The loud ringing echoed in Randi's ears long after the woman tossed the object back into the wagon.

The Quinter brothers walked around the wall simultaneously, and the breath stalled in Randi's throat. Walking side by side, the three men created quite a scene. Tall and muscular, with just enough swaggers in their strides to make anyone, man or woman, take a second look, each one was uncommonly handsome. Bug was the shortest, but only by less than an inch or so. His dark eyes and hair made him look like a cousin instead of a brother.

Not that she knew much about cousins, never having any herself, but the way Howard and Snake resembled each other, there was no doubt they were brothers. Snake was a touch shorter than Howard, who walked in the middle, talking to a brother on each side. Howard and Snake both had blond hair that wasn't curly but a touch more than wavy. Their eyes were a unique gray-green. Silently, she decided it was the way Howard's eyes danced that made his face more handsome. He was also broader than his brothers. Snake and Bug weren't skinny, but they weren't as bulky as Howard. There was no doubt to the amount of strength in his arms, she'd felt the hard muscles yesterday and the protection they offered last night.

Something tingled in the root of her stomach. She lifted her eyes. Howard's gaze captured her like a rabbit in a snare. Her face sizzled as if she'd been standing over a hot stove. A wide smile formed on his lips, displaying a straight line of white teeth. Her heart jolted, and her knees wobbled. Thankfully, the pan of potatoes in her hand didn't land on the ground.

Randi squared her shoulders and sucked in a deep breath. She turned back to the food. Life certainly had thrust her into an unknown plane. Focused on feeding the brothers, the cooking managed to keep her feet on the ground and head out of the sky, until Howard spoke.

Clasping her hands to her chest, against the pitter-patter, she turned about. "Excuse me?"

He waved a hand toward the table. "Aren't you going to join us?"

"No, no, go ahead and eat. I'll get something after you're all done." She moved to the fire to transfer the pot of coffee.

"I'll get it. You go sit down," Howard said from near her elbow, his fingers already grasping the handle.

"No, really, I'll get it." She reached for the pot, but was too slow. He quickly snatched it out of her reach.

With one hand carrying the coffee, he turned her about with his other hand, and then folded the arm over her shoulders. "Come on. The boys won't bite."

"What?"

"My brothers, they won't bite you." A crooked grin creased his face, and his eyes twinkled down upon her with more sparkle than the Christmas Star.

"I didn't think they would," she admitted as a warm mellow commotion wafted through her chest. She would like to ponder on how he did it, how he made her feel comfortable and at ease with a simple look. But couldn't, because his nearness also sent her heart racing. It was all quite perplexing and wonderful at the same time. They sat and soon the chatter and companionship at the table drew her in. She'd never enjoyed a meal so immensely.

Empty plates sat before them, and while Bug entertained everyone with a tale of how one of the workers had nailed his own shirtsleeve to the wall yesterday, squeals interrupted their small group. A shiver rippled Randi's shoulder, and she turned to stare down the road. The screams were female and very hostile.

"Sounds like someone ain't happy down at Danny J's," Snake said seconds before a gunshot sliced the air.

Randi leaped to her feet, hitched her skirts, and without further thought or ado, took off in a dead run.

For a split, dazed second, Howard watched

Randi leaping over sticks and larger patches of tall grass before he jumped and took off after her.

"Randi!"

She could outrun a deer, but luckily, he caught up with her on the road, before she barreled into the middle of two women tearing at each other like mountain cats. He grasped her by the waist, but her feet continued to run in the air near his knees.

"Whoa, up!"

She twisted about like a squirming fish. "Corrine! I have to help Corinne!"

Howard wrapped one arm around her waist and plucked her under his arm like a sack of feed. He took a few steps away from the dust being stirred by the fighting women rolling across the dirt in front of the gate surrounding Danny J's big house.

Beneath his hand, her heart pounded faster than a caged rabbit. He set her on her feet and kept a tight hold on her, while he turned to the screams and screeches. The blue silk and long ringlets of one of the wrestling women did resemble Corinne Martin.

Danny J, dressed as always in a black velvet jacket with tails that fluttered behind his knees, tugged at his lapels as he walked into the middle of the road. "Girls!" he shouted. "Girls!"

The two women, Corrine Martin, and Danny's other number one gal, Opal Smith, didn't even acknowledge the man had spoken as they wrenched one another's hair and scratched with long nails. Jagged, bleeding abrasions covered their arms and faces as they continued to scrape and scuttle, howling and yelling at each other.

Danny J should have known this day was coming, Howard surmised. No man can have two number one women. It had been a conversation held by several men, himself included, once or twice over the past few years.

A crowd had formed, besides men from his work site and women from Danny J's, several town folks ran up the street to gawk and cheer. Howard twisted about, looked for someone he could pass Randi to. He figured he'd better step in and put a stop to Corrine and Opal's battle before they blinded one another with their nails.

Both of his brothers were on the other side of the women. He tried to catch their attention, but their gazes were glued to the billowing petticoats and long legs of Corrine and Opal as they rolled around the ground.

Opal scrambled to her feet, stumbling to gain her footing. The next instant, she squared a little pearl-handled derringer at Corrine's heaving bosoms.

"No!" Randi yelled, and Howard had to increase his hold to keep her from leaping forward.

"Opal! Put the gun down!" he shouted above the roar of the crowd.

Danny J stepped forward, stationing himself between the two women. "Opal!"

"Move out of the way, Danny! You was mine long 'afore she came along!" Black kohl smeared across Opal's face made her look like a raccoon. A very pissed off raccoon.

Danny held up one hand. "Opal—"

"No, I've had enough! She's gotten away with enough!" The gun shook as Opal shouted. "I told you about that gal she was hiding in the alcove, but you didn't do nothin' about it. All I wanted was a new red dress, Danny. A red one, not some blue thing she picked out!" Her eyes settled on Danny. "Move or I'll shoot ya both!"

"Opal, you're not gonna shoot anyone!" Danny yelled.

Corrine sidestepped around Danny, a matching derringer clutched in her hand. "We'll settle this fair and square, Opal."

"No!" Danny reached out, but Corrine was quicker, ducking away from his grasp.

The gun in her hand waved at the other woman. "On the count of three, Opal. One, two—"

A shot rang out followed by a loud, pain-filled wail. Smoke swirled from the end of Opal's gun.

With a terrorized scream of her own, Randi wrapped both arms around him and buried her head deep into his chest. Holding her tight, Howard brushed her billowed hair away from his face to see who'd shot whom. Wide-eyed with shock, he watched Danny J slither to the ground. Both Opal and Corrine threw their guns to the dirt and flew to Danny's sides, screeching and howling all over again.

Chapter Eight

Howard guided Randi into the tent and assisted her to sit on the edge of the bed. "Are you doing all right?"

"Yes," she half-mumbled while bobbing her head.

The tent flap slapped open before he had a chance to say anything more. Ma looking more flustered than a startled grouse flew through the opening. "What the devil was goin' on out there? Who got shot? Are they dead?"

"Ma—"

She didn't stop talking to listen. "The caterwauling was enough to make skin crawl, and I couldn't see past the crowd. Speak up now, who was it?"

He walked over and twisted her back toward the door with both hands. "Just some girls down at Danny J's. Bug and Snake can tell you about it." He gestured toward Randi with his head.

Ma's eyes grew wide. "Oh, all right," she whispered, but before she stepped out of the tent she added, "Her folks are here to see her."

A stream of ice water ran through his veins, and a twitch formed in his cheek. He flinched at both. "We'll be out in a minute."

Ma nodded and tugged the canvas flap shut behind her exit. Howard ran his hands over his face. Not only had he barely slept last night, his body still ached from holding Randi's lush, perfect body for hours, and now he had to deal with her irritating father again. He took a fortifying breath and was about to turn around when the flap opened again.

A hand holding a folded telegram stretched into the space. "This just arrived for ya," Ma said, waving the note.

He took it, and her hand disappeared. Unfolding the paper, he quickly read a single line. 'Looking forward to meeting your in-laws stop Skeeter stop.' A smile tugged on his lips. *Perhaps there is a God, and he loves me.* Howard tucked the paper into his pants pocket and turned to Randi.

Expectant brown eyes gazed at him. He mustered up a smile, just for her, one that came from the center of his chest.

"Doing all right?" he asked.

"Yes," she said and scooted over as if to make room for him to sit next to her.

He crossed the room and sat in the space. For lack of anything better to say, he said, "I'm sure Corrine is just fine. There's no need to worry."

"I imagine you're right." Her gaze floated around the room.

"Do—"

"I—"

They started simultaneously, both stopping so the other could speak. "Go ahead," he encouraged after a moment of silence.

"I was just going to ask if fights like that happen a lot," she said.

"I don't rightly know. That was the first one I saw."

She gave an agreeing nod. "Me, too." Her head began to shake negatively. "I can't believe Opal shot Danny J."

"It was just a flesh wound. He'll be fine."

Her gaze settled on the far wall, and she nodded again.

Another long silence ensued. He swallowed, rubbed his chin, swallowed again, and then finally said, "Well, I guess your pa is here to see you."

She didn't make a move to rise. "Yes, I heard Ma say that."

"You don't have to see him, if you don't want to."

"Yes, I do." Her shoulders slumped as she let out a long sigh.

He wrapped an arm around her, and her head slipped onto his shoulder as if it belonged there.

"No, you don't. I can tell him you're not up to it."

"He'll just wait until I am up to it. Besides, he expects me, and no one keeps Thurston Fulton waiting." A grain of aggravation flavored her words.

Howard wasn't sure how to respond. He'd be happy if he never had to see Thurston Fulton again, happier still if Randi never had to see the man again. But he was her father, and if there was one thing Ma had instilled in her sons, it was that family was all a man had in the world. A heavy weight settled on his shoulders. Like it or not, it appeared Thurston Fulton was now his family as well. He leaned over to press his cheek against the top of her hair.

His mind was flapping about like a tweety-bird in a wind storm. What surfaced and came out his mouth almost surprised him. "Randi, do you want to stay here? Want to help get the hotel and restaurant started?"

She went stiff in his hold.

He held his breath. Would he ever master the ability of small talk? Probably not, his big old mouth just took to spurting when it wanted to. But damn if his heart didn't want to know her answer.

"Yes. Yes, I do." She hesitated for a moment before asking, "Do you want me to stay?"

The air locked in his lungs slipped out, and he closed his eyes. "Of course I do," he admitted, knowing he'd never said a sentence that held more truth in all of his life. The whole thing was complicated, had him twisted in more knots than a rope ladder. It was almost as if he couldn't imagine what life had been like without her and really didn't want to return to a life without her. And damned if he didn't know how it all had happened.

"I…" She shook her head, as if to stop herself from speaking.

"You what?"

She didn't move.

"You what?" he repeated.

"Well, I just don't want my being here to interfere with your plans." She bit her lip. "My—uh—family can be a bit tiresome. I don't want them to interrupt your work."

He slipped his other hand into his pocket, pulled out the note, and flipped it open with his thumb. "Well, about that," he said. "I have a plan."

"A plan?"

His lips brushed the fluff of her hair before he sat up straight. "Yes, a plan." It was a gamble, he knew, him against her father, but he took the bet and held the note before her eyes.

She scanned the telegram. "Meet your in-laws?" Her gaze moved to his face. "Skeeter? Your brother who lives out by the badlands?"

He nodded.

"He wants to meet my father?"

Not wanting to influence her decision making, he didn't speak, just nodded again.

The most adorable sparkle he'd ever seen appeared in her eyes.

"Tell me your plan," she whispered with a hint of delight.

A chuckle rumbled up his chest, but he quelled it. He had to tell her the truth.

"I have to warn you, Skeeter doesn't think much of politicians."

She grimaced. "He doesn't? Why not?"

"He's had to deal with a lot of politics with his fossils."

"Oh." A thoughtful frowned formed on her face. "Will he hurt them?"

"No, not physically anyway. Lila won't let that happen, but Skeeter might mentally badger them, and his friend, Buffalo Killer, might frighten them."

Her brows formed perfect arches. "They know about us, about the-the marriage?"

"I sent Skeeter a wire yesterday."

"Why?"

"Because it's going to be hard for me to get things done with your father and Belinda here," he said, hoping she didn't see through his somewhat white lie. "Your father said he wanted to meet the rest of my family."

"What about Belinda?"

"She'll go with him."

Her lips quivered and puckered, as if she was fighting a grin from forming. It finally won out.

"For how long?"

He shrugged, tried to look as if he didn't relish the thought of getting rid of her father and the irksome Belinda.

"As long as they want."

"And that will give you time to focus on your hotel," she said, clearly a thought coming out aloud. She stood up and smoothed her skirt with both hands before she held one out to him. "I believe I like your plan." As her fingers wrapped around his, she added, "I believe I like this plan very much."

Hand in hand they left the tent, and Randi fought hard to keep her wondering mind at bay. He'd said he wanted her to stay. And if her father and Belinda left—went to see Skeeter, she would have time to concentrate on helping with the hotel. She could cook, and help Ma sew, and she wouldn't have to worry about Belinda putting a stop to it all.

****

Her father and Belinda didn't stay long, especially not after they heard of the invitation to travel to the badlands. While Howard explained traveling directions to her father, Belinda took her arm, forcing her to walk to the black rented carriage. They stopped near the gray mare hitched to the buggy, standing in a small amount of shade from one of the only trees about, a lonely elm with tear drop leaves.

Randi stared at the branches, having no idea what Belinda wanted, but instantly braced herself for whatever was about to come. She could only imagine it would be how she must never be seen wearing an apron or serving a meal. It just wouldn't be seemly for the next governor's daughter to look like hired help. She'd heard it all before, too often to forget.

Belinda glanced about, assuring their privacy no doubt, and then took a step closer. She raised one long finger and pointed it sternly at Randi's face.

"You better not ruin this."

Randi lowered her gaze to her toes, wondering exactly what *this* she pertained to this time.

"You almost ruined your father's chance at becoming governor by running off. Edward Keyes had already paid a tidy sum to wed you."

"What?"

"You heard me. We need a goodly sum to repay him, and it's up to you to get it."

"Me?" A glob of dread settled in Randi's stomach.

"Yes, you. You better make sure the Quinter family forks over a hefty donation to your father's campaign."

Randi glanced around, spied her father and Howard still standing near the outdoor table.

"What if they don't have the money?"

"Don't have the money?" Belinda let out an evil laugh. "Don't you know who you married?"

Of their own free will, Randi's shoulders shrugged. Whether it was out of confusion or to chase away the shiver rippling up her back, she wasn't quite sure.

Belinda rolled her eyes and let out a long exasperating sigh. "Kid Quinter's ranch is one of the largest in the state, and Skeeter is a millionaire because of the fossils found on his property."

"But I'm not married to Kid or Skeeter," Randi explained.

Belinda lifted a hand, and Randi flinched, ready for the slap. Her stepmother must have had second thoughts, because she lowered the hand without striking.

"Nonetheless, you married a Quinter, and you will get that donation for your father. A very large one." She whipped around and climbed into the buggy.

Before Randi had a chance to reply, a hand settled on her shoulder. She glanced up and met Howard's gaze. A frown tugged his brows tight.

"Are you all right?"

She nodded, but couldn't speak. Could do little more than offer a small wave as her father climbed in the buggy. She watched as he and Belinda drove away. *How much money constituted a very large donation?*

****

Two weeks flew by faster than Randi could blink. From the time the sun rose in the morning until it set in the evening, Howard, his brothers, and a flock of workmen, sawed, pounded, and mixed mud, creating a magnificent brick building that had created a buzz rolling through the streets of Dodge louder than the ever present rail cars. Every day people, some just moseying by to look, others stopping to sell wares and services, and some hoping to find work, flocked to the area.

Randi was busy as well. She not only fed her husband and his brothers three meals a day, but also provided the noon meal for the workmen. The work kept her active, and besides cooking, there was the constant trail of people who, for the most part, stopped by the tent instead of the building site to ask questions. By the time night rolled around, she was exhausted and usually fell asleep long before Howard stepped into the tent. However, the moment he did, a sixth sense would rouse her enough to move over, give him the warm spot on the bed, and wait for his arms to mold her back against his chest before allowing her to fall asleep again.

Now, during an unusual lull, her gaze automatically went to the building where men stacked dozens of rock-red bricks on top of each other, plastering thick mortar between each one. She twisted slightly toward a silent draw. Howard stood on the front steps, and their gazes met. A very familiar stir rolled across her stomach, filling her insides with pleasure she'd become accustomed to, and yet, one she wondered about steadily. It was an extraordinary mixture of joy and longing—quite perplexing.

Howard tipped the brim of his hat, a simple social gesture that tickled her from the inside out. As natural as breathing, she lifted a hand, responded by wiggling her fingers in a downright silly wave that made her giggle aloud.

"If'n ya don't quit makin' googly-eyes, your bread's gonna be burnt crisp," Ma Quinter's gruff voice broke the silent communication and made Randi twist about to glance at the Dutch oven holding two loaves of bread for supper.

When the heat in her cheeks cooled enough to promise she was able to speak, Randi assured, "It's not going to burn," then added for good measure, "and I wasn't making googly-eyes at anyone."

Ma gave out a guffaw. "Yeah, and I ain't got five sons either." She grabbed Randi's arm. "Come take a gander at the curtains I just finished. They're some of my best work, if I say so myself."

Randi paused at the doorway, unable to follow the other woman into the tent due to the remembrance of yesterday flashing before her eyes. The breakfast dishes had been done and water for laundry heating over the fire when Ma had said if Randi wanted a bath she should do it before they started washing clothes. Determining the men wouldn't return to the camp for several hours, she'd accepted the invitation and quickly set about dragging the large tub into the center of Ma's tent and filling it with buckets of water.

The other woman had stood guard outside the tent, and Randi had taken her time washing away the fine sand the non-stop wind settled into her hair. She'd completed bathing and had just stood to retrieve a towel when the flap had slapped open. Assuming it was Ma, she'd stretched over to pick up the cotton when a startled, "Sweet Lord," rumbled the interior.

Looking much like a startled deer, Howard had stood in the doorway, his eyes glued to her breasts. She'd been just as shocked and just as incapable of moving. Then he'd twisted about and bolted. The entire tent had shuddered and flapped. His feet had become tangled in the canvas of the doorway. She'd grabbed the towel and leaped out of the tub as the tent came crashing down around her. It had been difficult, but she'd managed to garb herself while crouching next to the tub. By the time she'd crawled out of the tent, Ma had stopped shouting at Howard long enough to assist him in repairing the toppled center pole.

He'd left the camp without a word, his face prickled red. Ma had giggled half of the morning, but thankfully when it was time to serve lunch, she'd quit sniggering, and Howard seemed to have dismissed the encounter, for he was as polite and kind as always during the meal.

"You coming in or not?" Ma poked her head out the flap.

"Yes, I'm coming," Randi said, hoping her blistering face didn't give away her thoughts and ducked into the tent.

Yards of deep blue fabric covered every spare inch of the small area. Drapes, fringed with long tassels and gold ropes were spread out on all three cots.

"These are beautiful." Randi moved forward to run a finger over the thick velvet.

"Yeah, they are, aren't they?" Ma picked up another bolt of cloth, gold brocade with swirls of blue velvet. "This here is what I'm using to make the tablecloths."

"Oh, my. It's gorgeous." Randi glanced about. "What about napkins? We could use both blue and gold. Wouldn't that be pretty?"

"Hey, good idea. I'll go down to the mercantile and see if'n Mr. Street can order me in some. I hadn't thought of the napkins yet."

"It's going to be wonderful isn't it? The hotel, I mean. It will surely be the best one in the world."

"Yup, I'm thinking so."

Randi continued to finger the material, completely caught up in the thought of the fancy restaurant and hotel. The opening date was getting closer every day, and her hopes that her father, well mainly Belinda, would stay away at least until she had a chance to see it all in operation grew stronger every day. The peace and harmony her life held was so wonderful. She never wanted it to end, but the reality that hung out in the back of her mind told her it would as soon as her family returned. Then, of course, there was the fact she was expected to secure a large donation.

She tried to ignore the nagging tension tugging at her, the one that said get the donation or else. She knew the or *else*. Had seen the wrath of her father before, but it had never been directed at her. Her mother, no matter how worn and ragged by the tuberculosis, had always found the energy to put herself in the path of Thurston Fulton, protecting Randi until the day she died.

Randi let out a distressing sigh. The loss of her mother had the capability of infusing raw pain in an instant. She pressed a hand to the burning behind her eyes, realizing it wasn't just Mama's death plaguing her. She wanted to stay here. Stay in Dodge and help Howard with the hotel. Prove to him, and maybe to herself, that she could become a wife, possibly even a mother someday. She and Howard were getting along just fine and dandy. However, it wasn't like they had a real marriage, one with all the amenities. She dug the heels of her palms into her eyes, somewhat embarrassed to admit, even just to herself, that she and Howard weren't intimate.

Problem was she was at a loss as to how to rectify the situation. It wasn't right, she thought, to want to further their relationship in the marital way, but she had to. She had these wonderful happy dreams where she was pregnant and Howard promised he'd never send her away. In those dreams she had the family she'd always longed for.

She'd even gone down to Danny J's, hoping her aunt would have some insight as to what she could do to spark Howard's interest, but both times the woman answering the door had said Aunt Corrine was indisposed and couldn't be disturbed.

Her stomach churned with a sick feeling, one that said her plan was deceiving and unjust. A consoling touch fell upon her shoulder.

"Are you all right?" Ma asked, concerned.

Randi nodded with false confidence, not trusting her ability to speak.

"Well, then let's check the bread, if'n it's done we can head to town," Ma said.

Randi took a deep breath, willed strength to keep her voice from cracking. "I'll see to the bread. You go ahead and go to town to see about the material for the napkins and the other items."

"Don't you want to go to town with me?"

The opening of the tent had been tied back, letting the sun and warm air flow in. Randi paused in the doorway and let out a heavy disgusted sigh.

"What for?"

"I don't know. Ain't you needin' anything?"

Her gaze floated across the way, settled on the big building. "No, I don't think I can buy what I need," she mumbled.

"When are you two gonna quit your tomfoolery?"

"What?"

Ma Quinter stood beside her, arms folded over her bosoms. "When are you two gonna make that bed you've been sleeping in a real marriage bed?"

She pressed a hand to her hot cheek, completely wondering if her mother-in-law had read her mind.

"Ma," she groaned.

"What ya so embarrassed about? I'd say the way you two are carrying on should be the embarrassing part."

"Ma—"

"Quit Mawing me! You sound like a sick calf." Ma waved a hand toward the building site. "What's wrong with that son of mine? I can tell the two of you are head over heels within' each other."

"Ma," Randi said sternly. Shaking her head, she

walked on somewhat shaky legs to the fire pit. "There is nothing wrong with your son." The need to come to Howard's defense was too strong to hold in.

"Then why ain't you two shaking the mattress?" Ma had followed, standing inches behind her.

"Ma!"

"I said stop that." Ma grasped her arm, forced her to twist about. "Talk to me, girl, tell me what's wrong."

"There isn't anything *wrong*," Randi said, shaking her head.

"Oh, yes, there is. Those boys of mine are as hot blooded as their pa."

Randi choked on the lump in her throat, had to swallow hard to keep from fully gagging. She couldn't possibly tell Ma how she thought about their marriage bed almost nonstop lately. Her body ached with a need eating her from the inside out. A natural, inborn sense told her what she hungered for, but Howard seemed perfectly content to just hold her during the long nights. It wasn't a woman's place to be forward, to talk about such things, yet the fact he didn't want to do those things with her was also something she worried about—constantly.

Ma took her hand, leading her to the table. Randi sat down and covered her face with both hands, hiding her blazing cheeks, but also to keep the tears from sprouting. She wasn't a wife. She was little more than something else for him to take care of—at a time when Howard had more than enough to worry about. That's all she'd ever been to anyone—one more thing to worry about. She most likely was a disappointment to him, too. And then of course there was the donation.

"What's wrong, Randi?"

The kindness in Ma's voice made her stomach sink to her shoes.

"Come on, sweetie, you can tell me," Ma

encouraged.

"I can't—" a hiccup interrupted her.

"Can't what?"

She shook her head, tried to come up with something to say. "We aren't really married."

"Ain't really married?" Ma sounded shocked. "What you talking about? That was a real preacher Bug hauled in here."

"No, I mean we *are* married. But only because we were forced to be." She let out a burning sigh, and quivered. "When my father returns, I'll go back to Topeka with him and Belinda."

"Over my dead body!" Ma slapped the table.

Randi wiped the moisture from her eyes. Building the restaurant and hotel had to be so expensive. There was no way she was going to beg money from him. Not for any reason.

"Howard has so much on his mind with the restaurant and all. I completely understand. And I'm very thankful he's let me stay here this long." A clump of regret the size of a cast iron kettle settled in her stomach. "I guess I'm just a failure at everything I try."

"A failure? Poppycock! If that boy of mine—"

Randi laid a hand over Ma's. "Please, Ma, please don't say or do anything. I don't want him to do something he doesn't want to just—just for my sake."

Like a fish out of water, Ma opened and closed her mouth several times. Her cheeks grew bright red before she said, "I'm going to town."

"Please, Ma?" Randi begged with her eyes. "Please don't say or do anything."

A loud huff floated from her lips. "I ain't gonna say or do anything. I don't know what's goin' on in that pretty head of yours, but in my mind it's a crock of gobbly-gook." With a huff she turned about, and arms pumping at her sides, Ma stormed down the trail to the road. The stiff heels of her men's work boots stirred up plumes of dust with each step.

Randi bowed her head. There had been plenty of times when she'd wished there was a way to turn back time. If there was she'd go back to the farm, where it was just she and Mama. Or maybe go back farther, and completely erase her miserable life from existence. That would be the only way to save Howard, protect the entire Quinter family from her father.

****

Howard watched his mother march away from the campsite. A deep frown tugged on his brows before he turned to the tents. Randi rose from the table and meandered over to the fire pit like the weight of the world bore down on her. His nostrils flared. What had his mother done? He should have known everything had been too smooth. Ma wasn't always the most couth person. There were times when he'd seen her be downright rude to folks. But to be honest, those folks normally had it coming.

His gaze turned once again and followed Ma's trail. She seemed to like Randi, fluttered around her like a mother hen, and he really couldn't remember a time when she'd been impolite or bad mannered to his sisters-in-law. Then again, neither Kid nor Skeeter would ever allow someone to mistreat Jessie or Lila. Was that it? Had someone been rude to Randi and he hadn't seen it? Hadn't been there to protect her?

He searched the building site, letting his gaze jump from man to man. There wasn't one he could think of that had done or said anything. His roaming eyes moved to the road, settled on Danny J's. Ire coiled in his guts like a snake.

Opal had left the day of the shooting. Sporting a black eye and with deep scratches still bleeding. Danny J had ordered her out of town. The man's silver snuff box had stopped her bullet from doing any damage. Randi had been down to see her aunt a couple times, and he, too, had gone to see Danny J and knew the man was doing fine. His hand went lax, and the hammer tumbled to the floor.

Danny had told him when he was tired with his new wife to let him know, had said if he'd seen how beautiful Randi was before she ran away, he'd have never let her go. Howard had laughed it off, assured Danny he had no intentions of ever growing tired of his wife, but had Danny or Corrine asked her to move back in? Was she considering it?

His hands balled into fists. He squared his shoulders and ignored the fact his march resembled his mother's as he stormed across the yard toward the road. *Damn that man!* He'd let the man know just how serious he was when it came to Randi. No little snuff box would save Danny J this time.

"Howard?" Her soft voice called. The sound made him cringe slightly, but wasn't enough to make him forgo his mission.

Her soft fragrance filled his nose even before she arrived at his elbow. "Where are you going in such a hurry?" she said, slightly huffing.

Little more than a slight grunt exited his throat, partially because her nearness, as usual, made his heart flutter until he was afraid it would jump right out of his chest. It was as if a full-blown thunderstorm erupted inside him with all the snapping and cracking. And, also as usual, his heart found a way to get itself tangled around his throat. In that instant, while he was just about being choked to death, he couldn't quite remember where he'd been going.

Her fingers settled on his arm, the light touch brought his feet to a halt.

"Where are you going?" she repeated.

"I-uh." His gaze settled on the big house at the

end of the road, and he swallowed, sent his heart back down to his chest where it burned from the striking lightning bolts.

"I was going to see Danny J."

"What for?"

He folded his arms, blood pounding in his neck. "Has he asked you anything?"

"Danny J?" she asked, brows furrowed.

"Yes," he said a bit harshly. The toe of one foot tapped the ground.

Her gaze went to the house. "No, what would Danny J want to ask me? I've never even spoken to the man."

Foolishness showered him like a spring rain, and his neck became warm as blood rushed to his face. A response didn't form in his mind.

She glanced back to him and rubbed her hands over her arms. "And I hope to keep it that way. He scares me."

Those big brown eyes held a gaze that rippled right through him, and his hands rose to caress her upper arms.

"There's nothing to fear. I won't let anyone harm you."

"I know," she murmured and took a step forward. Her head nestled against his chest. "I just wish I wasn't such a burden to you."

He took a step back, forced her to look up at him. "Did Ma say you were a burden? 'Cause if she did—"

She pressed a finger to his lips, and her chest heaved with a sigh. "No, Ma didn't say anything. I just know I am. I've always been a burden. Ask my father. Ask Belinda, or Aunt Corrine." Her eyes glistened with unshed tears.

A familiar wave of dislike roamed up, made his lips pucker and the urge to wring Thurston Fulton's neck struck him like a snake bite. "Your father doesn't—"

Her finger increased its pressure. "Please. I don't want to argue about my father."

He didn't want to argue about her father either. The touch of her finger, though slight and truly insignificant, had lit a flame of desire in the pit of his soul. The fire rising up his loins could set the warning bell off at the newly built fire station down on Front Street. Before he could fathom a reason not to, he folded his hands over her cheeks, held her face still, and pressed his lips to hers.

It had been weeks since he'd kissed her—really kissed her, tongue and all. The taste, that irresistible sweetness, was like the first bite of a luscious dessert and instantly made him want more.

She tilted her head, and he took it as an invitation to delve deeper. His hands, while roaming her back, pulled her close so their bodies, from knees to shoulders, could merge. Her arms wrapped around his waist and featherlike touches floated up and down his back. The effect sent waves of pleasure gushing hard enough to make his head swoon and caused his manhood to stand upright and throb.

Chapter Nine

A rumble of a wagon or maybe the hooting of men made Howard lift his head. It took a moment for the haze to clear enough for him to see the group of workmen whooping and hollering from the building site, and the wagon carrying Randi's Aunt Corrine rolling up the road.

"Good-afternoon, Mr. and Mrs. Quinter," Corrine Martin said as she waggled her fingers. The wagon rolled completely past, and Corrine's high giggle, wafting in the air faded, before he pulled his eyes to Randi. The last thing he wanted to do was embarrass her and making a complete spectacle in the middle of the road, had to top the cake for embarrassing moments.

Her face wasn't red with anger or embarrassment. Instead her eyes shone with something he could only interpret as merriment. Actually, her whole face glowed as if she'd swallowed the sun. Happiness flew about his insides like a flock of butterflies.

She slipped her hands away from his waist.

"Well, I suppose I should let you get on your way," she said, her eyes following the wagon.

"Uh?"

One of her hands rose, a finger pointed at the big house down the road. "You said you were on your way to seeing Danny J. Looks like he and Corrine are back now."

"Oh, it wasn't important," he said.

They stood in the road for a moment, each glancing about before their gazes met and held onto one another for an extended length of time. The chirps of birds flying overhead and the pounding of the men, who'd forgotten the show and returned to work filled the warm air.

"I—uh, I have bread to check." She twisted, pulled her gaze from his, but didn't move.

"I'll help you." He took her elbow, and together, companionably, they walked across the area. There was something comforting and gratifying about walking beside her, almost as if she were a very dear friend.

She was a dear friend, more than a dear friend. He'd already concluded that. Problem was he really didn't know what to do about it. The thought of marriage had long since settled, and he had to admit, he liked the notion. Liked waking to her every morning, liked sleeping with her every night, other than the fact sexual tension was driving him insane. He'd even contemplated making a mid-night trip up to Danny J's, but knew that would be extremely awkward if anyone found out, which was sure to happen no matter how discreet he tried to make it.

Besides, it wasn't just sex he wanted, he wanted his wife—*his wife*. Damn if that wasn't an overpowering thought. Randi was his wife. He glanced her way.

She'd said she wanted to stay, wanted to help with the hotel, but she'd never said she wanted to be his wife. And he couldn't force her to—that certainly wouldn't be right.

"Howard, can I ask you something?"

She stood beside the fire, replacing the lid after checking on her bread. Her cooking skills even surpassed his, something he'd realized after that first day. He'd not only accepted the fact, but liked it.

"Never mind," she said.

106

"No," he said, comprehending his delay in response was the reason she retracted her question.

"No, go ahead, ask anything you want."

Nibbling on her bottom lip, she shook her head. "No, never mind," she said nervously.

He stepped forward, took both of her hands. Caressing the backs with his thumbs, partial to the feel of her skin, he said, "No, I mean it, ask anything you want."

"No—"

"Randi," he interrupted. "Ask me."

Randi froze, couldn't even swallow around the lump in her throat. How could she have thought about asking him such a thing? It was foolish, so very stupid. Of course he regretted marrying her. The bravado, the boldness his kiss had instilled, washed away and left behind nothing but idiocy.

"Randi?" he repeated.

"I was just wondering how the building was coming along," she lied.

His brows pulled together, and she stilled her breathing, hoping he wouldn't see through her fib and force her to tell the truth.

"The building site?" he asked with disbelief.

"Uh-huh." She nodded, trying to act nonchalant, making her fib more believable.

His gaze bounced between her and the building before he said, "Come on, I'll give you a tour."

"You will?" A sense of excitement rose beyond the regret shrouding her. She'd wanted to see the site, but hadn't dared to ask.

"Sure, take your bread off the fire, and we'll go."

Regrettably, she had to answer, "It's not done yet."

"The Dutch oven will keep it cooking, by the time the oven is cool, the bread will be baked." He moved over, and using the hot pads lying nearby on the table, he removed the large cast iron kettle from

107

the flames.

"Are you sure?"

"Yes, I've done it a million times over the years."

"You have?" she asked as they started to walk toward the building.

"Yes, I have. I've always liked cooking. That's why I decided to build a hotel and restaurant. At first I was going to write cookbooks, but realized I like the actual cooking more than writing down the recipes. What about you, what did you want to be when you grew up?" He took her hand as they walked side by side.

Puzzlement twisted her face. He likes to cook? No one had mentioned that. His gaze continued to stare at her, and she shook her head, clearing the shocking thoughts in order to answer his question.

"I don't know. I never thought of it," she admitted truthfully.

"You never thought of it?"

"No, maybe when I was really little, but all I thought about was taking care of Mama." *And later, hoped her father wouldn't come home.* Guilt tightened her throat, remembering the first time she remembered seeing him. She'd been thirteen and wondered who he was. The man was her father, and she hadn't known who he was. That is until he left. Her mother, exhausted, had slept for days afterwards, completely worn out. That had been the only time he'd come to the farm without Belinda. Since then, they'd stopped by two or three times a year, and each visit had seemed to exhaust her mother more, which made his visits even more distasteful and destructive to Randi. It took Mama longer to recover after each visit, a fact that built a dark loathing deep in the confines of her stomach. It rose again now, made her grit her teeth.

Even after she'd wired Mama had died, it had taken him almost five months before he came home.

During that time, Randi had grown used to the idea of living alone on the farm. It couldn't really be called a farm, she silently admitted. Though she'd paid taxes on close to a hundred acres surrounding the small clapboard house, they'd never planted any crops, nor owned any more than a batch of chickens and a milk cow. The property had been her grandparents, and truth be told, the only way they'd been able to pay the taxes was because of the money Aunt Corrine sent.

When her father and Belinda arrived that day it had been bitterly cold. That visit had proven to be the most distressing one ever. He'd sold the farm. The new owners arrived the following day. Randi had been unable to do anything except pack a small bag of clothing, forced to leave the only home she'd ever known. Another wave of guilt flushed her system. She'd failed her mother, too. It had been Mama's last breath, torn with labored breathing, she'd begged, *Don't let him have the farm.*

"Hey, why the terrible frown?" Howard asked. "Don't you like the bricks?"

Snapped back to the present, she let a blurred gaze wander from the ground to the roof, taking in the entire height of the structure standing before them. And she'd have to leave again. She took a deep breath, tried to find an ounce of courage.

"Maybe I should have just used wood, but bricks are more solid," Howard said.

"No, I mean, yes, I like the bricks. I was just thinking about something else for a moment."

"Not still worried about the bread, are you?"

She couldn't bring herself to meet his gaze, he sounded so caring, so concerned. "No." Pointing up the front steps, to the framed in doorway, she asked. "Can we go inside?"

"Sure." He took her arm and immediately began to explain the layout. "There'll be a wide balcony here with tables for people to dine outdoors if they wish." Entering the building, he continued, "This'll be the front foyer, over here will be the desk, and glass paneled doors over there to separate the restaurant from the hotel."

Fresh cut boards, still sparkling white, greeted them on all sides, but Randi could picture things in her mind just as he described and allowed the images to wash away the disturbing thoughts that had been consuming her. The wood would be stained a deep mahogany, or at least she hoped.

"Will the wood be stained?"

"Yes, I'm thinking dark mahogany, along with the floors. The rugs I've ordered are the same blue as the material Ma's using for curtains."

She pressed a hand to the excitement pounding in her chest, clearly picturing the hotel complete and busting with customers. Women in fancy dresses, men wearing smart three-piece suits would fill the rooms, raving about the beauty and comforts of the accommodations.

"Oh, Howard, it's going to be so beautiful."

He took her hand and led her through rooms framed in with thick beams. "This is the dining room and through here the kitchen."

"What's the large hole in the floor for?" she asked, stepping closer to a big square open space.

"That's the well. The pipes should arrive any day now, along with a plumber from Wichita."

Her eyes bugged. "You mean you'll have indoor plumbing?"

"Yes, just like the fancy hotels back east."

The delight and pride in his eyes made the beats of her heart double up. If she were granted one wish, it would be to stay here long enough to see his dream a reality. It felt almost as if it was her dream, too. The excitement was too much to contain. With an overjoyed yelp, she leaped forward to wrap her arms around him.

He caught her, held her in a tight embrace with her feet dangling somewhere around his shins. Their laughter echoed in the empty space as he twirled her about. The moment passed slowly, giving them both time to fully enjoy the thrill and enchantment. When Howard did lower her to the floor, his gaze locked onto hers, and as if he read her silent prayer, he leaned down to caress her lips with his. The kiss was gentle, benevolent, and more empowering than the heated one in the middle of the street had been.

The contact ended. Eyes closed and still swimming somewhere in a heavenly pool, she couldn't stop the words from emitting, "Oh, how I wish I was your wife."

One of his hands cupped her cheek. She lifted her lids and met the gaze of silver-encrusted green eyes fastened on her.

"You are," he said.

An enchanting spell still circled around her, making her thoughts turn into words on their own accord, before her mind had a chance to quell them.

"No, not really."

"You could be." His voice was as soft as hers.

At that moment, she concluded she'd do anything to make sure his dream came true. Even marry Edward Keyes. Then her father wouldn't expect money from him. He needed it all. This place must cost a fortune.

"When my father returns, I'll go back to Topeka with him," she said aloud and shuddered since the very thought caused her stomach to ache.

He flinched, it was slight, but she felt it nonetheless.

"Do you want to return to Topeka?" he asked.

"No," she admitted in the softest whisper.

"Good, 'cause I don't want you to."

"You don't?"

111

He ran a finger over her cheek. "Randi, would you like to make our marriage real? I mean I know it's real. But how would you feel about staying here, being my wife forever?"

She closed her eyes at the glob of regret plugging her airway. "I can't," she muttered.

"Why not?"

Randi owed him an explanation, she knew that, but saying it aloud would make it so real. She pulled in air, tried to breathe.

"R—"

"My father," she interrupted.

He grabbed both of her shoulders with a stern hold. "I don't give a damn about your father," he snapped, giving her a small, firm shake. "I only care about you."

Her mind was a mess, swirling and twirling.

"What do *you* want?" His hold softened, and an almost pleading glint appeared in his eyes.

The sight made her mind stumble, halt. Something warm and soft settled in her chest.

"To stay," she whispered.

He met her gaze eye for eye, looked at her deeply. "And be my wife? In every sense?"

Her heart was ready to burst right out of her chest and thoughts flew about fast enough to make a bird dizzy.

"Yes," she said.

"Yes?" he asked with a touch of skepticism.

She held her breath, praying with all the faith she ever hoped to have that what she wanted was possible. Unable to speak, she gave a nod of agreement.

"I'm talking forever," he said somewhat roughly. "I want this marriage to last. No second chance. No skipping out later on."

The room filled with a light so bright, it was almost blinding. It was a second or two before she realized the light was coming from inside her.

"Me, too," she admitted. "I want to stay, here, with you, forever."

He tossed his head back, and a moment later his laughter rippled the rafters like a ricocheting bullet. While it bounced about overhead, his lips came down to connect with hers. She wrapped one hand around the back of his head, kept him from breaking their contact until the air in her lungs burned with need to be released. The space surrounding them practically sizzled when they separated. He tucked her head beneath his chin, wrapped her in a tight hold.

His heart pounded below her ear. She closed her eyes, listened to the steady beat, knowing it was the most reassuring sound on earth. Another silent prayer formed in her mind. *Please don't let me disappoint him, please.*

A workman or two, she wasn't necessarily sure, entered the room. Howard responded to their questions, which she heard, but didn't bother to decipher, before he gently pushed her from his chest.

"Come on, let me show you the rest of the building."

She nodded, and as his arm circled her shoulder, hers wrapped around his waist. Arm in arm they strolled across the room. At that moment, bordered by his dream, which had become hers, she recognized the floating on air feeling she felt was love. True love, an emotion she comprehended to be so strong, so real, there would never be a time she'd stop loving him.

They roamed through the rooms until Randi felt as turned around as if she'd been wandering in a fairytale forest. Then again, the fact Howard would sneak a kiss whenever they entered a room that didn't contain workmen, and she'd let him, is more likely what had her head reeling as if she were

Cinderella herself. They were back in the foyer, a few minutes after he stole a final kiss, when she realized he'd spoken.

"Excuse me?" Another blush made her cheeks tingle, this time because her mind had been too busy relishing his latest kiss for her ears to comprehend his question.

"I said it's up to you."

"What's up to me?" she asked sheepishly.

He kissed the tip of her nose and proved once again the most simplistic touch could send her reeling.

"If we live at the hotel or if I have the workers start building us a house."

"Oh, here. Definitely, here," she responded without an inkling of doubt.

"Then here it is," he said, sounding as happy as she felt.

A remarkable sensation settled in her chest, warmed her blood from tip to top as they walked hand in hand back to the camp. It wasn't until he left her to return to work, after a mouth-watering, parting kiss, did she understand that hope had entered her life. The optimism of living as Mrs. Howard Quinter the rest of her born days made her steps lighter and everything around her appeared brighter and almost dreamlike. It was also powerful, as if she could conquer the world and come out unscathed.

The afternoon moved into evening, and her good mood must have been contagious, because even Ma's weathered face broke into a grin now and again as they prepared supper. When Howard and his brothers wandered in, they too, seemed carefree and excited. Randi's disposition continued to shine, especially since Howard never left her side, other than the short time all of the men were taking a quick bath in the stream near the trees on the back of the property.

Throughout the meal, one of his hands rested somewhere on her body. While he helped carry the meal to the table, one hand had settled in the middle of her back, as if guiding her footsteps, and as they ate, one hand rested on her knee. The constant touch heated her body to the temperature of morning coffee, and the effect so pleasing she questioned if it was real, or if she was entrenched in some kind of a mystifying daydream.

Ma's voice rumbled from the end of the table. "You boys can do dishes tonight." She waved her spoon toward the brothers. Perplexed frowns covered both Snake's and Bug's faces, but before they had a chance to utter a protest, Ma continued, "Randi had a long day."

"No—" Randi started.

"Yes," Ma interrupted. "You deserve an evening off. Washin' dishes ain't gonna hurt these boys none. They've done 'em most of their lives." Ma set down her spoon and took a long swallow of coffee ending the conversation as quickly as she had started it.

Baffled, Randi glanced to Howard, looking for either an explanation or support to go against his mother's declaration. One corner of his mouth curled into a little grin that made him all the more good-looking and sent her heart pitter-pattering.

His fingers squeezed the sides of her knee. "Ma's right. You deserve a night off." He rose and curled his hand around her elbow. "Would you like to see how much we got accomplished on the hotel today?"

Yes, she wanted to shout, but the table held the complete array of the meal.

"I really should at least help put away the food."

"The boys and I will get it, you two go on." Ma waved her hand again.

A flutter of guilt made her face twist, and she glanced to the boys. They had worked all day and shouldn't be expected to clean up. Both brothers met her gaze with bright smiles.

Bug winked one sparkling eye. "Go on. Check out the stairway railing I finished." He elbowed Snake. "We don't mind cleaning up. Do we?"

Snake gave a shake of his head. "Nope, don't mind at all." A sincere smile covered his face. "After a meal this fine, cleaning up is the least we can do."

She really wanted to see the inside of the hotel again. All afternoon her mind had conjured up ways to arrange furniture and decorate the interior of the building. The earlier tour had given her a connection to the hotel, and she couldn't deny the excitement at being a part of it all. Moreover, the thought of spending time alone with Howard made her completely jittery with anticipation.

"Well, if you're sure," she muttered, but her gaze had returned to Howard.

"They're sure," he answered.

His slow, low whisper made her bones turn liquid and luckily his other arm slipped around her back to hold her upright as her knees wobbled. Incapable of speaking, she nodded and didn't even look back as he led her away from the table.

Music from the many establishments lining Front Street, boisterous enough to reach the edges of town, floated on the air like a faraway songbird. Not loud enough to really decipher, the lively sound gave the air a tender thrill. The heat giving sun had long since set, and the farther they moved away from the campsite, the chillier the air became. An unexpected shiver slithered across her shoulders.

"Are you cold?" Howard asked, tugging her closer to his side.

"No." She fit her shoulder beneath his. "Well, maybe just a touch," she admitted, not wanting to leave the comfy position of snuggling beneath the curve of his shoulder and wide arm.

"Shall we stop at the tent and get a shawl or one of my flannel shirts?"

"No, it'll be fine once we're out of the wind."

He didn't say anything more, and she didn't expect him to. She'd already recognized how he didn't often say a lot, yet she had a feeling his mind was forever working. The strong, silent type is what her mother would have called him, and a new awareness wafted over her, made her smile. Her mother would have liked him.

He chose that moment to glance down and caught her gazing up at him.

"Happy?" he asked.

She had to process the question. No one had ever asked her that before. The answer made her lips separate into a full-blown, open-mouth, smile.

"Yes, yes, I *am* happy." *And it feels wonderful.*

"Good," he said with a single nod of his head. His wide palm ran up and down her upper arm, completely dismissing the early chill and holding her tight to his side as they walked up the outdoor stairs.

When had the transformation happened? This afternoon? Yesterday? A week ago? The day they married? She couldn't pinpoint the moment, but somehow happiness, an emotion she hadn't experienced very often, had taken up residence in her soul.

"Wait here," he instructed, leaving her inside the threshold and disappearing into the darkness. The roof and upper floor had been completed, making the inside darker than a cavern.

Moments later he returned carrying a lit carriage lantern. The tiny flame fluttered behind the glass and cast shadows to dance on the walls surrounding them. He lifted the light higher, eliminating most of the shadows and filling the area with enough light to see the progress of the day.

The double-wide staircase had been lined with finely carved spindles and long handrails. If there truly was a staircase to heaven, this is what it looked like.

"Oh, my," she sighed.

"Looks good, doesn't it?"

She stepped closer, ran a hand over the big knob at the bottom of the rail.

"Careful." He laid a hand on top of hers. "The boys still have some sanding to do. I don't want you to get a sliver."

"Oh." She lifted her hand, and his hand slipped beneath hers. Palm to palm, his fingers laced with hers. The contact sent a lightning bolt up her arm, straight to her heart. Her knees melted, and she had to tighten her leg muscles to keep from slithering to the floor.

He tugged her toward the left. "Let's start in the kitchen. The first load of furniture arrived today. We still have quite a bit of work to do before we can assemble it, so for now we put it in there."

They walked across the foyer into a large room. Big, square, and slatted crates were stacked along the far wall.

"What is it?" she asked.

"Tables and chairs."

The heat of his gaze was hot enough to singe the side of her face. She twisted her neck to see why he stared so hard. His eyes held more light than the lantern. Pale green had turned completely silver. A soft rumble rolled about in her stomach. His gaze floated over her face until it locked onto her lips. The action made her emit a slight gasp and sent her heart racing. They stood like that for several moments, his eyes kissing her lips.

When the need to feel his lips on hers was so strong she wanted to cry aloud, beg him to kiss her, his head lowered. With painstaking slowness, he drew closer and closer until their lips connected. It was an awakening of emotions. Her heart swelled from its rapid beats, her head swirled, and every muscle from head to toe tingled. His hands never moved. One held the lantern and the other still clutched her palm, but it was as if she became completed gloved by his aura. Her eyes fluttered shut, and she let herself float on a cloud as they kissed.

Tenderly, his lips ran over her upper, and then her lower lip. The gentle, easy actions kept her immobile. Not because his arms held her tight, but the tantalizing sensations of his kiss prevented her body from being able to do anything except stand still and absorb the slightest touch. When his lips started to slip away, she leaned forward, following them.

She completely lost her balance, toppling into Howard's chest. His arms wrapped around her waist. A rumble vibrated up her cheek at his low chuckle. She glanced up and tried to focus on his face as the world spun.

His smile slipped away; his features became serious.

She wrapped both arms around his waist, and breathless, as if she'd just run a mile, begged, "Please take me to the tent."

The arm around her tightened and something flashed in his eyes. "Randi—"

"Please," she interrupted. Never a daring person, she questioned the courage that made her continue. "I know what I'm asking." And before he could respond, she reached one hand up to pull his face toward hers. A final plea slipped from her mouth into his when their lips met.

"Please, Howard, take me to bed."

Chapter Ten

Howard lost control and devoured her mouth, drinking the sweetness like a man who'd been without water for a month. The blood surging through his veins could hold a candle to the Mississippi and was hotter than lit gun powder. It was Randi who broke the kiss. A glow brighter than the stars emitted from her face. She grabbed his hand and towed him to the door.

A light, carefree giggle faintly filled the air around them, and he tugged, forcing her to pivot about so he could see if it was really her laughter he heard. His heart leaped to his throat, and then burst open. His laugh met hers and hand in hand they ran down the steps of the building, leaving the echoes of their merriment to rise into the night sky.

Once inside the tent, he set the lamp on the trunk and pulled her close with both hands. Her lips met his with a demand that almost surprised him—almost because he was demanding just as much. The kiss was rewarding and leading at the same time. A need filled his system, one he knew only she could fulfill. He lifted his head, had to make sure she truly wanted what was about to happen.

"Blow out the lamp," she whispered, brushing little kisses along his neck.

His head spun with such speed it might twist right off and float away.

"What?" he mumbled.

"Blow out the lamp." She took a step back and began to pull the pins from her hair. "You know. The shadows." Her head tilted toward the lamp as she plucked pins, tossing them onto the trunk.

A tiny bit of common sense filtered into his dizzy mindset. He quickly dowsed the light before she finished with the pins, wanting to be the one to pluck the final few and to smooth the long tresses over her shoulders. Darkness filled the tent, but her outline was still there, just a step away. Gently brushing her hands aside, he combed his fingers into the chestnut colored fluff, searching for the tiny bits of metal. He removed each one, letting them fall from his fingers and bounce across the trunk or onto the floor with abandonment.

"You are so beautiful," he whispered.

"So are you." Her fingers began to slip the buttons of his shirt through their holes.

The last pin landed on the top of the trunk with a tinkle. A thick heavy veil of silky hair tumbled through his hands like snow falling off a rooftop. He bent to thoroughly inhale the flowery scent. The tightening in his groin let him know the full effect she had on him.

She finished with the last button and pulled his shirttail from his waistband. Her hands went to his shoulders and pushed the material aside. He'd never been undressed by a woman before, and the act was enough to drive him to the brink. Searching for restraint, he stalled her hands by grasping her elbows and leaned down for a kiss.

His mind became completely befuddled, because kissing her made his britches tight enough to cut off his blood flow. Somehow her fingers still managed to push the shirt off his shoulders.

Piece by piece their clothing floated to the floor and their bodies found the bed. Howard held his breath, experiencing a ritual that fleshed out more emotions than a man had a right to experience. A groan rumbled his voice box and made his mind focus on her. With skill and due diligence, he tuned into making her feel as wonderful as he did.

He led the way, gently at times, forceful at others until together they climbed to the top of the earth. It was there they completed the ceremony, gave themselves to one another with explosive abandonment. Howard held her close, his heart full, as they tumbled back down to earth.

And that was just round one. Hours later, when early birds twittered outside the tent announcing morning would soon arrive, Howard wondered if they'd slept a wink. He wasn't tired, just the opposite in fact. His body felt so satisfied he probably had more energy than a dozen men. She let out a little moan and wiggled closer into his embrace. He lowered his head to run a trail of kisses down the side of her face.

"Mmm, I like that," she mumbled in his ear.

"Hmm, so do I," he admitted against her skin.

"I like you," she said, kissing the side of his ear. "I like you very, very much."

He tugged the blanket down exposing two spectacular breasts, which he promptly began to caress. Trailing his kissing down her neck, along her collar bone, he asked, "I like you very, very much, too. But how about I show you, instead of telling you?"

"Oh, I think I'd like that, very, very much," she said.

He liked it, too, to the point that later, when they both lay flat on their backs, panting, and sunlight filtered through the thick canvas, he hated the thought of crawling out of bed. As if she read his mind, she rolled onto her side and cuddled her head into the crook of his shoulder.

"Do we have to get up?"

He brushed a kiss to her forehead. "I'm afraid so." His sigh lingered in the air. A giggle shook her body. A scowl tugged at his face, and he glanced down. "Just what do you find so amusing?"

A wide smile made her nose wrinkle and sent tiny sparks dancing in her eyes.

"You." She inched up and kissed his chin.

Her breasts teased his skin, made him want her all over again. The thought of getting out of bed became quite horrendous. He grabbed her and lifted her to lie on top of him from hip to shoulder. Running his hands over the silky skin of her back, he asked, "And what about me is so amusing."

She flipped her head, tossing her hair out of her face. "Everything," she said. "Everything about you makes me so happy I can't stop smiling. I just want to giggle with delight."

The admission filled him with joy. He kissed the tip of her nose. "I know the feeling."

The bang and clang of pots and pans made them both turn toward the side of the tent. Neither could see anything, but he imagined her mind conjured up the same as his, and simultaneously they began to laugh.

Happier than a daisy in the sun, Randi planted a wet, promising kiss on Howard's lips, and then with a touch of regret, rolled off his chest. "I believe that is your mother calling for my help." The night had been extremely fulfilling and far more pleasurable than she'd ever imagined.

He followed her to the edge of the bed. "I believe you're right." His hands wrapped around her waist from behind. Wide fingers met in the center of her stomach while his lips kissed her back, from shoulder blade to shoulder blade.

"You keep that up, Mr. Quinter, and I'll never make it out to help her." The boldness she'd found last night still lingered, and the power it brought was wonderful.

"Really, Mrs. Quinter?" His kisses went lower.

She giggled and pried his fingers apart so she

could rise.

"Yes, Mr. Quinter." Still holding both of his hands, she twisted about, feeling no embarrassment standing naked in front of him. Tugging, she took a step backwards and insisted, "Now come on before she sends one of your brothers in here to get us."

He stood, and her eyes couldn't help but move up and down so she could drink in his magnificent body. She stepped closer and lifted her face.

"Kiss me one more time, and I'll help you get dressed."

One brow rose, and a hint of mischievousness flashed in his smoldering eyes. "You will?"

"Of course. I helped you get undressed, the least I could do is help you dress." She let her fingers walk up his arms, but really wanted to push his dangerously appealing body back onto the bed and have her way with him.

"Am I really married to you, or is this some kind of a dream?" he asked.

She had already wondered that same thing and stretched on her toes to let their lips meet. "If it's a dream, please don't wake me up. Please don't ever wake me up."

They lingered over the kiss, and another, and yet another as they helped each other recover garments strewn about as if a miniature tornado had set down in the tent the night before. By the time they were presentable enough to exit the tent, Randi's blood was hotter than the coffee pot perking atop the camp fire.

If they knew what had transpired the night before, neither Ma nor either of the brothers said a word and breakfast happened just as it had every morning since she'd arrived. Except for the fact her heart sang, and her body played a harmonic tune that reached to the sky and encouraged the sun to brighten its shine. There was also the fact that

Howard delayed leaving until after the boys had traipsed off to the building and Ma had secreted herself into her tent. As the hum of the treadle sewing machine emitted through the flaps, he pulled Randi to the backside of the storage tent to steal a few kisses, which she gladly gave.

With her heart flying about inside her ribcage faster than bees gathering pollen, Randi waved good-bye as he scooted off to meet a man climbing down from a large wagon. She lifted her skirt and twirled around until the world spun before her eyes. It was as if the universe had opened up and filled her soul with something so good and bright it was impossible for her to fathom it all. Giggling with delight, she skipped back to the fire pit to clean up the breakfast dishes and begin preparations for the lunch meal.

****

The week passed with glorious bliss, but more than that Randi found strength and determination with her new status. Not only was she Howard's wife, in every way, which was utterly splendid, it was as if he also shared his willpower and grit with her. She felt driven, as if there was nothing or no one who could shatter the perfection of her world.

The man in the large wagon had proven to be the plumber Howard spoke of, and the man had been busy installing pipes, sinks, tubs, and all other sorts of things. She could hardly wait to see the finished product and to test out one of the porcelain bathing tubs the boys had hauled into the hotel.

Somewhat lost in the thought, she entered the supply tent in search of a new bottle of ginger. She was crouched over a large box when familiar hands grasped her hips. In one swift movement she was twisted about and kissed until her head spun so fast she thought it might jump off her neck and sail away.

She giggled, and then whispered against her husband's lips, "Hello."

"Hello, my sweet." Howard trailed kisses along her chin.

"And to what do I owe this unexpected pleasure?" she asked, totally enjoying his action.

"I want to show you something." He lifted his face and met her gaze.

Her breath caught as she spied the excitement in his eyes. She wrapped her arms around his waist, ready and willing for whatever was to come.

"What is it you want to show me?" She ran her nose along the underside of his chin and placed a tiny kiss right in the hollow of his throat.

His hands roamed from her lower back to her shoulders and back down again. Every stroke kindling the fire he'd set to forever glow in the pit of her soul.

"It's a surprise," he said in his husky tone that made the flames leap a bit hotter.

Her tongue darted out to catch a taste of his neck as she continued to nuzzle. "I like surprises." She stepped closer and rolled her hips across the front of his britches.

One of his hands settled in the small of her back, holding her hips firmly against his groin. With a low, husky chuckle, he said, "Some days I can't believe you are the same shy, little girl I found in my bed one morning." A touch of apprehension made her lips stall for a split second. Then he added, "I'm so lucky you got over your shyness."

"And I am so lucky it was your bed I crawled into that night." She nipped at his neck with her teeth and rubbed her breasts across his chest.

His hands grabbed her waist, and he lifted her into the air as if she weighed no more than a feather pillow. Her hands flew to his shoulders and held on while she looked down upon his superbly handsome face. Nothing had ever filled her with such immense joy as simply looking at him did. Suspended in air, she leaned down to capture his lips in a perfect union.

He lowered her to the ground and held her close until the merger ended. By then neither of them could breathe. Their teasing had turned into a raging fire of need.

"I think we should go see your surprise before I decide there's plenty of room in this tent."

"Plenty of room for what?" she asked innocently, pretending to glance about at the boxes, crates, and gunny sacks full of food stuffs and cooking supplies.

His laugh sounded like it was filled with a growl. "As if you don't know my sweet, little vixen." He gave her rump a playful slap, and then tugged her toward the door.

March had flowed into April, and the wonderful smells and sights of spring filled the air. Randi lifted her face to the sun, thankful for not only the warmth and brightness, but also for the way it appeared springtime was inside her, too.

"I don't have a clue as to what you mean," she said, glancing back to the tent. "There's barely room to turn around in there."

"I know," he laughed, wrapping an arm about her shoulders.

She laughed, too and wrapped an arm around his waist as they ambled toward the building site. Snake waved to them as they grew closer. He no longer spent his time building, instead he'd set about preparing the ground for a lush lawn complete with rose bushes, a lilac hedge, and several fruit trees. Already tiny sprigs of grass covered the turned soil, and large stepping stones had been placed so customers would be able to take evening strolls through the grounds.

"What's he working on today?" she asked,

waving back to the brother.

"I'm not sure. He said something about a fountain." Howard frowned.

"Really? A fountain. Will it have a fish pond as well? Could we get some of those little gold fish to swim around in it? Wouldn't that be wonderful?"

"Would you like a pond with gold fish swimming in it?" he asked.

"Yes, wouldn't you? I bet it would be the only one in Kansas." She added the last part hoping it sounded less frivolous and possibly more focused on drawing in customers.

"If you want a fish pond, I'll have him build you a fish pond." His tugged her closer. "Is there anything else you want?"

She laid her head against his shoulder and kept it there as they walked from one stepping stone to the next. "No, I think I have more than I ever imagined having," she said honestly.

No one had ever asked her what she wanted, nor asked her opinions on things, yet Howard did. Every night, cocooned in their bed, sedate and satisfied, he'd tell her what had arrived that day for the hotel, ask her opinion on how rooms should be set up and decorated, or question her on what she thought they still needed to purchase to make the hotel the finest around. It all had increased her self-esteem to the point some days she felt downright shameful of how boastful she'd become.

They climbed the back steps, which now hosted a spacious porch, complete with handrails. Once inside, Howard swung her about to settle both hands on her shoulders.

"You're also much more than I ever dreamed of."

The seriousness of his tone made the smile slip from her face. His gaze seeped into her with all the heart-filled passion she felt lying beneath the comfort of his weight every night. She reached up and ran a hand deep into his blond, tousled hair. Words seemed insignificant, so she put all of her emotions into one very long, extremely meaningful kiss.

The embrace wasn't like the ones in the tent, it wasn't meant to ignite fires in her veins, instead, it was intended to tell him he was her world, without him she was nothing, like that shivering girl he'd found in his bed weeks ago. It was the kind of kiss that said I want to be yours forever, and I want you to be mine forever—the kind of kiss she'd never known existed until this moment.

When their mouths separated and he tucked her head beneath his chin, they weren't gasping for air, but simply absorbing life from one another.

After a few stilled moments, Howard said, "Are you ready for your surprise?"

She glanced up and noticed not only happiness on his face, but a gleam of satisfaction had settled deep in his eyes. It made her smile.

"Yes, I'm ready for my surprise."

He kissed her forehead. "Well, turn around then."

She did, but didn't see anything out of the ordinary. The backdoor led into the kitchen, which was still used for storage of the crates of furniture that arrived on a daily basis. Her gaze made it about halfway around the room when something slid over her eyes, and she reached up to tug it away.

"Oh, no, none of that," he said near her ear.

She fingered the bandana he'd settled over her eyes and proceeded to tie in the back of her head.

"What are you doing?"

"Blind-folding you so you can't peek." He tugged the cloth. "How's that? Is it too tight?"

"If I say yes, will you take it off," she teased.

"No, but I'll loosen it."

"It's fine," she admitted. He was full of

surprises, and she loved it. Having no siblings, she'd never played games such as blind man's bluff and had told him so the other night.

He took her hand. "All right, then, come along."

She stepped carefully, the blindfold made walking a precarious event. Her other hand reached over so both of hers held onto his. "Where are we going?"

"Upstairs."

She paused for a moment. "I don't think I can climb stairs without seeing where I'm going." The thought made a touch of fear tickle her spine.

"Sure you can. I'm right beside you and won't let anything happen to you." He wrapped his other hand around her back.

The action and words chased away her fear. He'd said that to her the first day they'd met, and he was right. With him around nothing bad could ever happen to her.

"All right," she said, stepping forward.

He counted the stairs for her as they climbed, encouraging each step. The staircase off the kitchen, she knew, rose to the second floor and the private apartment being built for them. She'd seen it a couple times, but it had been nothing more than two-by-four stud walls and open spaces where windows eventually would be. Perhaps that was it. Windows had arrived a few days ago, maybe he wanted her to see how nice they looked.

They stopped at the top of the stairs, and his hands left her for a brief moment. She heard a faint sound, like a door opening before he once again took her hand to lead her forward. Within a few feet, the clicks of her heels become muffled, and the floor softened as if she walked across a plush carpet, but he didn't stop. The floor became wood again and another door opened before he brought her to a halt.

"I thought I'd show you this room first." His

fingers loosened the blindfold, but he didn't let it fall away from her eyes. "Are you ready?" he asked, kissing the side of her neck.

"Yes," she laughed, rubbing against his touch.

After one more kiss, the blindfold fell away.

It took her eyelids a moment to open, and when they did, she blinked, stared, and blinked again. Her heart flapped about, somewhat out of control, and her mind had gone blank. Before her stood a shamefully, gorgeous hotel suite with a four-poster bed the size only kings and queens slept in. Draped with a burgundy brocade bedspread and topped with enough gold, green, and burgundy silk pillows to fill their tent. The bed, which was framed with matching bed tables and lamps on both sides, should have dwarfed the size of the room, but it only took up a small portion. Curtains, matching the bed covering, were drawn back with long gold tasseled sashes letting the sun fill the room with natural light. In front of one of the double-paned windows was a long chaise lounge, decorated again with a pile of silk pillows. A table and two large leather chairs were grouped in the corner on the other wall.

She had to turn to take in more of the room. A tall dresser, complete with a framed oblong mirror stood beside a shorter dressing table that also held a huge round mirror, and a matching bench sat in front of the table, as if awaiting a grand lady to sit upon it as she pinned her hair or dabbed on perfume.

"Oh my word!" Randi finally gasped, breathless.

"What? Don't you like it?"

The sound of his worried tone made her spin all the way around. Behind him, next to the doorway, two wide doors stood open, and she moved to peer inside. It was a built-in closet, two actually, a his and a hers. Her eyes strained, and she squinted to make sure they weren't playing tricks on her. Nope, those were her clothes hanging on the high bar, and her traveling bag sat on the floor beneath.

Howard stepped around in front of her and laid a hand on her arm.

"Randi? Don't you like it?"

"Like it?" she asked with disbelief.

He gave an adorable if not somewhat unsure little, questioning nod.

"Howard, it's the most beautiful room I've ever seen." She reached out to point at her traveling suit. "But what are my clothes doing in the closet?"

"It's our bedroom. Where else would your clothes be?"

"Our bedroom?" She flipped back around to once again gape at the magnificent area.

"Yes, our bedroom. Don't you like it?"

He sounded so worried, despite the shock still rippling her frame she had to smile.

"Like it? I love it! I never thought our rooms would be this...luxurious." She twirled around but was unable to settle her pointing finger on any one item. Everything was too spectacular. "This is like something they'd have in New York, or Philadelphia, but not Dodge City, Kansas."

"You've been helping me plan it. You've seen it all along. You even helped Ma pick out the material for the curtains."

She pivoted to look at him. "I know. But I just..." With a single leap she was in his arms. "It's absolutely fabulous! Isn't it?"

"So, you like it?"

"Yes, silly, I like it. I love it. I can't believe we're going to live here." She peeked over his shoulder. "Are the rest of the rooms done?"

He set her on the ground and took her hand. "The rest of our rooms are done. But not the guest rooms. I wanted to move you out of that tent as soon as possible. It's stifling our style." His eyebrows lifted in a very provocative way.

Warmth pooled deep in her belly, and she gave him a coy look. "Stifling our style? I don't think anything has been stifled."

"Maybe not, but I'd still like a bit more privacy than what the tent offers." He led her out of the room. "Let me show you the rest."

Her degree of shock rose another ten degrees when he led her into the sitting room, complete with an oil burning parlor stove so they wouldn't need to carry logs up the stairs. A settee and several chairs as well as tables, decorated with potted plants sat about, and again several long windows framed with thick curtains, filled the room with light. Three doors lined the walls.

"Where do those go?" she asked when she'd caught enough air to speak.

He crossed the room and pointed at the first one. "This one goes into the hotel hall." Moving his hand, he continued, "This one goes to our second floor. Those rooms aren't done yet, but up there will be three more bedrooms." His eyes settled on her stomach. "For future use."

She pressed both hands to her middle, warmed by the thought of someday having children. His children. Their children. Already she dreamed of a little boy with blond curly hair and a little girl with silver-green eyes.

"And this room," he said, drawing her attention back to where he stood. "Is your bathing chamber."

"My what?"

He pulled open the door and waved a hand for her to enter. She flashed him a questioning gaze and slipped into the room. If the other rooms had been a shock, this one was absolutely death defying. A huge porcelain tub sat front and center in the room. Sparkling, a large gold-colored spigot curved its way over one edge. Too curious to control herself, she walked closer and turned one of graceful handles.

Water instantly shot out the spout.

"Oh!" she squealed, quickly turning off the spigot.

"Hot and cold running water," he said proudly.

"Land sakes! I never," she stammered, not knowing what else to say.

He walked behind a small partition wall. "And back here is an indoor privy."

"A what?" She scurried across the room for a look. Sure enough, there stood a round porcelain chamber pot decorated with blue flowers and stationed high on the wall was a holding tank with a long gold chain dangling down. She pressed a hand to her mouth to hide a short fit of giggles.

"People are going to come for miles around just to try these."

"I don't care what brings them here, as long as they come," Howard said, joining her laughter.

She weaved her way back around the tub, twisting the knob to watch the water burst out one more time, and then meandered out into the other room.

"Howard?"

"Yes," he said near her shoulder.

She jumped a touch, surprised he was so close, and then smiled, comforted to know he would always be close.

"What's behind that door?" She pointed across the room to a door next to the one that led downstairs.

"That's my office." One hand settled in the small of her back to steer her across the room. He opened the door and again waved an arm for her to enter first. A large desk, several shelves, and a table and chairs were assembled to make the room look very professional. A woven rug similar to the one in the sitting room covered the floor.

She crossed the room, ran a hand over the desk

top, and then moved to the window. The tent they'd been living in for several weeks flapped in the wind yards away from the hotel. A happy smile filled her face, and she flipped around.

"When can we move in?"

He was right there, not more than a few inches away, and reached out to take her hands. His fingers, calloused, yet soft, caressed the backs of her wrists. A smile rolled his lips away from his straight, white teeth.

"We already have."

The ripples of pleasure running up her arms made thinking a bit difficult.

"Excuse me?"

"Your clothes are in the closet, remember?"

She nodded, more intrigued with the sensations of his touch than his words.

"That's your surprise. Welcome to your new home. Our new home." He pulled her close and covered her mouth with a decidedly reverent kiss.

As his lips lifted, she whispered, "I can't wait until tonight."

He wrapped one arm around her shoulders, crooked the other behind her knees and lifted her. Cradling her in his arms, he turned toward the open doorway.

"Who said anything about waiting?"

Chapter Eleven

An hour later, Howard didn't want to, but knew
he had to get back to work, so he left Randi after he
watched her lower her graceful, delightful body into
the deep bathing tub. She'd denied her want to try
out the tub, but he could see it glistening in her eyes
and insisted she take a bath, claimed the plumber,
Joe Smallish, would want to know that everything
worked properly. Once she thought her activity
would assist with the building, she readily agreed,
and completely in the buff, all but flew to the
bathing room.

At this moment in time, completely satisfied
from head to toe, inside and out, nothing could erase
the smile covering his face. A joyful tune floated
around in his head, and he began to whistle it as he
pranced down the stairs. The backdoor, still open, let
the sounds of the day float in; men pounding,
sawing, shouting orders, and asking for directions,
along with traffic on the road, birds in the trees, and
the happy overall sounds of life. Howard took a deep
breath, let it fill his lungs completely, and
determined life was perfect.

Bug's head popped in the doorway, and he
graced his youngest brother with a wide grin.

"Hello, little brother."

"Uh, Hog?"

"Yes," he answered, his grin never faltering.

"Um…" Bug's cheeks puffed as he dragged a
long sigh out.

A chill made Howard's shoulders quiver and his
smile fade.

"What?"

"Randi's folks are back."

He kicked a block of scrap lumber lying on the floor. The small chunk of wood flew across the room, hit one of the crates with a solid thud.

"Aw, shit," he muttered.

"Yeah, that's what I thought," Bug admitted.

"Where are they?"

Bug pointed his thumb over his shoulder. "Over by the tents."

Howard didn't look. Maybe if he pretended they weren't here they'd go away. He rubbed his face, knowing Thurston Fulton would never disappear.

"When did they get here?"

Bug shrugged. "'Bout half an hour ago. Maybe longer."

Dread washed away the last bits of the bliss he'd lived in the past few weeks. He'd forgotten the raunchy dislike Thurston Fulton ensued in the pit of his guts. Randi had been so happy lately, the load her father thrust on her shoulders from the time she'd been a young girl should be illegal. From what he could surmise, by all she'd told him, the man had deserted her and her mother not long after she'd been born. The farm they lived at had been purchased by Randi's maternal grandparents, decedents of the ones who owned the hotel back east, yet as soon as her mother had died, Thurston had swooped in, sold the place, and pocketed the money for his political campaign.

He gave a low, slow shake of his head. The man also had a hold on Randi that Howard hadn't yet figured out. She talked of the years she and her mother lived alone, and he heard the disdain she felt. He knew she had grit, he'd seen how hard she worked, how tirelessly she helped, but whenever she thought of her father she grew as weak as a featherless bird.

There was no doubt that Thurston Fulton was crooked and most likely as mean as a wild cat. The man was true trouble with a capital *T*. And of course, there was the overall knowledge that any connection with a Populist was sure to kill Howard's dream before he'd even served his first customer. He wanted to have the man investigated, but knew it wouldn't be favorable for him to even look interested in Fulton.

"Anything you want me to do?" Bug said.

Howard spun about having forgotten his brother still hovered in the doorway.

"Wait here for me would ya? Don't let anyone upstairs. Randi's trying out that new fangled bathing tub with running water."

Bug glanced at the stairway. "I can't wait to try one of those out myself."

Howard frowned.

"Not now. I happen to like my life just fine."

He shook his head, tried to catch the meaning of Bug's words. "What?"

"I said I happen to like my life."

"Yeah, what's that suppose to mean?"

"It means, I ain't gonna go messin' with your wife, or any other man's wife. That's the fastest way to find yourself dead." Bug stepped into the kitchen.

Howard had to nod in agreement. He'd easily shoot a man if he found them messin' with Randi.

"I'll clean up the scraps and stuff in here. Want me to send her over to the tents when she comes down?" Bug asked.

"No, I'll come back for her. I don't want her running into her father when I'm not around."

"You really don't like that man do you?"

"Nope, I really don't."

"Why? You're not one to take a disliking to anyone."

"Honestly," he shrugged, "I don't know. From

the moment I met the man, I got this feeling that he's bad. Just flat out evil." Howard hadn't admitted his instincts to anyone else, certainly not Randi. His gaze went to the stairs. "Don't tell Randi I said that."

"I won't. But that has to be hard."

"What?"

"Hating your wife's father so fiercely."

Howard rubbed his forehead. "It ain't easy, I'll give you that." He tugged his hat low on his brow. "I'll be back as soon as I can. Don't tell her they're back."

"I won't." Bug started sweeping odds and ends of wood shavings into a pile with a whisk broom.

Howard checked his shirt, assuring he'd tucked it in straight while dressing a short time ago, and made sure his waistband was even, then lowered his hands to check his gun belt. His steps slowed. He'd left the whole thing, gun and all, hanging on the back of one of the chairs in their new bedroom.

He shot a glance over his shoulder wondering if he should retrieve it but ultimately determined he wouldn't shoot Thurston Fulton, not today anyway. Taking a deep, fortifying breath, he marched out the door and across the new green grass of the yard.

Belinda Fulton's sickly-sweet voice vibrated the air long before he entered the campsite.

"Oh, Howard, it is so good to see you!" she screeched, and lifting a gaudy green dress high enough to show a good six inches of pantaloons, she raced toward him.

Moments before she arrived in front of him, she released the dress to throw her arms up in the air. Howard side-stepped, and a smile tugged on his lips as she flew passed him, arms flaying and feet stumbling.

A twinge of guilt crossed his chest, but not enough to stretch out an arm. *Simpleton!* Why would she think he'd welcome a hug from her? He'd rather snuggle up to a rattler. He watched, wondering if she would take a nose dive into the dirt. She didn't and another twinge of regret tickled his chest.

There were few women he'd taken a liking to, outside of his wife, that is. There was his Ma, of course, and his sisters-in-law, and family friends, Willamina and Eva, but beyond them, he could only recall a gal or two down at Danny J's, and they'd just been 'cause he needed to appease his manhood. He'd never had time for silly or uppity ways, and Belinda Fulton took the cake when it came to uppity.

Her red lips were pulled into an ugly pucker as she snapped her skirt and twirled around to sneer at him. He raised one hand, touched the brim of his hat with a mocked greeting before he turned and strolled toward the camp. Her huff vibrated the air but slid off his shoulders like water on a duck's back.

"Mr. Quinter," Thurston Fulton said, one hand stretched out.

Howard thought about refusing the handshake, but decided he'd best try and get along with his father-in-law, for Randi's sake. If it was just him, he'd chase the repulsive man and his dim-witted wife clear back to Topeka.

"Mr. Fulton," he greeted, pumping the man's hand with more force than necessary.

Thurston flexed his fingers several times when they released their shake.

"We had a wonderful time at your brother's place. Didn't we, dear?" Thurston turned to Belinda, who flounced up beside them like a one legged goose.

"Yes, Mrs. Quinter is remarkable. And their children are such darlings," Belinda remarked, the whole while her hooded eyes wandered from his boots to his hat.

A quiver raced down his arms. Howard shrugged it off and directed his question at Thurston, "You just stopping in on your way to

Topeka?"

"No, no, we wanted to be back here in time for your grand opening." The man's beady eyes went to the hotel. "You've made remarkable progress while we were gone."

The couple's presence even dimmed the pride he felt every time he looked at his accomplishment. That irritated Howard even more. The hotel was something to be proud of. At three stories tall, it was three times the size of anything in the state. Not even a building in Wichita, Kansas City, or Topeka could compare to the empire he was building. Some folks thought his plan crazy when he first started talking about it, but Lila and Skeeter hadn't. Lila swore the hotel would bring in people by the droves, travelers heading to Denver or farther west, those going all the way to Sacramento, would relish the idea of a touch of luxury while crossing the otherwise desolate plains.

At the sound of his brother's name, he snapped his head back to Thurston.

"Excuse me?"

"Your brother, Steven, and his wife, Lila, they, too, plan on being here for the opening. They'll arrive in a week or so," Thurston said.

Howard nodded, he'd expected as much. After all they had invested a lot of money in his undertaking. Kid and Jessie should be arriving around then, too; his other financial backers.

"Oh, I can't wait to see their younguns," Ma said, setting a pot of coffee on the table. "It's been a coon's age since I seen my babies."

"Well, let me assure you, those children are doing just fine. Full of spice and vinegar, both of them," Thurston said with a strained smile.

The comment made Howard frown. His niece, Kendra, wasn't even three yet and his nephew, Charles, was just a baby, both children were too small to be considered full of spice and vinegar. A smile tugged at his lips. The man had never seen children at their best. He and his brothers had some tales that would singe the small amount of hair Thurston Fulton had clear off his round skull.

A hint of orneriness crept into Howard's mind and made him ask, "Is Buffalo Killer coming with Skeeter and Lila?"

The way Belinda sucked in her breath was more of an answer than he needed.

"I certainly hope n—"

"They didn't say," Thurston interrupted. "He, Buffalo Killer, had returned to his tribe before we left."

"How's he doing?" Ma asked. "Buffalo Killer? He's like one of my boys, ya know."

Belinda turned a pasty white, and the color of Thurston's face wasn't far behind.

The man cleared his throat and answered nervously, "He appeared to be fine."

Howard couldn't wait for Skeeter to arrive and learn what had actually transpired on the Fulton's trip to the Badlands. The thought made his mind circle about. Quickly it returned to the amount of work he still had to get accomplished before the grand opening of the hotel.

"Well, I'm sure you're here to see Randi. She's at the hotel, I'll go get her."

"At the hotel? Is it habitable? Is that where you're living?" Belinda's eyes gazed at the brick building like a child stares at a candy jar. "We'll, of course, be booking rooms there."

"The rooms aren't ready yet, just our living quarters," Howard said.

"But their tent's empty if'n you want to bed down there," Ma supplied, and Howard loved her all the more for her comment. The way Belinda gasped one would have thought she hadn't breathed for hours.

"Oh, well, thank you, Mrs. Quinter, but we'll get rooms at the Dodge House. Our last stay was quite comfortable there," Thurston said.

Ma shrugged. "Well, I got some sewing to do. Ya all are welcome to join us for supper if'n ya want." With a parting nod, she ducked inside her tent.

Howard watched her depart with a frown. He couldn't very well ask them to wait here alone while he went to get Randi. Damn, if he had one wish it would be to shove Thurston and Belinda back under the rock they'd crawled out from under. A new twinge of guilt tickled his insides. His mother would be appalled if she knew his roaming thoughts centered on the hatred eating at him. Just as Bug had said, it was out of character for him to feel and act this way toward someone.

"Thurston, I'd really like a bath. We can see Randilynn later," Belinda said.

"Yes, of course, my dear." Thurston once again stretched a hand forward. "Mr. Quinter, will you please tell my daughter we'll be back later?"

Once again, somewhat remorsefully, he shook the other man's hand. "Certainly."

"Or perhaps, you and Randi could join us for supper at the Dodge House." Belinda turned to Thurston to add, "I would like to eat indoors." She sent a nasty glare about the campsite. "I've had enough of the wilderness for awhile."

Thurston patted his wife's shoulder. "Of course, my dear. Would that be all right with you, Mr. Quinter?"

Howard shrugged. "I'll have to ask Randi. It'll be her choice." It was obvious his answer didn't settle well with Belinda, who rolled her eyes and let out another huff.

"Yes, yes, we men must please our wives, mustn't we?" Thurston said, yet his tone didn't quite match his words.

Howard almost felt a tinge of sorrow for the man. Almost, being the critical word.

"Yes, we must," he said. Out of politeness, or perhaps because he wanted to make sure they left, he waited until their wagon rolled down the road before he turned to make his way back to the hotel.

A sixth sense made him glance up. Randi's silhouette stood behind the window of his new office on the second story. His heart plunged. Was she wondering why her father hadn't stayed long enough to see her? Damn that man. Howard picked up his pace as she turned away from the glass.

Without a nod, nor glance toward Bug, he leaped up the stairs and seconds later thrust the door open. A sweet rose scent, most likely from the little tin of soaps he'd purchased, lingered in the air, and after a quick glance in his office, he moved toward their bedroom. She sat on the little stool in front of the lady's dressing table combing her long hair with a silver handled brush. Her gaze found his in the mirror above her head.

"Hello," she said. The soft smile curving her lips appeared genuine, but he had to wonder.

"Hello. How was the bath?" He moved closer, watching her in the mirror.

"Wonderful," she giggled. "I've never used so much hot water at one time. It's almost sinful."

He took the brush from her hand and ran it down the wet tresses, gently smoothing away the twists formed from washing. She wore her yellow dress, and his stomach fluttered a touch. With her deep brown eyes and dark hair, she reminded him of a sunflower dancing about in a field. It was a delightful sight, one that made his loins stir. A few short weeks ago, he'd thought he didn't have time for a wife. Now he'd trade his dream, the hotel, restaurant and all, for her. Not that his dream had completely dissolved, he still wanted it, still worked to make it happen, but somehow that dream had shifted, became second fiddle to her.

His smile continued to sparkle in the mirror. The dream had also become hers—no theirs—and he enjoyed sharing it with her. It had come to the point where he didn't make a single decision without consulting her. Even their apartment, he'd asked for her opinion on every piece of furniture. She just hadn't known it was for her, because he wanted to surprise her. He'd instructed the men to finish this space first and set it all up, so all she had to do was walk in and see it completed.

"My father and Belinda are back," she said, somewhat dully.

The brush stalled for a split second. He grasped the handle tighter and continued to run it from her scalp to the middle of her back, not once glancing to the mirror.

"Yes. They had to go check into the Dodge House." He tried to sound non-judgmental.

"Will they be back?" There was a slight crack to her voice.

He gathered all of her hair into one palm and concentrated on brushing the ends.

"Actually, they were wondering if we'd care to join them at the restaurant in town for supper." He snuck a peek.

A frown pulled her dark brows down until they almost met above the bridge of her nose.

"Really?" she asked, rearranging the things on her dressing table.

"Hmmm," he muttered, holding in any other comment that might like to be heard.

She twisted her neck to look up at him. "Are we going?"

He set the brush down on the table top, next to several other bits of necessities his mother thought he needed to purchase. A glass bottle of perfume, a tin of talc powder, a container of hair pins, and some other items he didn't even try to assume he knew what they were.

She wrapped her fingers around his before he lifted them away from the brush handle.

"I don't mind that you don't want to go."

"No." He shook his head. "It's not my decision. It's yours. If you want to go, we will. If you don't, we won't."

Her gaze met his as she rose to stand. She plucked at the button of his shirt. "My decision?"

"Of course."

She stared at his buttons for an extended length of time. "Well, then, I think I'd like to go."

"You would?" He hadn't meant to sound surprised, should have known she'd want to see her father. No matter how much he disliked the man, he was her father and always would be. The thought made his stomach curdle like old milk.

She laid her head on his chest and wrapped both arms around him.

"Yes, with you beside me, I can face anything."

He was reminded of that first day, when Belinda had chastised her for wearing an apron, and when Randi had choked at the table.

"We don't have to go."

"No," she said. "I want to go. What time are we to be there?"

"They didn't say."

She leaned back in his arms, gazed up at him.

"Well, Belinda insists a person should eat before six, so their stomach has time to digest before going to bed."

Feeling as defiant as a ten-year-old, he said, "Then I'll have one of the men take a note to the Dodge House telling them we'll arrive by seven."

Randi couldn't control the giggle that started in

her heart. As it slipped out, she said, "That will be perfect."

The dread that had settled on her shoulders when she looked out the window and saw her father and Belinda at the campsite flew away as if it had wings. Perhaps it did have wings, or maybe she had wings, or at least the ability to send the anxiety away, for that is more how it felt—like she had the power to decide if her father and Belinda would intimidate her, or if she would refuse to be threatened by them.

She leaned onto Howard's chest, hugging him with all her strength. Her life had become so perfect there was no way she was going to let it be ruined. Though Howard had never said anything since that first day, she knew he'd never wanted a wife, never wanted the extra responsibility. But yet, she also knew he cared for her.

He was extremely busy getting the hotel and restaurant up and running. She'd tried to be an asset to him, instead of a burden, and would continue with all her might. And that included not asking him for money. No matter what her father or Belinda wanted.

Tonight, at her husband's side, she'd tell them so. She wrapped her arms tighter around Howard's waist as a new fear began to take shape.

A tight knot formed in her stomach, squeezing the breath from her. They—Belinda and her father— had the ability to destroy it all, wipe Howard dry without him even knowing it. She'd seen it over the years with her mother. Every possession worth an ounce of gold had been sold off the past few years to finance her father's political career. Thoughts tumbled, rumbled about in her mind. Why hadn't she realized it before now? It was evident Howard's family had money, and if there was one thing her father was good at taking from people—it was money.

His hold tightened to keep her close as she dragged in a fresh breath of air, trying to rid her body of the sinking feeling in her stomach. It was as if a big day-old clump of bread dough had risen in her stomach. She swallowed, vowing, if she had to die trying, she'd save Howard from her father.

As if he knew fear gripped her, Howard brushed a kiss over the top of her head.

"We don't have to go if you don't want to."

She straightened, thrusting her shoulders back. "Yes, we do." Determination filled her, and she pulled a smile from the depth of her strength. "I thought you had work to do?"

A little scowl formed on his face. "I do, I did…" he stammered.

"Well, then you best get to it. We don't have time to waste if this place is going to open on schedule." She took his hand. "And I have to get supper started."

He walked beside her to the doorway. "You don't have to cook supper. We are going—"

She interrupted, "I know." Tugging him through the door, she continued, "But I already have steaks in a marinade sauce. It won't take any time to cook them up for the boys and Ma."

Chapter Twelve

They separated in the kitchen where Bug asked about some things that needed to be uncrated. Randi took her time walking across the yard, checking on the shrubs and bushes Snake had planted. Needing the distraction, she imagined how beautiful the area would look when everything was full grown and in bloom.

"Want to see the fountain?"

She pivoted and smiled at Snake standing near the back side of the hotel.

"I'd love to," she replied honestly.

Snake motioned to her with one hand. "Come here. I'm just getting ready to test it." He waited until she drew closer to add, "I hope it works like I believe it will."

"I'm sure it will," she said as they began to walk toward the large pond he'd created in the center of the back yard with bricks identical to those of the hotel. He'd used mortar to bond the bricks into a beautiful oval shape about eight-feet long and four-feet wide. In the center stood a large concrete pole about four-feet high and holding three brass saucers of various sizes. The top one was the smallest, with each one below relatively larger.

"Where will the water come from?" she asked, stopping near the pool's edge.

"I've created an aqueduct system from the creek," he said.

He'd already lost her, but not wanting to sound stupid, she simply replied, "Oh."

He nodded and pointed across the yard. "I also

built a windmill."

"Oh, that's what that is." Randi stared at the large tripod that held an unusual looking ball of iron with metal flaps encircling it.

"Yup, it's a windmill. The crank shaft will pump the water into the pond from the underground system. When I'm done, I'll plant morning glories to climb up the legs. It'll look like a tower of flowers all summer long."

"That'll be pretty," she admitted.

"There's a hole under the windmill where I dug a reservoir and put in decline platforms. Through the series of platforms I've channeled the water into a pipe that runs under the pond and up the center of the pedestal in the middle." He glanced at her and smiled. "So, if it goes as I've planned, water should spout up the middle and cascade down, over the three basins, and into the pond. I also put a small pipe in the bottom of the pool to drain the water back into the reservoir, so it won't overflow and stay clear."

Still confused, but excited to see the water bubbling out of the pedestal she said, "How do you make it start flowing?"

He winked one eye, and the action reminded her very much of her husband. "I also installed a cistern pump to fill the reservoir this first time. I figure I may have to pump it up once a day for the first few days to keep the pressure up and the flow moving. But afterwards, the windmill should be enough to keep it moving."

Again, "Oh," was the only thing she could think to say. All three of the brothers amazed her with their knowledge. Snake seemed to know everything about gardening, and it appeared water systems, and Bug had insisted Howard use oil burners, like the little parlor stove in their apartment instead of depending on wood for heat. He even said the stove

Howard had ordered for the kitchen would be oil burning. Bug continually insisted oil was the way of the future.

She turned to Snake. "How did you learn so much about all this?"

He shrugged. "I guess mainly from our brother, Kid. When he built his house he wanted indoor plumbing and bought every book he could find on it. That's where I read about aqueducts and such."

"Really? Kid's house has indoor plumbing?"

"Yup, Skeeter's too."

"I guess I thought only big mansions and such had indoor plumbing."

"Lots of places out east have indoor plumbing. The White House has had indoor plumbing since the eighteen-thirties." Snake pointed to the pedestal. "I'm going to go start pumping, you tell me when the water starts coming out."

"All right."

He walked toward the windmill. "I made this here door to cover the hole under the mill, so no one will fall in."

"That's a good idea."

Snake glanced back over his shoulder. "Wish me luck."

She laughed. "I wish you all the luck in the world. But I know it's going to work."

He lifted the door and pushed it aside, then disappeared into a hole in the ground. She glanced back and forth between the pedestal in the pond and the spot where he'd disappeared under the windmill. Within minutes, a gurgle sounded and then water began to bubble out the top of the pedestal.

"It's working!" she shouted excitedly. "It's working!"

Water quickly filled the top basin and began to cascade into the second, and then the third before it flowed onto the bricks covering the bottom of the pond. Snake didn't crawl back out, so she moved closer.

"Snake? I said it's working!"

"Great!" echoed out of the hole.

She walked over to peer down the hole. It was fairly deep, and he crouched atop a large barrel, pumping a hand pump.

"Don't you want to see it working?" she asked.

"I have to keep pumping until it fills up the first time."

"Oh." She glanced back to the pond where water continued to flow over the three basins. It was too bad Snake couldn't see how well it worked. After all he was the one who built it. Gathering her skirt, she plopped onto the ground and lowered her legs into the hole. "Here, let me pump for a bit so you can go check to make sure it's working properly."

He glanced at her, excitement shining in his eyes, but instead of agreeing to her request, he grimaced.

"I don't think Hog would like that."

"Don't think he'd like what?" She landed on top of the barrel beside him.

"You in this hole for one. Pumping water for the other." He pointed to the ladder she'd used to climb down with his free hand. "You best climb back out," he said without slowing the rhythm of the pump handle.

"Oh, for heaven's sake. I've been pumping water since I was three." She took a hold of the handle and started to pump. "Go on now, go see how it looks."

He glanced to the top of the hole, and then back to her.

She could tell he fought a hard battle. He really wanted to go see it but didn't know if he should.

"Go on," she encouraged.

A smile that made his eyes snap filled his face. "All right. I'll be right back, just keep pumping, slow and easy." He watched her motions as he pulled his hand away.

"I've got it. Go on!"

"Thanks, Randi." He scrambled up the ladder and over the edge.

"You're welcome!" she shouted, figuring he was already halfway to the pond. Leaning back against the wall that had been reinforced with bricks, she continued lifting the handle up and down. The round windmill was directly above. Metal bars had been bent and intertwined like a skein of yarn. The wind flaps were spooned to catch the smallest of breezes. As she watched, it took to flight twirling and twisting. It was uniquely lovely, and once again, she found awe in Snake's knowledge.

He was so silly, thinking Howard wouldn't want her pumping water. Good Lord, she'd helped do everything else, why on earth would he care if she helped with this?

The thought had no sooner formed when a dark shadow fell over the opening above. She glanced up and smiled at the man staring down at her.

"Hello," she said with all the brightness she felt in her heart.

"What the hell do you think you're doing?" Howard literally growled.

The sound shocked her and made her nerves go raw at the same time.

"Excuse me?" He'd never used that tone with her before.

He crouched, stretched a hand toward her. "Get out of there."

She kept pumping. "No, I'm helping Snake."

"Snake doesn't need your help. There's a yard full of men he can ask." He waved his hand. "Now come on, get out of there."

"No." The tips of her ears were on fire, and her breath intake increased. She really had no idea why she was so angry with him, other than his tone, and the fact he told her to get out of the hole.

Why would he tell her to get out of the hole? The past few weeks he'd made a point of asking for her opinions, asking for her assistance. She glared up at him, pumping the handle with hard thrusts.

"Snake asked *me* to help him, and *I am*."

He jumped into the hole. "Not any longer, you're not!" He grabbed her around the waist and shoved her upwards.

She screeched, and her arms flayed.

Snake caught her upper arms and tugged, lifting her out of the hole.

"Sorry, Randi, I didn't think he'd like it."

Her hands balled into fists, she planted them on her hips. "I don't really care what he likes and doesn't like."

Howard appeared before her eyes, as if he'd leaped out of the pit in a single bound.

"Oh, you don't do you?" His face had become extremely red.

"No, I don't!" She twisted, trying to break the hold he all of sudden had on her arm.

He drew a ragged breath through his nose. The sound filled the air snapping around them. His lips parted, and he blew the air out slowly.

"Ran-di," he said, drawing her name into two very long syllables.

It reminded her so much of how Belinda said her name, the frustration burning her chest emitted with a loud, "Ohhhhh!" She met his dagger-filled eyes with matching ones.

"Let go of me this instant, Howard Quinter, or you'll be sorry."

He lifted an eyebrow in a very mocking way. "I'll be sorry?"

She raised her knee and drove it between his legs. It didn't make a direct connection to his groin, but was close enough to make him release his hold.

"I warned you," she shouted, hitching her skirt and running as fast as possible to the campsite.

Near Ma's tent, she chanced a glance over her shoulder and saw him talking with Snake. They weren't really talking. Howard was waving an arm toward her and shouting at his brother. She paused, questioned if she should run back to protect Snake. Before she made up her mind, Snake threw his hands into the air and climbed back into the hole. She twisted and stomped into the tent.

"Land sakes, girl, what happened to you?" Ma's startled gaze settled on the front of her dress.

Streaks of green and brown covered the entire front of her yellow dress.

"Oh!" she screeched with frustration and frantically wiped at her bodice with both hands.

"You're only making it worse." Ma stood from her stool and grasped her wrists. "Stop, you're smearing it all over. What happened?"

Randi squeezed her eyes shut, refused to let her anger turn her into a blubbering idiot. It didn't work, the tears pushed their way out and with a mewing sound she crumpled onto Ma's cot.

Ma sat beside her, rubbed her back until the tears flowing from her eyes slowed.

"There, now, feeling better?"

"No," Randi declared.

"Want to tell me what happened?"

"I don't know." Randi shrugged.

"I'm a good listener," Ma said, still rubbing her back.

Randi gave a half-hearted smile. "I mean I don't know what happened. I was just helping Snake, and he yelled at me."

Ma stiffened. "Snake yelled at you? Why that little whipper-snap. He knows better. I'll—"

"No," Randi supplied, "Not Snake. Howard."

"Hog yelled at you?" Ma sounded like it was unbelievable he'd do such a thing. "Why?"

"I don't know. I was down in the hole, pumping the water for Snake."

Ma held up a hand. "Down in what hole? The one Snake dug for the windmill?"

Randi nodded.

"Honey," Ma started, handing over a handkerchief embroidered with yellow flowers. "Dry your eyes, and let me tell you a little bit about men."

Randi attempted to keep a startled look from racing across her face. It didn't work.

Ma, all five feet of her, shook with good humor.

"I not only raised five good men, I was married to the best one that ever stepped foot on this earth." She nodded. "Land sakes, that man made my heart sing, and all it took was the faintest smile, or to see a glimmer in those big brown eyes of his and I was quivering in my boots."

"You were?"

"Yes, I was. We women are funny that way, how we let a man get so deep in our hearts it practically bleeds just for them." She patted Randi's hand. "But let me tell you, men are worse."

"They are?"

"Yes, they are. Men got this way of thinking that they have to protect their woman all the time. And if Hog yelled at you 'cause you were down in that hole, he was most likely scared you'd get hurt."

"Hurt? I was perfectly safe."

"You knew that, but he didn't. He was probably conjuring up all kinds of things that could happen to you. Snakes could have been hiding down there, or some nasty spiders. One of the water lines could have broken, or that pump spring let loose."

"I never thought of any of those things," Randi admitted.

Ma nodded. "Most likely, none of them would

have happened. But you see, a man likes to know his woman is safe all the time. When something happens to her, whether he could have prevented it or not, he blames himself. Loving you is still new to Hog, and he's still learning the ins and outs, but I gotta say he most likely won't get any better. His pa never did. That man watched me like a hawk from morning 'til night. Probably the whole time I was asleep as well. God, I miss him. Suspect I will 'til the day the Good Lord takes me to meet up with him."

The words of Hog loving her had caused all the air to leave her lungs, and Randi had to rub her chest to get the organs moving again. When air seeped in, and she found her voice, she said, "Hog loves me?"

Ma frowned. "Yes, he loves you."

"He never said he loves me."

"So?"

"So?"

"Randi that man loves you as much as his pa loved me. No, the man didn't say it constantly, not with words anyway. Didn't have to. The look on his face said it loud and clear every day."

Her heart was thumping so hard, she wondered if there were two of them beating in her chest. Randi frowned.

"He yelled at me because he loves me?"

"Of course. Do you think he would have yelled at any other woman for being down in that hole?"

She shrugged.

Ma shook her head. "He wouldn't have. I know that for certain."

"Why didn't he just ask me to climb out?"

Ma let out a guffaw. "When a man thinks his woman is in danger, his instincts take over, kinda like a cornered wolf. I think something inside their brain just snaps or maybe quits working."

Randi let the words sink in, wondering for a

moment before she asked, "Is it that way with all men?"

Ma shook her head. "Nope. Just the good ones. The bad ones, they don't care about anyone 'cept themselves. Not even their women."

A chill ripped up Randi's spine, and she glanced at Ma, somehow knowing they both had thoughts of her father.

Ma patted her hand. "I gotta say something here, child."

Randi nodded, clenched her hands.

Ma took a deep breath, gave her head a quick shake. "My Hog loves you. Won't ever let anything happen to you. And you got yourself a passel full of brothers now, who love you just as if you were born their sister. But not all men are as good as my boys. There's some mean ones out there. I think there's been one whose been a hurtin' you for some time now. So, I want you to stick close by, make sure one of the boys is always near ya. That ways you'll be safe." She patted her hand. "With my boys around, you'll always be taken care of, darlin'. Always."

Randi shivered as if a goose had just ambled over her grave.

****

Sweat poured down his back. Howard shifted the load on his shoulder and marched up the flight of stairs. Huffing in air, he paused on the landing to catch his breath. Dang it, all he had done was told her to get out of that hole. Hell, anything could have happened to her down there. Snake should have known better than to ask her to do something like that. And he'd better never do it again. No one had, he made certain of that, he'd told them all she wasn't allowed to help at the hotel, at all.

"Geez, Hog. I would have helped you carry that. Those rugs are as heavy as a load of bricks." Bug walked out of one of the rooms at the end of the hall, striding toward him. "Let me help, what room are you going to?"

"I got it," he grumbled.

Bug paused, his face flashed confusion for a moment. "Which room?"

Howard nodded toward the closest room. All of a sudden the rug had become extremely heavy. Bug leaped forward, opened the door, and stood aside for Howard to carry in the load.

He dropped it onto the pile of several others, and then bent forward. Pressing both hands to his knees, he drew in several long breaths, wishing he could gain control of his heart as easily as he could his breathing.

"You carried all of those up here?" Bug asked, pointing at the mountain of rolled rugs.

"Yes," he huffed.

"Why?"

He straightened. "Because they're the rugs for the rooms on this floor."

Bug nodded. "I know, but they didn't all need to be carried up right now, did they?"

Howard glanced to the rugs. He'd wanted something physical to do, needed to burn off his annoyance. Hefting the huge rugs up the stairs seemed like a good idea at the time.

"Yes, they did," he said, trying to convince himself as much as his brother.

Bug rubbed a hand over his chin. Though the youngest of the five brothers was now twenty-one, Bug had that pretty little-boy appearance and didn't look much over sixteen.

"I see," Bug said.

Howard glared. "You see what?"

"You and Randi had a tiff, did ya?"

"No, we didn't have *a tiff*."

"That's not what Snake says."

"Ya, well Snake better keep his trap shut if he

knows what's good for him."

Bug sat down on the heap of rugs and patted the space beside him. "Have a seat."

Howard frowned. Who did Bug think he was? He wasn't about to sit down and listen to what the little snap had to say. He moved over to stand by one of the framed in window spaces, hoped the breeze would cool his sweating body.

Bug patted the rugs again. "Come on, have a seat."

Not the faintest breeze entered. Where was the wind Kansas was so known for when he needed it? Howard ran a hand over the back of his neck, where the muscles were stiffening from the strain of carrying so much. A brief rest couldn't hurt. He moved across the room and plopped down beside his brother.

Still miffed, he bluntly said, "We didn't have a tiff."

Bug bobbed his head up and down several times. After a few stilled moments, he said, "These are nice rugs. Gonna look real fetchin'."

"Yeah," Howard mumbled.

"I got the last of the closet doors installed." Bug let out a low whistle. "Built in closets in every room. Folks ain't gonna know what to think when they see them. You really think Lila knows what's she talking about?" He waved a hand about the hotel room. "Built in closets, a private bathing station in each room," he turned, lifted an eyebrow, "room service?"

Howard shrugged. "I believe her. They all sound like things people may want while staying at a luxury hotel."

"She's probably right. Women usually are. Guess it's instinct or something. Men are the hot headed ones. We spout off without thinking, just jump into action. Where as women, they're always thinking."

A shower of cold rain couldn't have been more awakening. Howard took a deep breath.

"Are you saying Randi's right, too? That I was just spouting off?"

Bug stood up. "I ain't saying nothing. But I'll tell you Randi carried an armload of clothes up to your rooms a short time ago. And Ma said the two of you are going out to have supper in town tonight."

"Shit!" Howard leaped to his feet. "I forgot. What time is it?"

Bug pulled a watch out of his front pocket. "A little after six."

Chapter Thirteen

Howard eased the door off the hallway open and peeked around the edge before stepping into the empty sitting room. Closing the door behind him, he turned to slip into the bathing chamber.

"Howard?"

One foot stalled mid-air at the sound of his name. She was in the bedroom, the tone of her voice was light, not laced with anger as it had been before—after he'd thrust her out of the hole. A heavy sigh left his chest. Had he heard the tone right, or was it just wishful thinking? He lowered the foot to the floor and quivering like a kid in trouble, walked to the doorway.

As earlier, she sat at the little table, this time she poked pins into the back of her hair. He moved farther in so he could peer in the mirror. He loved the way she made her hair billow out from her face and situated tiny curls to hang down at her temples and in front of each ear.

His heart stopped as their gazes met. One corner of her lips barely inched upwards.

"Hello," she said.

"Hello," he croaked, unable to swallow the frog in his throat.

"I laid clean clothes in the bathroom. That is if you still want to go." She lowered her arms and twisted about to look at him.

"Yeah, sure," he answered, a touch apprehensive. "If you still want to go."

"I do."

"All right." He pointed to his shirt. "I'll go get

162

cleaned up."

She stood, and every muscle in his big frame pulled tight. The gown she wore fit her like an old glove, so snug every curve of her body was highlighted. The raven-black material had tiny silver stitches running along a very low neckline, drawing his eyes directly to her cleavage. The firm mounds popped out of the material as if they wanted to play a game of hide and seek with him.

He gulped. "Y-you look incredible." The word was inferior, didn't begin to describe how beautiful she looked, but it was the only one his fumbling mind could come up with. She must have liked it because a faint pink blush lit up her cheeks.

"Thank you." She stepped closer, and her sweet unique scent, which always reminded him of vanilla, filled his nose. "About this afternoon," she started, lowering her dark lashes. "I—I'm sorry. I-I over reacted."

Repent flooded his system, made him feel lower than an ant. "No. It was my fault. I'm sorry, I—uh spouted off without thinking." Bug's words seemed a fitting explanation. She was close enough to wrap his arms around, but he couldn't, sweat still trickled under his arms. He held up both hands and took a step back.

"I gotta get cleaned up, or we'll be late."

Her top teeth bit her bottom lip so hard the area turned white, and her gaze held a touch of uncertainty. She dipped her head.

"Of course."

He couldn't resist and leaned forward to brush a kiss to her forehead.

"I won't be long, I promise."

Less than fifteen minutes later, he, too, decided running water was a remarkable discovery. After buttoning the tan silk vest with tiny brown diamond shapes weaved in the material, he grabbed the jacket hanging on the hook on the back of the door and left the room.

"Randi? Randi? Where did these new clothes come from?"

She twisted her elegant neck to gaze at him from where she sat on the settee in the front room. The sight had the ability to puff his chest with stalled air. He'd thought of how she'd look, sitting in the middle of this room while he built it, but the real sight was even more charming than when he'd imagined it. She was as well-designed as her surroundings—a queen in a royal court.

"Does it fit?" she asked.

"Uh?" It took his wandering mind a moment to register what she asked. "Yes." He slid his arms in the black, silk-lined jacket. "Yes, they fit. Where'd they come from?"

"Your mother made them. She was going to wait until the grand opening to give them to us, but decided we should wear them tonight." With both hands, she lifted her alluring skirt, stood, and then walked around the furniture, meeting him in the middle of the room. Her fingers immediately went to his tie, deftly tied it into a knot—without choking him, a feat in itself.

"Turn around," she said. "I told her I'd inspect it, make sure it fits perfectly."

He did as instructed, feeling a bit foolish having a woman scrutinize him so.

"It's fine," he said, stopping so they once again faced each other. "Did she make yours, too?"

"Yes, isn't she talented?" She hitched her skirt off the floor and twirled around so quickly he barely caught sight of the dress.

He took her shoulders. "Do that again, but slower, let me inspect your dress."

Her smile hit his heart like a bullet. Slowly, she turned, whipping her head about so their eyes met for most of the time.

When she stopped, once again facing him, she asked, "So, what do you think?"

"I think you're the most beautiful woman I've ever seen." He couldn't wait any longer, not without dying leastwise. Without further ado he lowered his head and covered her lips with a smoldering kiss.

He'd much rather stay here, in their apartment, and slowly uncover the beautiful body beneath the attractive black dress, but knowing they couldn't, he raised his face, easing out of the kiss with several small pecks.

Randi sighed, a sound that made his groin quiver, and rested her head against his chest.

"Do we have to go?" she asked, breathlessly.

He chuckled, stepped back to lift her chin and gaze into her majestic eyes. That's it, he thought, the name of their hotel flashed across his mind, The Majestic. His chest filled with pride.

"Yes, my dear wife, we have to go. A few minutes ago you said you wanted to."

"I know, but that was before you kissed me."

Her eyes shimmered with such promise that he truly considered changing their plans.

"We'll leave early," he declared, brushing one more kiss over her lips.

****

The Dodge House was nice, but with black and white checkered tablecloths and heavy dull stoneware dishes, it held none of the elegance Howard's—no their—hotel would possess. Then again, maybe it was her. While walking to the restaurant Randi silently tried to boost her courage, ready herself to tell her father he wouldn't be receiving a donation from her husband—not if she had anything to say about it anyway. But the minute she'd seen her father and Belinda across the crowded room, her throat locked up tighter than if she'd eaten a batch of poison berries, and her toes began to tremble.

Randi smoothed the red plaid napkin lying on her lap and snuck a peek at her husband sitting beside her. Dashing, downright amazingly handsome in his impeccable new suit, there wasn't a man in all of Dodge who could compete with his attractiveness. Probably not one in all of Kansas, or the world for that matter, and the knowledge made her body sizzle, especially since he was hers—all hers. A touch of fortitude returned.

The Majestic. During their walk to the Dodge House, Howard had asked what she thought of the name for their hotel, and she'd quickly agreed. She loved it. The name not only described the hotel, it described him, and her life of late.

She didn't attempt to quell the smile forming on her face, there really was no use. She was just too happy and literally bubbling with joy that not even her stepmother could lessen the feeling. Her throat opened, and the newfound strength she'd possessed the last few weeks returned. She'd tell them there would be no donation, and that they should return to Topeka, post haste.

"You certainly seem smug tonight," Belinda said from across the table, her brow slightly elevated.

Howard reached over and captured Randi's hand. She flashed her smile his way.

"No, just happy," she admitted. "Just happy."

He squeezed her hand and winked. Belinda huffed. Randi chose to ignore it and rolled her hand to fit more snuggly in his. When she knew stepmother was about to make another snide remark, she pulled her gaze from her husband's and turned to her father.

"How was your trip to the Badlands?"

Her father, usually very composed, sputtered into the glass of rum held against his lip. After

166

swallowing a couple times, he answered, "Fine." He set the glass down, cleared his throat, and blinked his watery eyes. "Just fine. Steven and his wife, Lila, are remarkable people. And their home is quite lovely." Glancing to Belinda, he added, "Isn't it, dear?"

"Hmm, a bit unusual, but nice nonetheless," Belinda replied as if not really interested. Her eyes, darkly rimmed with kohl, had been roaming Howard ever since they'd arrived.

They sat at a square table, one person per side. All of a sudden Randi had a strong urge to make Howard switch seats with her to put more space between him and her stepmother. The sensation was odd, but very strong. As if he read her mind, he did, very discreetly, scoot his chair her way a touch. Belinda, of course, noticed and settled a disgruntled stare Randi's way.

She let her happy grin remain on her face, it actually had increased a mite by his actions. Well, that and the fact Howard loved her. The knowledge was enough to make her capable of conquering the world. Slowly, she turned away from Belinda, back to her father. She didn't want to just blurt out her decision and thought after a touch more small talk she'd ease into the subject of donations.

"And their children? Ma—I mean, Stephanie says they're very delightful."

"Oh, yes, yes they are quite delightful." Her father set his glass down. "The little girl," his glance once again went to Belinda, "what's her name, dear?"

"Kendra," Howard supplied.

"Yes." Belinda laid her hand on Howard's arm resting on the table. "Yes, Kendra. Such an unusual name. Don't you think?"

He removed his arm, settled his hand on his leg under the table. "No, I don't think it's unusual at all.

167

It was Lila's mother's name."

Randi kept smiling, delighted. She knew she was being spiteful, but Belinda had been rather nasty over the years and seeing the woman rebuked for once in her life was rather delightful. Or maybe she was just so cheerful everything about the night was enjoyable and knowing what would happen when they returned to their apartment was the most pleasing thought of all.

"Yes, Kendra, that's it," her father continued as if nothing had interrupted his report. "She already rides a horse, all by herself. And is very good."

Howard let out a low laugh. "I can believe that. Skeeter's had her on the horse with him almost since the day she was born."

Randi found herself wondering what kind of father Howard would be and instantly decided he'd be a wonderful parent. He'd been so kind and caring to her since the moment they met, he'd surely be just as loving to their children. While Howard and her father conversed about Skeeter's family, her mind took a different path. She marveled at how contently she looked toward the future, a future she knew she'd have with her husband. It wasn't just because she felt safe and cared for, but because it was what she desired above all else—a life with him—forevermore.

"I'd prefer not to discuss politics over dinner," Howard's statement yanked her back to the conversation. Randi held her breath, wondering what she'd missed. Had her father asked for money? Her knees began to shake.

Belinda let out a snide chuckle. "I'm afraid, Howard, that is quite impossible. Politics is all Thurston knows how to discuss. After all, he's been in politics for years, he knows what Kansas needs, and it is his foremost ambition to become the next governor."

Howard leaned back, giving the waiter room to set a dinner plate, piled high with a large beef steak and fried potatoes, in front of him.

"Thank you," he said to the young man wearing a white apron splattered with grease spots. Making no comment to acknowledge he'd heard Belinda, he lifted his silverware and waited for everyone else to be served before slicing into his meat.

Randi held in the shiver rippling her shoulders. She could all but see thick tension oozing off Howard. Why hadn't she been listening? How much had her father asked for? After glancing around the table, she followed suit, cut into her food, and tried to focus on the meal. The outside crust of the beef was charred stiff, and the inside seeped red juice. The food at their restaurant would be considerably better, she silently vowed as she raised her fork to her mouth. The meat was as tough as it looked and needed to be chewed an extended amount of time before she could swallow.

Evidently, every steak was tough because silence filled the table as everyone chewed. It was several minutes before her father took a sip of his drink.

"Howard, er, Mr. Quinter, I would think you'd be very interested in what's happening right now, especially with your new hotel."

Howard didn't respond, just cut another slice off his steak.

Her father continued, "If the current legislatures have their way, they'll be hitting you with a hefty tax bill. Now, the Populist Party, we believe in a graduated income tax. With our system you'd be allowed to keep a much larger portion of the income your establishment takes in."

Randi glanced to Howard. Her fork paused near her lips. He'd quit chewing, and the veins in his neck pulsated. She squared her shoulders and took a deep breath, readying herself to stand up to her father and his request. But Howard spoke first.

"Mr. Fulton," he said, not pleasant in any way as he laid down his fork and met her father's gaze with a solid, deep stare. "If you are unable to refrain from talking politics, I'm afraid, my wife and I will need to leave."

"Well, now that's just silly," Belinda said, once again reaching over to lay her hand on Howard's arm.

He pulled it away. This time a crystal clear understanding he didn't welcome her touch, but his gaze never left her father's. Randi laid her fork across her plate, a chunk of meat still stuck in its tines, and wondered if she glanced up if she'd see a storm cloud hovering over the table.

"No, no dear, that's not silly," her father finally said. "If H-Mr. Quinter doesn't wish to discuss politics, we won't discuss politics." He waved his fork around the table. "Please, everyone, eat your food before it grows cold."

The silence was as thick as the meat and just as charred. A clink of a fork, or thud of a glass being set down were the only sounds as the meal was consumed. Everyone's plate, minus Belinda's who'd ate as if nothing was amiss, held a large portion of their meal still sitting on them when the waiter removed the dishes from the table. Howard thanked the man for the meal, though Randi knew it was half-hearted and didn't have anything to do with the poor cooking.

Her father drew two cheroots from his breast pocket, offered one to Howard. He politely declined, which she was thankful for, having never liked the smell of the cigars. She reached over and laid a hand on Howard's.

He met her gaze, and then turned to her father. "I hope you will excuse us now, we need to get back to the hotel."

"So soon? I thought perhaps we could visit a while." Her father's gaze never roamed to her. "I really think you'd be interested in my reform package."

Howard pushed his chair away from the table and reached into his breast pocket. After laying several bills on the table, he stood and pulled her chair back.

"No, we need to leave now."

Randi rose and bowed her head in farewell. Her husband, who was normally so relaxed and friendly, was stiff and uptight, clearly very upset. As they walked through the dining room, she noticed all the eyes following them and immediately knew the churning in her stomach had nothing to do with the meal. It was as if a storm cloud hovered over the entire room.

Anxious, she all but bolted out the front door when Howard pushed it open. Randi took a deep breath, tried to chase away the heaviness in her chest. She'd apologize for her father's behavior as soon as they were alone. A short square man with a printer's cap and pen and paper in hand stopped them not two steps out the door.

"Mr. Quinter," the man began. "My name is Carl Robertson. I'm with the *Ford County Globe.*"

"I know who you are," Howard answered stiffly.

"Could you answer a few questions?" Carl Robertson asked, licking on the tip of his stubby pencil.

"No." Howard grabbed her elbow.

Randi double stepped, trying to keep up with Howard's long strides as Mr. Robertson followed at a quick pace behind them.

"Mr. Quinter, how long have you been acquainted with Thurston Fulton?"

Randi glanced over her shoulder, then back to

Howard, now almost running to keep up with him. Chin thrust forward and lips pinched tight together, Howard continued to pull her down the road.

After a few more attempts, Mr. Robertson gave up and turned around, making a beeline back to the Dodge House. Randi didn't comment, couldn't really since she was almost breathless. It wasn't until they came to the front of their hotel that Howard slowed his pace. A loud, ragged sigh left his chest before he led her across the front lawn.

Once they entered their rooms, Randi drew her own sigh of relief and turned to face her husband.

"I am so sorry."

He glanced up.

"I wasn't listening. I'm sorry for that too." She bowed her head. "How much did he ask for?"

"What? Ask me for what?"

"Money. How much money did my father ask you to give him?"

He frowned.

She stepped closer, rested her hands on his jacket lapels. "Please believe me when I say I didn't have anything to do with it. Please."

His hesitation let her know he struggled, tried to figure out what to say.

She stepped back, shrugged at the anxiety covering her shoulders. "I didn't think he'd asked you for it in the middle of dinner."

His frown grew deeper as he met her gaze.

"I thought I had time, I thought..." She huffed out air, not really sure what she thought.

Howard's head shook with an odd movement, like he checked his hearing.

"I didn't know Edward Keyes had paid to marry me. I didn't know things like that happen." She turned her back on him and continued, "I'm afraid I don't know much about politics and such. I lived my whole life on the farm, and Mama, well, she didn't like to talk about my father, so we didn't. After she died, I moved to Topeka." She shrugged again, knowing she had to tell him the truth. "I was only there for a few weeks before I left. When he told you I was a hostess for his parties, he lied. I've never attended a political gathering of any kind."

"You didn't know…you haven't—"

"Well, I'm not completely ignorant." She spun around, interrupting him. Attempting to make herself sound a mite more intelligent, she added, "I mean I read some things, I know some things about our government. And I can learn more. I can read very well." She turned about, unable to face him. "I've just never been interested in politics. I'm sorry if that's a disappointment to you."

He flipped her around. "Your father sold you?"

She blinked, thought about it for a minute. "Well, I guess you could say that. But I ran away before I married him." Ice-cold pin-pricks tickled her shoulders. "He was a creepy old man."

"So now your father expects me to pay him the same amount?"

"I don't know the amount. But Belinda said I had to get a donation from you to make up for—"

He held up one hand. "When? When were you told to get this donation?"

"When they left for your brother's," she answered, staring at her toes, unable to meet his steely gaze.

"You haven't asked me for any money," he said.

She twirled about again and wiped at the tears trickling down her cheeks. If she tried to talk, she'd most likely sob aloud, so she shook her head.

His hands covered her shoulders, and he used the hold to twist her toward him. "Why not?"

She shrugged, still unable to speak.

"Randi." He tipped her head up by placing one finger beneath her chin. His eyes were serious, extremely solemn. "I won't give your father one red cent."

She nodded. "I know, and I don't want you to. I'm sorry he asked. I was going to tell him not to expect anything, but I was too busy..." The blood rushing into her cheeks made her pause.

"Too busy doing what?" he asked.

"Thinking how much I love you. How wonderful my life is with you."

He didn't say a word as his finger traced the outline of her face. The touch, soft and caring, was enough to make the tears form again.

"I'm so very sorry," she said.

"You have nothing to be sorry about," he said. "Your father didn't ask me for any money."

"He didn't?" she asked, searching his face, looking for the truth.

His eyes, though still shadowed, held a touch of glimmer way in the back. "No, he didn't." He leaned forward, pressed his lips to her forehead. "I love you, too."

She leaned in, absorbing the warmth of his caress.

"I would give up everything I have for you." He set her back a touch, gazed down at her. "But not to your father. I can't support his political beliefs. I might as well burn down the hotel."

She bit her lip, not sure what to say.

He let out a long sigh. "But, that's not going to happen. And it's not for you to worry about. I'll take care of it."

Her mind spun a million miles an hour. If her father hadn't asked for money, what had he asked that had upset Howard so? "I wish I wasn't such a disappointment to you."

He frowned. "Nothing about you is a disappointment to me."

"What I said before is true. I've never hosted a

party."

"So? Neither have I. I'm sure we'll learn as we go." He pulled her close again, brushed a kiss to the top of her hair.

The simple touch, his nearness, made the walls of her heart swell. "Really?"

"Yes, really."

She pulled back a touch and looked up at him. "I do love you, and I'll do anything, everything I can to prove it to you."

His hands slipped from her shoulders, roamed up and down her arms, and the glimmer in his eyes grew stronger.

"You don't have to prove it to me. I know you love me. Just as I love you," he finished in a whisper, lowering his face.

His kiss consumed her, led her into a world where no one but she and he existed.

By the time the kiss ended, the Dodge House, her father, even Belinda had flown out of her mind, floated away like the seeds of a dandelion. She reached up, began to unbutton his suit jacket.

"I'm glad we came home early."

His fingers went to her hair, and one by one, he plucked out the pins, letting them fall to the thick carpet beneath their feet.

"So am I," he whispered before his mouth captured hers again.

Chapter Fourteen

Howard knew it would happen and shouldn't have been surprised, still the commotion outside jolted his body upright. Beside him, snuggled beneath the covers and encompassed in the haven of slumber he'd been in seconds ago, Randi rolled over. Flipping the covers aside, he padded barefoot across the carpet and out the bedroom door to one of the front room windows.

Throbbing, his gullet rose, blocking his windpipe while the heaviness of known dread covered his shoulders like a heavy winter coat. A good two dozen men had gathered below along with their horses and a few wagons. The street was full. They shouted amongst themselves, gesturing toward his building.

He twisted and hurried to the bedroom to get dressed before addressing his lynching party. It had been inevitable, so why was he shocked? In a matter of seconds, he was dressed and leaving the room. Howard paused for a split second, glancing back to the bed. It had been his choice, from the moment he'd realized Thurston Fulton was her father, he'd known if he stayed married to her this moment would come.

He pulled the door closed and moved across the front room to the door that would lead him below. It had been the right choice. She meant more to him than anything else on earth. If needed, they'd start over. Somewhere other than Dodge—that is if he lived long enough for their marriage to last longer than the past month.

Bug and Snake met him as he stepped off the

stairway, the back door still swinging open from their rush inside.

"What's going on?" Bug asked.

He pushed his way around them, walking to the foyer.

"I'm assuming my dinner at the Dodge House with a member of the Populist Party made the front page of the paper this morning."

"Aw, shit," Snake said, walking beside him. "I wish Kid was here."

"Well, he's not," Howard said, wishing his oldest brother was here as well. "You boys don't have to come with me."

"Like hell we don't," Bug said, clicking open the chamber of his six-shooter and stuffing in brass plated bullets before sliding the gun back into his holster.

All three of them, shoulder to shoulder, walked out the double front doors and down the steps. The crowd, quite rambunctious, mellowed a touch, and Howard silently thanked his brothers for flanking him. Steps as sequenced as a line of soldiers, he and Snake and Bug strode to the edge of the street.

"Morning, George." Howard nodded to the ex-sheriff. George Hinkle was a friend of the family, and Howard was willing to accept any allowances the relationship may provide. Hinkle was a born peacemaker, and Howard felt the town had suffered a loss when George, after marrying the local school teacher, chose not to run for reelection. He had yet to meet Pat Sughrue, Hinkle's replacement, hadn't had a need—up until now that is.

George tipped the edge of his hat to each of them. "Hog, Snake, Bug."

"What's going on out here?" Howard asked, playing ignorance.

George stepped forward, handed Howard a newspaper.

The headlines, a good two inches tall, leaped from the page. *Owner of New Hotel a Populist.* His temples pounded. Howard handed the paper to Snake and turned to the crowd.

"Hell, George, you know me. You know all of us. Kid's the President of the Stockgrowers Association. You can't believe I'm a Populist."

George shrugged. "Thurston Fulton claims the Quinter's are his relatives. And some of his biggest supporters."

Howard clenched his jaw, there was no use lying. "Thurston Fulton is my father-in-law—"

The crowd began to roar, obscenities flew through the air. Men slapped their hats against their legs and overall let it be known how disgusting they found his statement.

Rubbing the back of his neck, George stepped closer and dipped his head.

"That's quite an alliance."

Howard grimaced. "You think I don't know that?"

"Could be enough to get yourself hanged."

"Yeah, I know."

****

Shocked to find half the bed empty, since the sun wasn't even completely filling the sky yet, Randi scooted out from beneath the covers.

"Howard?" she asked, walking toward the door. The eerie feeling of knowing she was alone in their room tickled her spine. She stopped before opening the door to quickly throw on her underclothes and a day dress.

Voices floated through the window as she stepped into the front room, drawing her to the panes of glass. A large crowd lined the street. Looking none to friendly, the group stood in the middle of the road, facing off against three men near the edge. Her heart somersaulted and landed in the pit of her stomach with a solid thud when the familiar shapes of Howard, Snake, and Bug registered.

Thrusting the door open, she tore down the stairs, stumbling to a halt only when she ran smack dab into someone.

"Hold up there, girl." Ma caught her with both hands.

Randi tried to bolt around the other woman. "What's going on out there?"

Ma held her ground, wouldn't let her pass. "Don't rightly know. But my boys'll take care of it."

Just then the back door flew open. Aunt Corrine, red curls sticking out in all directions and her satin, lacy dressing gown flapping like a cape behind her, rushed into the kitchen. Her bright, searching eyes landed on Randi.

"Oh, Randi! Thank God you're all right!" Arms stretched Corrine leaped across the room.

Randi had to lock her knees to keep from tumbling as Corrine landed against her chest and wrapped arms around her shoulders. She patted the other woman's back, and then pushed her aunt's flyaway red curls out of her face.

"Of course I'm all right. Why wouldn't I be?"

Corrine stepped back, pressed a hand to her bosom dramatically. "That mob for one!" Her other hand patted Randi's shoulder. "But don't worry, Danny's out there, he won't let them hurt Hog."

Air refused to move out of her lungs, no matter how hard she gasped, air wouldn't go in or out. Danny J hadn't been able to protect himself from being shot, let alone someone else. She glanced to Ma, wanting the other woman to say something, anything.

Air finally flowed in, and Randi grabbed Corrine's arm. "Hurt Howard? Why? Who?"

Corrine looked around the kitchen area still

very much under construction. "Is there a place we can sit down?" she asked, her gaze stopping on Ma.

Ma gestured toward the stairs and took Randi's arm. "Come on, let's go upstairs."

Randi shook her head. "No, I—"

"There's nothing we can do out there. Come on." Ma nodded toward Corrine who took a hold of Randi's other arm.

Between the two women, one tugging and one pushing, Randi didn't have a choice but to trudge up the stairs. Once they stepped through the doorway, she broke loose and ran to the window. The mob had grown, flowed a distance down the road. Howard, Snake, and Bug still stood near the front of the property, two other men, one she recognized as Danny J, stood near them. No one had their guns drawn, which she hoped, was a good sign.

Behind her Corrine screeched, "Oh, my goodness, Randi! This place is gorgeous!"

Pulling her gaze from the street, she twisted. "What is going on? Why are all those men here?"

Corinne patted the back of the settee. "Come sit down."

Randi shook her head.

Corrine held something out in one hand. Randi took a final glance out the window. No one had moved, so she walked across the room, took a newspaper out of Corrine's grasp. The large headline across the front made her plop onto the couch while she scanned the rest of the article. Her father was quoted as saying he was related to the Quinter family, and that they financially supported his campaign and his plans of reform including the alliance with the railroads.

Randi read the article a second time, but still didn't understand the crowd on the street. She lifted her gaze to her aunt.

Corrine frowned, her eyes extremely sad. "You

have no idea, do you?"

Randi watched as her aunt walked around to take the seat next to her.

"No," she admitted.

Corrine flounced her dressing gown, twisted and tugged on her pantaloons until everything was situated before she began, "I don't know what your mother told you over the years, but what I am about to say is the truth."

"Mama?" Randi asked. How could her mother have anything to do with all this?

One of Corrine's hands patted her cheek. "Your mother was so young when you were born, barely fourteen, much too young to have a child."

"No, she was—"

Corinne pressed a finger against Randi's lips. "Randilynn, what I'm saying is the truth."

Randi nodded, figuring it didn't matter how old Mama was, she was gone now.

Her aunt took the newspaper, pointed to the headline. "The real reason I had to hide you at Danny J's wasn't because I was afraid he'd make you work for him. Danny's not like that, he'd never make a woman do something she doesn't want to do. It was because of this. Being a Populist in Dodge right now is worse than being an outlaw. A horse thief is less likely to get hanged."

It was as if she went numb, completely unable to feel anything.

"Why?"

"Along with several other odd beliefs, the Populist Party claims the government should own all the railroads and their attempts to make it happen have started more than one range war. The cattlemen claim they already pay enough to have their cattle shipped east, and if the government owns the railroads they're sure to set more regulations and taxes on shipping, the costs will be unaffordable. New railroads are being built every day, and the Populist Party believes the rail companies shouldn't pay the land owners for their property when laying a new line. They claim the land owner should simply give it to the railroads as part of their citizenship."

Corrine put the paper down. "There's a lot more to it than that. Populists also want to abolish national banks and several other things I can't think of right now. I don't know much about it all, but believe me when I say the folks around here want nothing to do with them. Just six weeks ago there was a big shootout at George Hoover's place." She paused to explain, "He owns that big liquor and cigar place next to the Long Branch. Anyway, the shootout was between some cowboys and some men who were passing out literature on the Populist Party. It turned out the men were part of an outlaw gang."

"Really?" Ma asked, leaning closer from where she sat, perched on the edge of one of the tapestry chairs beside the settee. "What outlaw gang?"

Corrine shook her head. "I don't know. But Danny says outlaws across the state are following the Populists. He says the whole party is nothing but outlaws, renegades left over from the war. I guess they probably figure if the government owns the railroads and the banks it'll be easier to rob them. Danny also says this country will go to hell in a hand basket if a Populist gets elected. He says lots of the men claiming to be Populists rode with Quantrill during the war, and that's why they hate the government so much. They want the south to rise again and figure the best way to make it happen is to form their own party."

Randi thought she might swoon. She lowered her head and rubbed at throbs in her aching temples. It all seemed so convoluted. The crinkle of paper made her lift her gaze. Ma had snatched the newspaper from Corrine, and the more she read the larger her eyes became.

"This article says the Quinter's are Populists!"

Corrine nodded.

"So those men down there think my boys are outlaws?"

"Not necessarily outlaws," Corrine corrected.

"But in cohorts with 'em!" Ma slapped the paper against her knees. "I've never heard anything so harebrained!"

"Harebrained or not, people for miles around read that paper, and they believe what they read," Corrine said, her voice gravely serious.

Ma leaped to her feet and stomped to the window. "Gall-darn it, I left my shotgun in my tent!" She whipped her gray head around. "Hog got a gun in this place?"

Randi rose, tried to compose her jumbled nerves. "Ma, y-you can't shoot them all."

"No, but I could get a good dozen or so." Ma turned back to the window.

Twisting her clammy, trembling hands together, Randi walked across the room and stopped beside Ma to peer at the group below. A tall man with a large white hat that covered his face was talking to the crowd. He kept gesturing to the hotel and Howard.

"It's all my fault." Randi pulled her eyes away, unable to see through the tears. "It's all my fault."

"No, it's not," Aunt Corrine said, wrapping an arm around Randi's shoulders. "It's not your fault. It's Thurston Fulton's fault. He knew what would happen when he talked to that reporter last night."

Randi glanced to her aunt, ready to insist it was her fault. If she hadn't snuck into Howard's tent, he would never have had to marry her. The dark angry look in Corrine's eyes made her stifle her explanation.

"It's true, you know. What Danny says about Quantrill. Thurston Fulton rode with Quantrill on his raid of Lawrence," Corrine stated.

"The devil you say!" Ma's response was filled with disdain.

Randi may have lived at the farm all her life, but even she'd heard of Quantrill and his savage attack on the innocent town folks of Lawrence. The raiders hadn't stopped until almost the whole town was dead and every building burnt. She stepped back, let Corrine's arm slip away and walked to her bedroom. Not bothering to check if anyone followed, she closed the door and moved to the bed.

Wanting to do nothing more than flop down and bury her aching, pounding head in the mound of downy soft pillows, Randi took a deep breath before she trudged to the closet. She'd always known there were deep dark secrets mama didn't want her to know. Her father was one of Quantrill's Raiders. One of the most evil men to walk the earth.

Standing there, staring at her traveling bag, a knock sounded. She ignored it, and when it came again. It wasn't until the door opened that she pulled her eyes from the bag.

Corrine walked in, took her hand, and led her to the bed. "It's time you know the truth. The whole truth."

Randi didn't protest, she couldn't. Simply out of habit, she continued to breathe and her feet moved, but there were no thoughts, no awareness. It was as if she was half asleep. The thought of leaving left her numb to the world.

Once settled on the bed, Corrine began, "We had made the land run a year or so before. Our parents claimed the farmland and built the house. We were all quite content and things were going well. Then the raid happened. They killed father in the front yard, and after raping mother, over and over again, they shot her. It had been Quantrill. Well, not Quantrill himself, but a band of his raiders, including Markus Nolan."

Randi listened, but it was like she was someone else, no emotions wracked her body, it was too numb, she just continued to stare at Corrine.

"Quantrill's large group had split into several smaller parties that were raiding the countryside like a band of heathens. They stayed at the farm for a few days, and when they left, some riding west, others south, the southbound band took me with them. I don't know why they didn't take your mother, maybe because I was older, she was thirteen and I was fifteen. They took me to Mexico and sold me to a man down there. I was sold a couple other times, and then spent some time in Texas before making my way to Dodge several years later. That's when I ran into Markus Nolan again and recognized him as one of the men from the farm that day."

"Markus Nolan?" Randi barely eked out.

Corrine didn't answer, just continued talking. "He threatened me, told me I'd better keep my mouth shut. I was working in a different house then, and he'd cornered me in one of the rooms. Danny heard the commotion and rescued me, I've been working for him ever since. But, during the confrontation, I learned about you, and that you and Josephine still lived at the farm. I was in no condition to travel and see you, so I sent a message. I'd been told Josephine was dead by the raiders who took me to Mexico." Corrine raised a hand, wiped away the tears flowing down her cheeks.

"I tried to convince your Mama to come to Dodge, but she refused, said the two of you were getting along just fine, and that there was nothing to worry about. She wrote the same thing, over and over again for the next several years. I'm sorry,

Randi, I should have came and got you. Got both of you, made you leave."

Feeling was coming back to her body, slowly and painfully. Randi's insides had grown extremely cold and dark. "Don't—"

Corrine cut her off. "I do blame myself and will forever no matter what you or Danny say. You see, many men weren't ready to claim the war was over. Markus was one of them. They took to creating mayhem across the nation in protest to the government and proclaiming the south would rise again. After several years, when they figured out outlawing wasn't the way to regain their country, they decided to overthrow the current government. They've been trying for some time now, and with their new Populist party, they're making great movements. Leastwise that's what Danny says. The party consists mainly of men of low characters. Even the James and Dalton brothers have publicly claimed to be Populists." Corrine let out a loud sigh. "For all that he is, Markus isn't stupid. He knows he doesn't have a chance at the governor's seat without major backers and plenty of money. Clean money. No, he's not stupid all right. He knows others will follow if he has big names behind him. And Quinter is a big name, holds a lot of weight across the state."

"Who's Markus Nolan?"

Corrine took a deep breath. "Thurston Fulton is Markus Nolan. He was wanted for his outlawing days, so he changed his name, cleaned himself up, and is now running for governor."

"Markus Nolan is my father?"

Corrine wiped her damped cheeks and sniffled. "I hope not, but I honestly don't know." She took Randi's hand. "There so many of them. It's hard to say who actually fathered you. Fulton was our grandmother's maiden name so that's why Josephine gave it to you when you were born. She also pretended she married a man who died before you were born and started using the name Fulton herself. I don't know exactly what happened, other than her story backfired. Markus needed to become an upstanding citizen to run for governor. Somehow he learned about your mother's lie and claimed to be her long lost husband. He changed his name to Thurston Fulton. Overnight, he not only became a land owner but a husband and a father."

Randi felt as if ice cold rain showered her. Pictures formed in her mind of all the men hanging out at her father's house in Topeka. They'd stared at her with beady, steely eyes that made her want to hide. And she had. The couple of months she'd been there, she spent most of the time locked in her bedroom, only coming out when Belinda made her.

Corrine huffed out a long breath. "I don't know why your mother went along with it. I don't know what Thurston promised. Your mother never wrote to me about it. She just kept telling me to stay away." Once again tears fell from Corrine's eyes.

Randi tucked everything she'd heard into the back of her mind where she could bring them out later to fully assess; right now she wanted to focus on the most immediate concern—her husband.

"We have to tell the sheriff. Tell him Thurston Fulton is really Markus Nolan."

Corrine let out a fake laugh. "Thurston Fulton already covered his tracks. There's a man in Fort Leavenworth, serving a life sentence, who claims to be Markus Nolan. Danny thinks it's because the man had a choice to either hang or claim to be Nolan. He chose life in prison."

"There has to be something we can do," Randi said, head swirling.

"Thurston probably thinks he hit the mother lode when you snuck into Hog's tent."

"When I snuck into Howard's tent..." She

snapped her head up, glanced around the room. "Thurston couldn't have known I would sneak into Howard's tent."

Corrine shook her head. "No, he couldn't have. That was just luck, whether good or bad. But as soon as you left Topeka, he'd figure you'd come here. I was the only relative you had. He arrived the day after you did."

A new shiver raced over Randi's shoulders. "It was him that night at Danny J's, wasn't it? All the shouting?"

"Yes, Opal had told him you were there."

"So it was my fault Danny J got shot?" Randi said with a long, self-loathing sigh.

"No, Opal had her bloomers in a knot for some time. Good riddance to her," Corrine said, scooting off the bed. "Thurston had sold you to some old geezer who promised to finance his campaign."

Randi shivered from head to toe remembering how the old man's blood-shot eyes had shimmered when he looked at her. "Edward Keyes," she said. "He was with Thurston when he came to get me at the farm."

Corrine climbed off the bed and moved across the room to look out the window. The door opening made them both turn toward the sound. Shame forced Randi to lower her head, unable to meet her husband's eyes.

Howard stood in the doorway, took in the scene. Corrine Martin, dressed in her usual silk and lace, moved from the window to the bed.

"I'll stop in to see you later," she said, patting Randi's shoulder. Her gaze met his, and the sad, cheerless glint in her eyes made Howard's heart hang even heavier in his chest.

He tipped his head in a simple farewell and waited until she'd left the room before closing the door. Randi sat on the bed amid the tangled covers, with her legs crossed beneath her, chin lowered to her chest. He crossed the room, sat down on the edge of the mattress and used one hand to tip her face upward.

Tears streaked down her cheeks, leaving little shimmering trails. He rolled his hand and cupped the side of her face.

"I'm so sorry," she whispered.

"It's not your fault," he said.

"Yes, it is. It's all my fault." She moved away, scrambling across the bed to stand on the opposite side. "Everything's my fault."

He would have tried to reassure her again, but knew she'd just rebuke whatever he said. She moved toward the closet, wiping her face with both hands. Howard rose and followed her. When she bent to pick up her traveling bag, he asked, "What are you doing?"

"I'm leaving," she said with a finalizing tone.

Chapter Fifteen

"No, you're not." Howard stepped forward and laid a hand on her trembling shoulder.

She shrugged it away. "Yes, I am. And please don't try to stop me."

He laughed, not a humorous chuckle, but a snigger of disbelief that she could possibly think he'd let her leave. Reaching out, this time with both hands, he grasped her shoulders and spun her about.

"You *are not* going anywhere."

"I have too," she said, her eyes cast down at the floor.

"Why?"

Her face snapped up. "Why? Because if I leave..." she paused as if trying to figure out what to say next. "He can't..."

"Randi, your leaving won't solve anything."

"But if I'm not here—"

"I won't be able to figure out a way to get this all taken care of."

"Uh?" A frown formed on her forehead, making little tracks in the smooth skin.

"If you leave, I'll have to leave, too." He ran a finger down the side of her face.

"Why?"

"To find you and bring you back."

She sighed, shaking her head listlessly.

He let his finger trace all the way around her face, down one side and up the other.

"Randi, don't worry. I'll figure out a way to fix all this. But I can only do it with you here."

"But my fath—Thurston Fulton, he's ruining your life."

"And I'll find a way to get rid of him." Howard pulled her close, wrapped his arms around her shoulders. "Him, not you. Without you none of this would mean anything." He pressed his cheek to her temple.

"But the hotel, the restaurant—"

"Doesn't mean anything compared to you." He twisted, kissed the tears from her cheeks before moving down to capture her mouth. "*You* are everything to me."

Her arms wrapped around his back, and the kiss deepened, not with the heated passion of last night, but with the sharing of life and love. When their lips separated and she nestled into his chest, the exact spot he wanted her to be the rest of his born days, they clung to one another, drawing strength and power from that unknown force only married couples know exists. He would find a way, if he died trying— he'd find a way to make it all work out.

****

Howard stomped up the stairs of the Dodge House, knowing he should have come straight here when the mob left his hotel, but the need to assure Randi all was right had outweighed his need of kicking Thurston Fulton out of Dodge. Not that he had the authority to forbid the man from staying in town, but he had the steam, and his brother's had his back—between the three of them, Thurston Fulton would not spend another night in this cow town.

The steady thud of his boots echoed off the narrow hallway walls as he watched the little numbers on the doors float past. Stopping in front of number six, he raised a fist to pound hard enough to make the door bounce against its frame.

"Open up, Fulton!"

Nothing but silence came from the other side, and he pounded harder.

"Fulton! Open the door!"

He reached down and grabbed the knob. Expecting it to be locked, he twisted hard enough the knob almost broke off in his hand. Throwing the door open, he stared into the empty room. The bed, unmade, was the only evidence someone had been there earlier.

"Shit," he mumbled, stomping back down the hall.

At the front desk, he banged on the little bell until its silver top flew off and tumbled across desktop before crashing onto the floor.

"I heard you the first time," Marnie Austin said, eyes snapping as she bustled her way through the swinging door on the far side of the room.

"Where's Fulton?"

"You already looked in the book when you stomped in here a few minutes ago," she remarked, picking the broken bell off the floor.

"His room is empty," Howard growled.

"The rat. He said he was staying for a week." She shrugged her thick shoulders and managed to repair her bell before adding, "Oh, well, at least I got his money for last night before he skipped town."

Marnie Austin was as tall as a man and just as broad, and the way she eyeballed him right now, Howard could have sworn she was a man—at least half man for there wasn't anything feminine about her.

"Why you asking me where he is anyhow? He's your friend," she snapped.

"He's not my friend," Howard insisted.

"Yeah, well you was in here talkin' to him last night."

"Yeah, and I'm talking to you right now, too, but you're not my friend either!" Howard fumed. The insatiable urge to throttle something had his temper flaring, but knowing he couldn't very well strangle the woman, he figured insulting her was the next best thing. Without taking the time to relish the nail spitting glare she gave him, he turned about and stomped out the door, letting it bang shut loud enough to be heard in Indian Territory.

Snake and Bug, one on each side of him, met his strides as he clomped down the boardwalk. He wasn't quite sure where they'd been standing and for half a second wondered if he'd caught one of them with the swinging door of the Dodge House. Neither appeared injured, so he didn't dwell on it.

Wagon's rolled, cowboys rode, and an odd assortment of people on foot strolled past, but other than blurs in his vision, Howard didn't really see any of them. Thurston Fulton had left town, and that was a good thing, or at least it should be. Trouble was the man was worse than a liver-bellied rat, and just like a varmint, it was when you didn't see them, didn't know where they were, that they were the most dangerous.

Thanks to Hinkle, most of the crowd that had bore down on the hotel this morning now believed he wasn't a Populist, and those still pondering it, didn't reckon it was worth their efforts to protest. But none of that took care of Thurston Fulton. Howard knew he hadn't seen the last of his father-in-law. Even more, the notion the man wasn't done using Randi sent a fear like nothing he'd never known, nor could describe, to live inside his chest.

"You want us to go look for him?" Bug asked, without glancing his way.

"We can take a few of the workers, shouldn't take us more than half a day to track him down," Snake added.

"No," Howard said, hoping his fuming mind was capable of thinking straight. "I don't want him to think his shenanigans fazed us. The less effect he believes he has, the better off we are."

Bug hesitated and then caught back up with a quick double step.

"That's some darn good thinking there, Hog. Right conniving."

Snake raised an eyebrow and gave an agreeable nod.

"It could get nasty, boys," Howard clarified.

"I'm in," Bug said.

Snake replied directly, "Me, too."

"The less Ma and Randi know the better," Howard felt inclined to add. He didn't need his mother filling anyone full of buckshot, and he'd lock Randi in the upstairs of the hotel if it was the only way to keep her safe.

"That's always been my motto," Snake said.

"You know that! The less Ma knows the less likely we all are to getting shot," Bug illuminated.

"So what do we do now?" Snake asked.

"We got a hotel to finish building." Howard stopped and pivoted around on the heel of one boot. Front Street lay before him, a mile long and bordered with dozens of businesses. Buildings of every shape and size made of bricks, wood, and even a few tar paper and canvas shacks hosted the hustle and bustle of people scampering about. Dust hung in the air from the street traffic, and noise, everything from dancehall music, people shouting, cows bawling on the far side of town, and the train whistle screaming her arrival, filled the air.

"Boys," he said, quite thoughtfully, and not unlike Ma when she was pondering deeply.

"Yeah?" they asked in unison and filled with skepticism.

"We're gonna have us the biggest open house this town has ever seen." Howard flipped back around and slapped an arm around each of his brothers. "We're even gonna invite the governor."

"We are?" Snake asked, leaning forward to glance at Bug with a look that said their other brother may have lost his marbles.

Bug shrugged. "You know the governor, do you?"

Howard shook his head. "Nope."

"Does Kid or Skeeter?" Snake asked.

"Don't rightly know if they do or not. But I'd take a gander and say they know plenty of folks who do."

Bug stopped, took off his hat, and wiped his forehead with the crook of his elbow. "Big brother, has anyone ever told you more range wars have started up over politics than over cattle rustling?"

Howard smiled. "Yup, I've heard that. But can you think of a better way to assure the town folks we aren't Populists?"

"Well, no, but folks around here don't think kindly of any politicians," Bug explained, replacing his hat with such caution Howard almost laughed. His youngest brother had always been the most precautious, the one who'd do just about anything to keep peace.

"Exactly, so if the whole mess of them are at each other's throats, the rest of us will be able to have a good ole' time." Howard gave them each another wallop on the back before he turned about, and whistling, walked up the street.

He didn't have to turn around to know his brothers stood stalk still, staring at each other while the dust of the street swirled around their boots. They were both wondering if he'd lost his mind, or more likely, what they should have carved in his headstone.

The knowledge didn't faze him.

No siree, not one little bit.

The grand opening of The Majestic would be the biggest party the state had ever seen, hell, he might even invite the governors of Colorado and Nebraska, too.

After all, if you want to catch a rat, you gotta set a big trap.

Chapter Sixteen

Randi laid the pen down and flexed her fingers. The way the digits cramped they might stay in that position forever. She'd done little more than hold a pen, writing out invitations for more than a week. Most of the out of town folks had been invited via telegrams, which had taken her almost a week to pen as well. And poor Mr. Miller down at the telegraph office, he all but quivered the last time she walked into his office. His gaze had landed on the large stack of messages she'd carried, and his winkled face had taken on the look of a forlorn hound before he accepted payment and started to tap away.

The ones she wrote now were for the local folks. Howard had hired two scruffy-haired boys to deliver the notes post haste. A smile tickled her lips, and a tiny giggle did emit as she thought of the two boys now. Ma Quinter wasn't one for scruffiness no matter how down on your luck a person may be, and by the second day, the boys were delivering the notes dressed in bright blue knickers and red shirts, complete with little black arm bands. Their once unruly hair was also well greased and parted on the side.

Her darling husband, upon seeing three other boys—younger brothers of the invitation delivery ones—standing near the front gate, had quickly found jobs for each of them, and Ma had just as quickly completed uniforms for those three. One now stood beside her, he couldn't be more than seven or eight, and it had become his job to gather the return reply cards from the basket hanging on a hook near the front gate.

She looked over and met his sparkling blue eyes. "How many today?"

He handed her several notes. "Twenty-two. Add those to the others and we got us a total of over three-hundred."

Randi nodded, not smiling quite as brightly as the child. "I don't know where Mr. Quinter thinks all these people are going to fit."

Willie glanced around. "Whatcha mean? This place is big enough to hold pert near everyone in Kansas."

"That's right, Willie," Howard's voice sounded from the doorway. "And if we do run out of room, we'll just put the band in the street."

"The band? Is the Cowboy Band gonna play here?" Willie's eyes lit up like the sun on a summer day.

"Sure enough," Howard said, flipping a coin toward the boy, who caught it mid-air. "Quitting time, you find your brothers and run on home now."

"Yes, sir, Mr. Quinter." Willie paused in the doorway as if just remembering his manners. "And, thank ya, kindly, sir," he said, holding the coin up.

Howard nodded an answer, and Randi rose to meet him where he'd stopped beside her chair in his office.

"You, Mr. Quinter, are going to have more people here for this grand opening than you will know what to do with," she said teasingly.

He shrugged nonchalantly, while his eyes took on a bright, knowing shimmer. "That's all right," he said, lowering his head. His lips brushed against her ear as he whispered, "Because I have you, and I already know what to do with you."

That was really all it took to turn her into little more than a puddle, but Randi did her best not to melt and slapped his chest playfully. "You're incorrigible."

"Perhaps I am," he stated, nuzzling the skin behind her earlobe with the tip of his nose.

It was no use, and she was only making herself miserable. Slipping her hands around his waist, she gave in, liquefying against his solid stance.

"Delightfully incorrigible," she said before their lips met.

Thankful his arms held her up, she snuggled her head under his chin when his lips left hers. It took several minutes before she had her bearings back enough to stand on her own.

She lifted her head to ask a question she'd been pondering. "Shouldn't the Timmer boys be in school?"

"Not right now," he said, his hands roaming her back.

"Why?" The question was almost a groan due to the way his touch made her blood swirl with heat.

"Because school is closed for planting."

"Planting?" The room now spun around her.

"Yes, schools are closed so the kids can help with planting, once the crops are all in the school will open back up."

She tried to focus on the conversation, but her hands explored his back, massaging the hard muscles beneath his soft cotton shirt. The feel of him was tantalizing, the simple touch made her excitement thud in her veins.

"The Timmers aren't farmers?"

"Nope." He said, running soft kisses along her neck.

"What does their father do?"

He straightened and set her a small distance away. "I don't think they have a father, at least not one that lives with them."

The space or perhaps the thought made her

heart sad. "Oh, it's just all those boys and their mother?"

He moved to the desk, shuffled through the replies Willie had brought up. "Yes, but I think she has a couple of daughters as well."

"How does she feed them all?" Randi wondered aloud.

"She did some odd jobs, laundry and such," he paused and lifted his head to look at her, "but I've given her a job here, at the hotel." His voice held a touch of apprehension.

She read his eyes, realized he waited for her reaction. Her heart fluttered a touch. What did he want her to say? Her mind scampered about, searching for the right answer.

"Randi?"

The truth was all she had. "I think it's very nice of you to offer her a job. What will she be doing?"

"Cleaning. We might have to hire someone to assist her." His eyes floated nervously around the desk as his hands flipped through a few sheets of paper.

All of a sudden it hit her.

She held her lips tight, wouldn't let the smile form.

"How about her daughters? How old are they? Perhaps they could help, at least when they aren't in school."

His gaze locked with hers, and a twinkle sparked in one eye. His lips curled up, and he reached out a hand. "That's a good idea." He tugged her closer.

Randi went willingly, wrapped her arms around his waist. "You've hired a whole passel of workers, why were you nervous to tell me about Mrs. Timmer?"

He kissed her, a soft, loving kiss that made her heart sing with happiness. When he lifted his head, he explained, "They were all men. This was the first woman I hired, and I didn't want you...I hoped you...Aw, hell," he muttered, "I don't know what I thought."

The happiness bubbling in her chest grew. She framed his cheeks with both hands. "Did you think I'd be upset?" It was amazing, knowing someone loved her so much they worried about upsetting her. The thought also gave her a sense of power.

A faint blush rose in his cheeks as he admitted, "I hoped not, but I..."

She pressed a hand to his lips. "I love you," she whispered.

His eyes lit up like a match flare, and his hold on her tightened. "You do, don't you?" he asked, breathlessly.

A cascade of warmth rushed over her. She met his gaze, knowing her eyes danced as brightly as his.

"Yes, I do," she stated. "With all my heart."

His exhale sounded as if he'd been holding his breath for a year. "And I love you," he said, little more than a whisper. "With all my heart and soul."

The happiness racing in her veins made her giggle with delight, before a touch of seriousness tickled her spine. She cupped his jaw.

"I've told you before how much I love you."

His cheeks were bright pink. "I know, but with everything going on..."

She pressed a finger to his lips. "I think I've loved you since I woke up in your bed. And I'll never stop."

"Speaking of beds..." the words slipped out as his mouth met hers. He caught her up in both arms and carried her through their apartment to their bedroom without ever tugging his lips from hers.

It was sometime later, when they both had re-dressed and meandered arm in arm down the stairs that they realized company had arrived. Howard flashed a wide, bright smile and increased his footsteps, dragging her along beside him.

"Who is it?" she asked, not recognizing the red headed woman hugging Bug.

"It's Lila and Skeeter," Howard answered, his voice filled with happiness.

Though the sun was shining bright and hot, a cold breeze brushed over Randi, made her shudder with thoughts of what Thurston Fulton and Belinda may have done while staying with Lila and Skeeter. She hadn't yet told Howard about Thurston being Markus. After all, she really had no proof, and no idea what could be done about it. The weight of the world once again fell upon her shoulders. It had been one thing to know she was the daughter of a money-hungry politician, but to be the daughter of a corrupt outlaw somehow seemed even worse.

"Hello, little brother," a tall man, with a smile as wide as the Arkansas River, shouted as he walked towards them.

"Hey, Skeeter," Howard stretched his arm toward the man.

Skeeter brushed the hand aside and wrapped both arms around Howard. Along with a growling bear hug, Skeeter patted Howard on the back. When he released her husband, he turned to her.

"And you must be Randi."

Before she had a chance to speak, Skeeter grabbed her around the waist and squeezed the daylights right out of her.

Gasping for air, she laughed, "Hello."

"And I'm Lila, this ruffian's better half," a strikingly beautiful woman said as she stepped forward to wrap Randi in a welcoming hug as soon as Skeeter let her go.

"Hello. It's nice to meet you," Randi said, praying the blush heating her cheeks wasn't apparent to everyone. She glanced at both Lila and

Skeeter, trying to read behind their eyes, to see if there was some form of abhorrence or disgust lingering from their visit with Thurston and Belinda. Seeing nothing but bright, sincere smiles, Randi let a touch of her uneasiness melt away. Of course the comforting touch of her husband as he rested an arm around her shoulders helped chase the doubt away more thoroughly.

"I wasn't expecting you this soon," Howard said.

"We wanted to get here in time to help with the preparation," Lila said, glancing toward Ma's tent when a shriek sounded. "Dear, I believe that's your daughter," she said, flashing a bright smile at Skeeter.

"So it is," he said, brushing a kiss on his wife's cheek. "I'll be right back."

Howard grabbed Randi's hand. Yes, he'd known she loved him, but wouldn't ever tire of hearing it, and the way she'd repeated it over and over while they flounced around the bed had filled him with more satisfaction than if he'd just ate two Thanksgiving dinners. Now, seeing his older brother and family, just added to his contentment.

"Wait up," he shouted to Skeeter, tugging on Randi's hand. "We want to see the kids, too."

"Yes," Randi agreed, hurrying along beside him. "Ma has told us so much about the children. I can't wait to meet them."

"Come on." Skeeter waved, already rushing toward the tent. "Kendra gets a little nervous when I'm not around."

Howard stopped in his steps and turned to meet his sister-in-law's smiling gaze. "A little nervous when he's not around?" He frowned, wondering what had happened, his niece was too little to even know what nervous was.

Lila laughed and pointed to Skeeter who was ducking into the tent. "He has his daughter spoiled rotten." She tucked an arm into the crook of his free arm, his other one was right where it should be, holding Randi's hand. "And I'm afraid, Charles is right behind her." Lila's smile grew. "And I wouldn't have it any other way. Come on, let me introduce them to Randi."

Skeeter exited Ma's tent, a child on each hip. Kendra, with red curls that matched her mother's, and Charles, with blond ones to match his father's, each had their faces tucked tight to Skeeter's shoulders making introductions difficult.

In between kissing the tops of his children's heads, Skeeter explained, "They were sleeping when we arrived so I laid them down in Ma's tent." He planted another kiss on each set of curls before adding, "But they woke up scared not knowing where they were."

Howard almost laughed out loud. Half of him thought it quite amusing the way his older brother doted on his children like a mother hen, the other half of him felt a tinge of jealousy with it all. His gaze went to Randi. Her eyes shimmered, and he knew why. She was thinking along the same lines as he—the day when they would have little ones.

"I suspect a wet diaper might have something to do with it as well," Lila said, wrapping her hands around Charles. "Come here, big boy, let Mama change you." The baby snuggled into her breast, and she turned to Randi. "Care to join me?"

"Of course," Randi answered, and Howard couldn't help but give her a loving squeeze before she slipped away to enter Ma's tent behind Lila.

"She's a beauty," Skeeter said.

Howard pulled his eyes from Randi and reached a hand up to pat Kendra's tiny back. "Yes, she is, but I told you that the day she was born."

"Not my daughter, well, yes, she is, too, I mean your wife," Skeeter said, laughing at each word.

Howard could swear his face was sunburned by the heat eating at his cheeks, but he stared his brother down and proudly proclaimed, "Yeah, and she's mine, all mine."

Skeeter chuckled and slapped his back. Their laughing lasted until Skeeter grew a touch somber. "You made a good choice. I was a mite worried after meeting her pa and step-mother."

An icy chill, brought on by extreme loathing, rippled his spine, and before he had a chance to comment, Kendra lifted her face.

"Daddy," she said, pointing a chubby finger across the lawn, "water."

"Yes, sweetheart, that's a water fountain. Do you want to see it?" Skeeter asked.

"Uh-huh," she nodded.

"Walk with us." Skeeter slapped Howard on the back. "Where are her parents now?"

Howard, ambling beside his brother, let out a loud, tell-all sigh. "I don't know. They haven't been back since that newspaper article came out."

"Well, I wish I could say you've seen the last of them. But I think we both know you haven't."

"You're right there," Howard agreed, letting out a slight groan. "How much money did he try to weasel you out of?"

Skeeter let out a rough laugh. "I told him the only way he was getting any money out of me is if he'd take Buffalo Killer to Washington." He lifted both eyebrows. "The Fulton's left for Dodge the next day. Course by then, Buffalo Killer had already let it be known what he thought of politicians."

Howard joined Skeeter's good natured laugh, almost wishing he'd been able to witness just how Buffalo Killer had shared his thoughts.

They arrived at the fountain, and Kendra scooted out of Skeeter's arms when he knelt down.

"Not too close, now, sweetheart." He glanced up

to Howard. "So what's the plan for when they return?"

Howard shrugged. "I honestly don't know, I've been so busy getting this place ready for the grand opening, I haven't had time to figure one out yet."

Skeeter let out a low whistle and stood up. Keeping his voice low so Kendra couldn't hear he said, "I knew I should have let Buffalo Killer scalp him."

Howard would have responded, if he could have thought of something to say.

Kendra had knelt beside the pond. "Daddy, fish!"

Skeeter crouched down, splashed a hand in the water, and then gave Howard a baffled glance. "What kind of fish you got here?"

Howard knelt on one knee, fluttered his fingers in the water, showing Kendra she could do the same.

"Gold fish." Gesturing across the yard with his head, he added, "Snake ordered them from New York City for Randi to have in her pond."

Skeeter bellowed with laughter again. "And you thought I was crazy when I built a bar for Lila in our kitchen. I think little gold fish take the cake brother."

Howard sat down on the short brick wall surrounding the pond and patted the space beside him. "Kendra, tell Daddy to take off your shoes and socks. You can dangle your feet in the water." He glanced to Skeeter and then back to the red-headed angel between them. "These little gold fish won't hurt you none at all."

Kendra plopped on the ground and stuck both feet up to Skeeter, who was laughing like a jackal.

****

In the tent, Randi sat on the cot, cooing at Charles while Lila pinned a fresh diaper around his chubby waist.

"You're as handsome as your uncle," she said. When the baby smiled, she giggled and added, "Yes, you are, and you know it."

"That he does," Lila said. "Be careful, he's just as charming, too. In no time he'll have you jumping to his tiniest whimper."

"I won't mind at all," Randi admitted.

Ma stepped forward and gathered up the soiled diaper. "I'll take this outside and wash it out."

"I can do that, Ma, you don't need to," Lila said.

"I know I don't have to," Ma said. "I want to. You two stay here and get acquainted."

Lila chuckled as Ma disappeared out the door. "Sometimes I can't believe that's the same woman who tied me to a chair and made me marry her son."

Randi had to giggle as well. "I know what you mean." She tickled Charles beneath the chin. "I was practically naked when we got married. I didn't dare ask for clothes."

"No!" Lila gasped. Her green eyes wide, yet twinkling. "I didn't know that! You must tell me all about it."

"You wouldn't believe it," Randi said. Though she wouldn't change a thing about her life, she did have to admit her wedding was a bit unorthodox.

Lila picked up the baby and twisted him about so he sat on Randi's lap and sat down beside them on the cot.

"Trust me," she said. "I'm the queen of unbelievable stories." Tickling the baby's tummy, keeping him satisfied to sit where he was, she continued, "Come on, spit it out, and I want all the nitty-gritty details."

Randi wrapped her hands around Charles's pudgy waist, bouncing him about. Feeling as if she'd run into someone who'd been a friend her entire life, she started at the beginning, the point where she snuck out of Danny J's, and relived her wedding night for her new sister-in-law.

They were laughing to the point tears streamed down their faces when Ma and the men, Howard now carrying Kendra, entered the tent.

Wiping at the tears on her face, Lila whispered, "Oh, wait until Jessie hears, she is going to love that story as much as I do."

Indescribable warmth filled Randi, as if she'd drunk a full gallon of happiness. She'd never had anyone to laugh with, to share secrets or stories with, and realized it had been a great loss.

"What's so funny?" Skeeter asked. He stepped forward and with one finger wiped a final tear from Lila's face with pure endearment.

"Oh, nothing that concerns you," Lila said, winking at Randi, before she rose to kiss Skeeter flat on the lips in front of Ma and everyone else.

Randi tried to tug her eyes away, not wanting to gape at their open devotion, but she couldn't, a part of her wished she could be so bold. Sure she and Howard kissed a lot, but in front of others it was always a short, soft peck of affection, not the deep, engrossed kissing Lila and Skeeter were doing.

Howard glanced from her to his brother, and then slapped Skeeter on the back.

"Why don't you wait until you check into my hotel for that?"

Lila started laughing and pulled her lips off her husband's. "Aw, Hog, if you want us to see your hotel, all you have to do is ask nicely and say pretty please."

Randi felt her mouth drop. Lila didn't seem embarrassed in the least. Nor did anyone else, not even Ma. Her gaze settled on Howard. He was smiling at her, and his eyes held that sparkle that made her stomach roll with pleasure. He held out a hand. She stood, shifting Charles onto her hip as if it was natural, and took his hand.

"What do you think, should we show them the hotel?" he asked.

Unable to speak, since her mouth was drooling, wanting to be kissed, she nodded.

He led her out of the tent. Kendra in his arms, Charles in hers, they began to cross the yard, not once looking back to see if the other's followed—who of course did.

While they were several steps ahead of everyone else, he whispered, "If we weren't holding their children, I would have showed them how kissing is done. I'm sure we are much better at it than they are."

She started to laugh, and by the time they arrived at the hotel, the whole tribe was laughing and joking with such companionship the air itself seemed happy. Thrilled to be part of such wonder, Randi happily guided the large group on a tour.

Once Skeeter and his family were settled in one of the comfortably furnished hotel rooms, Randi set about making a meal fit for royalty.

The kitchen was still under construction, so the family was enjoying the benefits of her hard work on the outdoor tables near Ma's tent when another wagon rolled in. She knew even before the introductions started that it had to be Kid and Jessie. Ma's description of blond hair hanging past her waist and a smile as angelic as a child's, described Jessie completely, and the oldest Quinter brother was the spitting image of Bug, just a tad bit older looking. Their children, three-year-old Joel, and four-month old Winifred, gained as much attention as Kendra and Charles had before the family settled back around the table to consume the meal.

"Hog Quinter!" Jessie exclaimed, still swallowing her first mouthful of steak.

Chapter Seventeen

Randi peered across the table. The woman had another piece of meat dangling off her fork, and a distressed expression twisted her glistening blue eyes. Randi glanced at her own plate. Snake had planted a large patch of herbs for her, and she'd used some on the meat, along with mushrooms and a small amount of brandy. She tossed a look across the table, searching to see if anyone else was upset by the meal.

"What?" Howard answered, chewing with more show than politeness allowed.

"Why don't I have this recipe?" Jessie replied, poking the fork in her mouth.

Howard wrapped an arm around Randi's shoulders and showered her with a loving gaze. "Because," he said, "even I don't have it."

Lila giggled. "I wrote down every move she made. I'll let you copy it," she said to Jessie.

Jessie's brows furrowed. Her perplexed gaze went to Ma, who started laughing and shook her head. With a sweeping gestured, the older woman pointed across the table, pulling Jessie's eyes back to Randi.

A wide smile grew on the Jessie's face. "You made this?" she asked.

Randi wasn't sure if she wanted to admit it or not.

Howard's arm around her shoulders tightened. "She sure enough did."

Jessie started giggling, and her friendly smile landed on Randi. "This is absolutely wonderful," she said, pointing at her plate. "And I can't believe Hog married a woman who can cook. If he hadn't taught me to cook Kid would have died from lack of nourishment by now."

"And Skeeter," Lila was quick to add.

"Really?" Randi asked, looking at her husband, whose face had grown extremely red.

"Yes, really," Kid and Skeeter declared, bringing a round of laughter from the entire table.

"You told me about your cookbook idea, but you never said you *taught* others how to cook," Randi said, somewhat frazzled. She wasn't really sure why, but for some reason it concerned her. Her mind raced. Had he told her at some time over the past month and she'd forgotten? She did recall that he once said he liked to cook, that was why he wanted to build the hotel.

"No, no, I didn't," Howard admitted, sounding indifferent.

Unable to let the subject go, she asked, "Why?"

He laid down his fork, and right there in front of Ma, and a table full of others, he kissed her, deep and passionately enough to make her head swirl and her blood race. Besieged, she could do nothing but join him, match the fervor of his embrace with all the enthusiasm singing in her soul.

When he broke the kiss, and while the world was still a foggy, spinning haze around her, he said, "Because from the first meal you cooked, I knew you were a better cook than I could ever hope to be."

It took her a moment to gain her equilibrium and make sense of what he'd said. "Oh," she mumbled, mainly because she felt the need to answer in some mundane way.

The meal continued, and Randi tried to stop thinking about cooking, but a hole grew in her stomach. After everyone ate their fill, and the women started to clean away the dishes, Howard pulled her aside.

"Are you all right?"

She nodded. "Of course, I'm all right."

"You've been awfully quiet," he said, examining her from head to toe with a deep stare.

She bit her lip, not wanting to say something she might later regret.

He curled a finger beneath her chin. "Tell me."

"Tell you what?" she asked with feigned ignorance.

"What's wrong?" A deep frown tugged at his brows. "It's the cooking, isn't it?"

Her eyes went to the ground.

"Aw, sweetheart, I'm sorry. I can help. I thought it was something you liked to do. And you are so good at it. You should've said it was all too much."

"No, no, it's not too much," she admitted. "I like to cook. I always have." She had to swallow the lump rising up her throat. "But why didn't you tell me?" Biting harder on her lip, to keep it from quivering, she added, "You didn't need my help at all, did you?"

"Didn't need your help?" He sounded confused.

She glanced up, met his gaze. "I thought I'd been helping you. Thought you needed a cook, and would need one once the restaurant opened—" She had to stop talking. The lump had become too large and was burning her throat.

"You have helped. And I do need you." He wrapped both arms around her, pulled her close. "The fact you are an excellent cook, is wonderful, but Randi, I'd need you if you couldn't even boil water. You're my other half. You're the sunshine in my day. I can't imagine life without you."

She'd been transported again, to that wonderful, loving world that existed inside his arms. The only problem with the heavenly world he created for her was that her mind didn't always work while she was there.

He continued, whispering close to her ear. "I love you. I love your cooking. I love your smile. I love your feet. I love your—"

"Stop," she insisted, giggling. "I'm sorry. I don't know why I acted so silly."

Howard separated them enough so he could look at her. What he'd said had been the God's honest truth. There was nothing about her he didn't love.

"It wasn't silly. And I'm sorry I never told you about my cooking. I should have."

She tightened the arms wrapped around his middle and laid her head back on his chest.

"I love you, Hog Quinter. I love you more than I ever imagined a person could love."

He wrapped his arms around her, and since he really didn't care if there were things to get done, places he needed to go, they stood like that for a very long time. It was Randi, who, exhaling a deep sigh, finally stepped back.

"I need to help with the dishes," she said.

And he had to help Kid unload the wagon, get he and Jessie and the kids settled into the room beside Skeeter and his family, so therefore, he agreed.

"All right."

Randi lifted her face. It was an invitation he had no means to decline. So it wasn't until after a very satisfying parting kiss that he left her, wandered over to grab an armload out of the back of Kid's wagon, and instructed his brother to follow.

The next night, after another delicious meal prepared by his lovely wife and while the women were still clearing the table, an old, somewhat lopsided wagon, sporting a well-used canvas top rolled down the dusty road. Howard took a second look at the driver before he let out a bellow of laughter.

"Well, look there. It's Willamina," he said to the rest of the table occupants.

Kid nodded. "We stopped by her place on the way, asked if she and Eva wanted to ride with us, but she insisted they would bring their own wagon. She also told us not to tell you." Kid winked. "She wanted to surprise you."

Howard rose, as did his four brothers, and all five moved to meet the wagon before it rolled to a creaking halt.

"Land sakes!" Willamina, a woman who might be twice Ma's age, exclaimed, pointing at the hotel. "If'n that ain't the most highfalutin' place I ever seen, I don't know what is."

Howard reached up to lift her bent over, withered frame out of the wagon. "And I've been saving the best room in the house just for you."

"Aw, you always was a sweet talker," Willamina said, pinching one of his cheeks as if he was about five instead of twenty-five, while he lowered her to the ground.

He gave her a quick hug, and then did the same to Eva after Kid lifted her down.

"This is a grand surprise. The whole family is here now," he said.

"You betcha," Willamina said. "You didn't think we'd miss your big day, did you?" Before Howard could respond, she whipped her head around and continued, "Where is this wife of yours? Aw, that must be her."

Randi, flanked by Jessie, Lila, and Ma gathered around, and Willamina let out a screech. Then, laughing with glee, she said, "By God, you did learn something from your brothers, didn't ya Hog? Go straight for the best looking one around and snatch 'em up 'afore someone else does!"

Howard wrapped an arm around Randi. "That I did." When the laughter eased, he offered, "Randi, this is Willamina and Eva."

"Hello," she said.

"Hello?" Willamina stiffened. "Lawd, girl, that ain't no way to greet your aunt." Holding both arms wide open, she added, "Come here and give me a hug."

Randi laughed and complied.

As soon as the new arrivals were fed and settled into a room in the hotel, Willamina insisted Howard get out his fiddle. She said it was a night for celebrating, and the rest of the family readily agreed. He had no objections, and not long after the music filled the night air, Danny J and Corrine meandered down the road.

"Heard the music. Thought we'd walk down and be neighborly," Danny J said.

Howard, taking a break between songs, rested the fiddle on his knee. There was still a part of him that was wary of the man, a touch troubled that Danny J might have ambitions toward Randi. On the other hand, knowing the love they shared, he had to admit his apprehensions were unfounded.

"Sure," he agreed, "Glad to have you."

Willamina leaned forward from where she sat between Randi and Ma and squinted.

"Danny J, why you old scoundrel! Are you still hanging around these parts? I would have thought you'd have lit out by now."

"Willamina!" the dapperly dressed man exclaimed. "If you aren't a sight to see. Come here!" he demanded, arms wide.

Willamina jumped to her feet, hugging the man while jiggling with glee. "Just as handsome as ever I see." She stepped back, eyeing the man from head to toe. "And no worse for wear." Turning sideways, she acknowledged Corrine with a nod. "I hear tell you took over where I left off."

Corrine bowed her head slightly. "Someone had to."

Willamina opened her arms. "I'm right proud of

ya, gal. And owe you my thanks. I was worried about the younguns I left behind."

Howard felt his eyes grow wide. For years Willamina had rescued young girls who found themselves in the family way from having to resort to employment in one of the brothels. And it appeared when she left town, with the young Eva after the girl had been attacked and her father killed, Corrine became the mother hen. It appeared both Corrine and Danny J had benevolence that went much deeper than anyone knew. He glanced at Randi, sitting beside him. A frown pulled on her brows.

He leaned down and whispered, "I'll explain later."

Randi glanced toward Howard, nodding at his words, but more so taking in the kindness in his expression. Her heart started to pitter-patter, like it always did when he settled those sparkling green eyes on her. She met his gaze with a smile that radiated straight from her heart. He leaned over and planted a short, but sweet and promising kiss on her lips.

The action brought a tingle to her cheeks. It was amazing how all the Quinter brothers really didn't hold to propriety when it came to kissing in public. They just did it when and where the urge struck them. Jessie and Lila seemed to accept the fact whole heartedly, and Randi figured she'd best do so as well, for it didn't appear any of them were willing to change.

Ma chose that moment to make a demand. "Quit kissing your wife and play us another tune, Hog. We got company to entertain."

The round of laughter made Randi's cheeks burn hotter, but Howard's good natured chuckle, and the way he kissed her once more, most likely to teasingly defy his mother, made her join the glee as he struck the bow across the strings of his fiddle.

The tune was lively. With a whoop that sounded like an Indian on the warpath, Lila leaped to her feet and snatched Skeeter's hand. The two of them danced in such a way that Randi found she had to lock her jaw to keep it shut. They weren't touching as couples normally did, nor were they doing anything close to a Virginia reel or a square dance. Facing each other, and gracefully, yet shockingly, they moved to the music. Twirling and waving their hips, as well as other body parts, it was as if they talked to one another through the movements.

Randi felt the temperature in her body increasing as the movements became more and more seductive. The two never touched each other, but all the same Randi felt as if she was watching some kind of secret mating dance.

Since Howard was totally engrossed in creating the music, she leaned over and whispered to Jessie, "Did Buffalo Killer teach them to dance like that?"

Jessie giggled, shaking her head. "No, Lila taught Skeeter. It's amazing isn't it?"

Randi nodded, not really knowing what else to do.

"Kid refuses to do it, in public," Jessie leaned closer to reveal. "But we've done it in the privacy of our bedroom. It's quite intoxicating."

"I'm sure it is," Randi said, feeling her blush all the way to her toes, mainly because she found herself wondering if Howard would agree to try it with her. In the privacy of their bedroom of course.

Chapter Eighteen

The next week flew by faster than a flock of migrating birds. Randi found herself extremely thankful for the assistance her new sisters-in-law provided, as well as Willamina and Eva. Even her Aunt Corrine made daily trips down to help out. Every room had been completed, along with the kitchen and dining room, and all the little details which seemed to be never ending. Rugs here, curtains there, napkins ironed into crisp squares, dishes and glasses washed to sparkling freshness, and flower vases and potted plants arranged just so.

And then there was the painting. The day after Eva arrived Howard had insisted Randi dress in her black gown and sit in the parlor of their rooms for Eva to paint her likeness. Randi's objections fell on deaf ears, and afterwards she felt a little guilty for it had taken the young girl less than an hour before she proclaimed Randi could go change. The quiet girl, who rarely spoke unless spoken to, had secreted herself in her room each afternoon, when the light was best, Willamina explained, to work on the painting.

Randi had to admit, she was anxious to see it, especially after the way Jessie and Lila raved about the ones Eva had painted of them and their husbands. Yet, at the same time, she was curious as to why Howard hadn't sat with her. It appeared this painting would be just of her.

Her thoughts in a cloud, she crossed the massive, amazing kitchen to withdraw several pans of corn bread from the oven. She'd just set the fourth and final pan on the large work table in the center of the room when Howard stuck his head through the swinging door leading to the dining room.

"Hey," he said, grinning from ear to ear.

"Hey," she responded with a smile just as large. It never ceased to amaze her at how wonderful her life was. One look from her husband and happiness swarmed her senses like a warm summer breeze.

He held out one hand. "Come here. I have something to show you."

"Oh?" she asked, walking across the room. "What arrived today? I can't possible think of one thing that we don't already have."

If possible his grin grew, but she didn't have time to confirm the fact because he pressed a quick, tender kiss to her lips.

"Come on," he said afterwards, pulling her through the doorway.

A crowd had gathered, all the family members present, as well as Aunt Corrine and Danny J, who also had been over on a regular basis lately. They stood near the large brick fireplace in the entranceway. She glanced to Howard.

"What—"

"You'll see," he said, tugging her through the group.

Eva stood near the hearth, a large canvas covered shape rested beside her.

"Oh," Randi said. "You've finished the picture." A wave of apprehension showered her shoulders, and Howard wrapped an arm around her as if he'd seen her shudder. She twisted and looked up at him.

"Surely you don't mean to hang it down here," she whispered.

"Of course I do." He nodded to Eva.

Heat flushed Randi's face, but she squared her shoulders. She thought the painting would hang upstairs where just family would look at it. The thought of her likeness set out for everyone to view made butterflies take flight in her stomach. She'd never had a likeness taken, had really only seen a few, and found the idea of a replica a bit disconcerting.

Her mind was still twirling with thought when oohs and ahhs escaped from the crowd. She twisted and her gaze landed on the picture Eva had uncovered.

Her heart stopped beating.

The painting wasn't of just her. It was the two of them. She and Howard. They stood on the large front porch of the hotel. She took a step forward, had to touch his likeness because it was so vivid, looked so real, she wondered if he'd moved—had somehow jumped right onto the canvas. He was dressed in his black suit and looked extremely handsome, but it was his eyes that held her attention. Somehow, painted there on that canvas was the exact way he looked at her after they'd made love in their big bed upstairs. A sweet flood rushed over her system.

Her throat grew thick as her gaze went to her likeness. Her image, dressed in the black gown had her head tilted upwards, looking at her husband. It was indescribable, the emotion filling her chest at that moment, because her painted gaze was exactly what she knew he saw when she looked at him. It was there, as plain as the nose on her face, the deep, undying love she felt for him.

He brushed a soft kiss against her ear lobe. "What do you think?"

She opened her mouth, sucked in air. "It's—it's—" Turning to Eva she struggled to catch her breath. "It's the most beautiful thing I've ever seen. I—how—" She stopped trying to talk. It was useless since there were no words to describe how she felt.

"Thank you, Eva. Thank you."

After giving the girl a hug, she turned to her

husband, tears stung her eyes. He stepped forward, wrapped her with both arms, and settled his lips on hers.

Sometime later, when the kiss ended and she floated back to earth, Randi glanced around. "Where did everyone go?"

He shrugged, and then nodded toward the picture. "So, you like it?"

She twisted, once again in awe by the likenesses.

"Yes, I like it."

"I wasn't sure what to have her paint. Other than us, I mean." He stepped closer. "I told her I wanted the hotel and the fish pond."

Randi looked at the picture again, and this time forced her eyes to scan the rest of the painting. Sure enough, off to one side of the hotel was the fish pond, complete with cascading water. She squinted, moved closer to see what was in the background behind the pond. The images were faint, but she recognized the symbols.

"Is that a cemetery?" she asked, completely confused.

He laughed. "Yes, that's Boot Hill."

"Boot Hill?" She glanced his way, took in his smiling face. "Why did you want the cemetery in our picture?"

He took her by the elbows, drew her to stand before him. "Well," he said, "Kid calls Jessie his shotgun bride, because she shot some cattle rustlers with Ma's big gun not long after they were married, and Skeeter calls Lila his badland bride 'cause she blew up half the Kansas badlands shortly after they were married. And I," his cheeks took on a pink hue, "call you my Boot Hill bride."

"Why?"

"Because the morning we got married, I remember thinking if I didn't marry you, I'd most likely end up in Boot Hill."

"Oh," she said, having no clue as to how that made her feel—knowing he either had to marry her or die. A little gasp escaped her lips.

"I can have Eva change it. I shouldn't have asked her to paint it."

"No." She glanced back to the painting. "No. I like it just as it is."

With one finger, he tugged her face about. "I wouldn't change a thing."

She shook her head, but in agreement. "It's a beautiful painting."

"I mean about you and our marriage. I wouldn't change a thing." His hands slid to her waist, gently squeezed. "I'd marry you a million times over."

A nagging touch of doubt, mingled in her mind. "Even if," she glanced at the floor, "Boot Hill wasn't in the deal? I mean, even if you didn't have to?"

He pulled her tighter. "Yes."

She glanced up, looking to see if he told the truth.

His sincere gaze met her questioning one. "I love thinking of you as my Boot Hill bride. It's like I fought destiny and won." He cupped her cheek. "Think about it. If we hadn't been forced to wed, I may have let you go. And that"—he kissed her forehead—"would have been a tragedy. I can't bear the thought of living my life without you. I love you, Randilynn Quinter. And I always will."

She had to blink in order to see past the blur of tears. "I love you, too," she said, almost sobbing at the intensity flooding her system. "And I'd marry you all over again." Tilting her head upwards, an invitation to kiss, she added, "I love being your Boot Hill bride."

He accepted her invitation. It was several minutes before they separated and realized Kid, hammer in hand, waited to hang their painting.

****

Well over three feet square and framed with the same dark wood that decorated the rest of the hotel, the painting looked absolutely fabulous hanging above the huge fireplace. Randi, unable to control her gaze, caught herself stopping to stare at it every time she walked through the hotel foyer. And today was no different. The entire building buzzed with workers, dressed in their blue and maroon uniforms sewn by Ma. Servers, cooks, cleaning girls, and bell hops skittered and scattered, completing all the last minute tasks before the evening's grand ball would begin.

The hotel hosted over thirty guests, besides the Quinter families, and many more bustled in, expecting to book rooms. They were sorely disappointed, for all fifteen rooms were booked. Skeeter and Kid's families, as well as Willamina and Eva, had been moved from their rooms into the extra bedrooms above her and Howard's apartment to assure all of the guest rooms were available. Most of them had filled up yesterday. The two rooms left open were spoken for—one for the governor of Kansas, the other the governor of Colorado, both personally invited by Kid, and expected to arrive at any moment.

A gentle hand patted her back. "You're going to get trampled standing here staring at that painting," Jessie said.

Randi smiled. "I just can't help myself. Eva is so talented."

Jessie agreed with a nod. "I'm going to have to find a way for Willamina to let Kid add on to the soddy. Eva will need the space with the amount of requests she's getting."

"Aunt Corrine said Danny J is having her paint one for him."

"Yes, him and half of Dodge." Jessie's face

twisted with a frown. "Perhaps I can tell Willamina the soddy has to be upgraded or I'll lose it."

"What?" Randi asked, "You'll lose it?"

"I know it's a white lie, but she's so insistent Kid and I not help her. She even pays rent on a regular basis. Kid of course finds a way to give it back one way or another as a payment of sorts, he says to flat out give it back would hurt Willamina's pride." Jessie clapped her hands together. "That's it! We'll say it has to be fixed up, and tell her we're using her rent money. That way she can't refuse us, especially if she thinks the government says I have to fix it up, and Eva will have room to paint."

The word government hit Randi like a ball of lead shot into her stomach. She almost doubled over between that and the heavy weight of dread that formed when her thoughts instantly went to Thurston Fulton. He and Belinda hadn't returned to Dodge, but Randi had a niggling suspicion they'd appear for the open house.

Trying to hide her fears, she continued Jessie's conversation, "Wouldn't the government tell Willamina she had to fix it up?"

"No. It's my soddy. I claimed it before I married Kid, but Willamina and Eva have lived there for the past five years."

"It's yours?"

Jessie nodded, but didn't have time to answer because Lila walked up just then.

"What are you two doing? Besides gawking at that gorgeous painting." She let out a long sigh. "There are days when I swear I do nothing but stare at the one Eva painted for us. She is so talented. Kodak would never believe it's a painting and not a picture."

"Who?" Randi asked.

"Oh, no one," Lila answered, flipping her red curls over her shoulder. "So are you two about ready to go upstairs and start dressing? I still need to press my dress."

"Oh, yes, let's go up," Jessie said, excitement dancing in her blue eyes. "Randi will you show me how to put up my hair like you do? It looks so elegant."

Randi raised a hand, patting her hair. No one had ever said she looked elegant. Her hair was so thick, it was the only way she could keep it all in a bun.

"Oh, yes, and maybe between the two of you, you can help me figure out what to do with my unruly curls. I'll never get the hang of pinning it up," Lila said.

Randi glanced between the two women, and all of sudden, as if someone had just drilled a hole and hit an underground spring, water gushed out of her eyes.

"Oh, goodness. What did I say? I'm sorry, Randi. You don't have to help me. Skeeter likes when I leave my hair hanging down," Lila apologized, draping one arm over her shoulder.

The woman's touch, as well as the concern filling her green eyes, made the tears flow faster. Randi tried to quell them, but it was as if they had a will of their own, and that will was to fall down her face as fast as possible.

"Come on," Jessie said, looping their arms together.

With Lila on one side and Jessie on the other, they led her up the wide staircase and down the long hall to the end door that opened into her and Howard's rooms. Randi gave up trying to wipe away the steady steam flowing over her cheeks. Once settled on the divan she bowed her head and sobbed into her palms.

The girls, again, one on each side, patted her back.

"Randi, what's the matter? You can tell us," Jessie said, handing her a kerchief.

"I don't know," Randi sobbed. She really had no idea what had overcome her.

"It has to be something," Lila offered, "besides the thought of my hair."

Randi had to smile, even though the tears still trickled. She wiped at both cheeks with the handkerchief. "I—I guess it's the thought that you two both brought so much to your marriage. I didn't bring anything to Hog except trouble."

Jessie and Lila both started to laugh. Not giggle, but all out laugh. Randi buried her face in her hands again.

Jessie, tugging Randi's hands aside, said, "Oh, goodness, Randi. You can't honestly believe that."

Randi nodded. It was true, she offered Hog nothing. She had nothing to offer any man. Belinda had told her so many times, but most recently when the marriage to Edward Keyes had been announced.

"I've been nothing but a problem since I arrived in Dodge. Before then even. Since I was born," she sobbed.

Jessie took the kerchief and dried both of Randi's cheeks. "You want to talk about bringing trouble to a marriage? Kid had to marry me to keep my brother from hanging for horse theft. Believe me, a wife, who couldn't even cook was the last thing he wanted."

Randi felt her jaw drop. "He did? Horse theft?"

Jessie nodded. "And there was a gunslinger after me."

Randi gaped.

"How about me?" Lila asked. "Skeeter had to marry me because I was pregnant when we met. And I had a mad man stalking me, too. Talk about trouble."

"You were pregnant?"

"Yes, with Kendra."

"Kendra isn't…" Randi's cheeks were on fire, she couldn't finish her sentence.

"Isn't Skeeter's?" Lila asked, and then continued answering her own question. "Not biologically, but bless his heart, in his eyes, and mine, she's his daughter in every way." Her gaze went to Jessie. "I was raped. Jessie killed him."

This time Randi's eyes all but popped out of her head. "Killed him?"

Both of the women nodded. Randi swallowed, her gaze bouncing between the two women. "Ma had said both of your weddings were arranged, but I had no idea of the circumstances."

"Arranged?" Jessie giggled.

"What did she say?" Lila wanted to know.

"I don't really remember, it was right after our wedding, and I was quite upset. She was trying to ease my fears."

"They were arranged all right," Jessie laughed. "By her shotgun and several feet of stiff rope."

Randi looked at Lila. "The first day you arrived. You said you couldn't believe Ma was the same woman who tied you to a chair and made you marry Skeeter. I thought you were teasing."

Lila shook her head. "As soon as she discovered I was pregnant, she sent," Lila paused as if remembering, "I think it was Hog, to get the preacher."

Jessie piped in. "It was Hog who got the preacher for us too." She giggled again. "Who fetched yours?"

"Bug," Randi supplied. By now her tears had dried up, left her face feeling dry and her eyes puffy. She rubbed at them. "But my problems go deeper. My fath—"

Lila pressed a finger to Randi's lips. "Your father is nothing Hog can't handle. Trust me, the

Quinter boys are invincible. And they love their women deeper and stronger than God Almighty."

Jessie laid a hand on Randi's knee. "We know your father's a Populist. And the trouble he's caused. But none of us, including Hog, hold that against you. You can't control what your father does. Nor are you responsible for his actions. You have no control over any of that. But, you do have control over what you do. How you support your husband and his dream." She stood, pointed around the area. "Look at all this. Look at what you and Hog accomplished." Her gesture, one finger pointing, landed on Randi. "I said you and Hog because that's what it's been, right from the beginning you've been beside him, helping him. Don't let anyone take that away from you. Stand up and be proud of it. Be proud of your husband." Jessie planted her hands on her hips. "And fight like hell if anyone tries to come between the two of you."

Lila leaned over, close to Randi's ear. "The Quinter men may be invincible, but you'll never find a fiercer woman than those of us brave enough to stay married to one of them. Listen to Jessie, she was the first and blazed a trail for the rest of us to follow."

Jessie's eyes bugged, and her stern, fierce look dissolved as a fit of giggles rippled her trim frame. She fell to her knees, wiping the tears of laughter from her eyes.

"Do I remind you of Ma or what?"

Randi and Lila looked at each other, and jointly burst with laughter. And that's how Skeeter found them. She and Lila sitting on the couch, Jessie crouched on the floor, laughing so hard tears streamed from their eyes.

"Lila?" he asked, very apprehensively.

"Yes?" she responded, still giggling out of control.

"I—ah—You all right?" he asked, glancing around.

She stood and stumbled toward him, holding her stomach against the mirth still spewing out her mouth. "Yes, my dear husband," she managed to say. "I'm—we're just fine." She wiped her face with both hands and then kissed him, long and deep.

"What did you need?" she asked.

Jessie climbed up to sit beside Randi on the couch, and the two of them, as if it was totally their business to know, looked at Skeeter and waited for his reply.

His gaze bounced around the room as if looking for whatever made them behave so silly. He shrugged and held up a tiny pair of shoes.

"Kendra got her shoes wet. Did we bring an extra pair?"

"No, I didn't. I just brought those," Lila replied. "Where is she?"

"Out by the pond with Kid and Joel." He looked at Jessie. "Joel got any extras?"

"No. He grows so fast it's impossible to keep him in one pair let alone two," Jess answered.

He nodded. "Well, then, Kid and I are going to town. We'll take Kendra and Joel with us."

A small puddle had formed on the floor beneath the shoes he held.

"Were the children walking in the pond?" Randi asked.

"Yes. We took their shoes off." His face grew red as he spoke. "But they threw them in."

"Were you playing in the pond as well?" Lila asked, pointing to his pant legs, which were wet up to the knees.

"I have extra boots," he said, smiling at Lila. "I'm thinking we need to have Snake come build us a pond like that. Complete with the little gold fish. Kendra loves it."

"Oh?" Lila asked with a smile.

"Yes, it's not very deep so both she and Charles could play in it. Especially on hot days. We could put it out back by the—"

Lila stopped his explanation with another kiss. This time Randi and Jessie looked away, letting the couple have their privacy.

A few minutes later, Skeeter said, "Do you ladies need anything from town?"

"No," Randi and Jessie answered in unison.

As he left the room, Eva came down the stairs from the rooms above, carrying little Winifred. Patting the baby's back, she said, "She just woke up from her nap, I changed her, but I think she's a wee bit hungry."

"Thank you," Jessie said, moving across the room to take her daughter. "We're going to do each other's hair. Do you want to join us?"

Eva shook her head. Her long, straight brown hair fluttered in front of her face. "No, thank you. I won't be attending the dance tonight."

"Why not?" Randi asked.

The gaze from Eva's brown eyes remained locked on the floor. "I'd prefer to watch the children. So you can all attend."

"Mrs. Timmer, the head of housekeeping here at the hotel has two daughters and Howard's already asked them to watch the children tonight." Randi stepped forward. "We really would like you to attend, Eva."

"Please do, Eva," Lila said. "We all want you to."

Eva blushed a delicate pink. "I—um—"

"Please say it's because you have nothing to wear," Jessie said from the settee where she nursed Winifred. "Because I brought along half of my closet, since I didn't know what I wanted to wear. And if you borrow something, Kid won't be able to grumble about hauling it all back home."

"Well," Eva said, twirling one toe over the floor.

"Please say yes," Randi begged.

"Yes, please, Eva," Lila added.

"I suppose I could," Eva answered quietly.

The other three of them were not quiet at all. Their screeches of glee woke Charles who had been sleeping upstairs. The sound of his cry sent Lila skittering up the steps to retrieve him.

The busy actions downstairs were nothing compared to the controlled havoc caused by four women upstairs preparing for the grandest ball any of them would ever attend. Even Ma and Willamina lit out of the area as fast as they had arrived, each one carrying a baby and laughing at the chaos in their wake.

Chapter Nineteen

Their trials and errors paid off, and Randi knew the exact moment. Dressed in her black gown, with her hair pulled into a perfect coiffeur, per Lila's determination and decorated with tiny white flowers stuck in with several additional pins, Randi was putting the final touches to Eva's hair when the door to their apartment opened.

The men, Howard, Kid, Skeeter, Snake, and Bug, laughing about something, filed into the room. Their chuckles turned into gasps as their feet stuck to the floor, and they ran into one another like a flock of sheep trying to walk into the same barn stall.

The women, Jessie, dressed in a stunning pink gown decorated with tiny pearls, and Lila, wearing a deep purple creation that was simply cut and adorned with a large bow in the back but looked absolutely spectacular on her, as well as Eva, clothed with a pale mint-colored chiffon ensemble that made her look like an angel who'd floated down from heaven, all turned to greet the men.

"Damn if we ain't gonna be the envy of every man from Mexico to Canada and back again," Skeeter, the first one to catch his bearings, said. He crossed the room, arms spread wide to encircle Lila.

Kid didn't say a word. He just swallowed several times, and his eyes never wandered from Jessie as he moved forward to gently fold her into his arms.

Bug was next in line. He blinked several times, and then rubbed his big brown eyes as he stuttered, "E-Eva?"

Snake elbowed his younger brother. "Yes, it's Eva, you idiot." Snake sauntered across the room. "You look right pretty, Eva."

Eva pulled her eyes from Bug and turned a sweet smile Snake's way. "Thanks," she murmured.

Randi glanced back to Bug, wanting to see his reaction since she thought he was sweet on Eva, but her gaze was caught by the final man in the room. Howard's stare blazed down on her with all the heat of the sun and struck the core of her being with more power than a lightning bolt. He started to move forward, and she dropped her hands from Eva's shoulders. They met in the center of the room, drawn together by some invisible tether.

"You're gorgeous," he said. At least that's what she thought he said, but since her ears were ringing she couldn't be sure. Her mind had traveled back in time, to this afternoon, when Jessie had demanded that she fight like hell if anyone ever tried to come between the two of them. Standing here, being showered by his love and feeling the shelter of his strength surrounding her, she determined that was exactly what she would do—tonight and every other day and night of her life.

****

The party was in full force, and Howard, though part of him was floating on cloud nine, kept a wary eye on the doorways. He knew Randi's father would show up, the problem was he didn't know if the man would walk in the front door or sneak in the back like a weasel. Walking through the crowd, he nodded, accepted congratulations, and paused to share a few words with one guest or another while making his way to the kitchen—the last place he'd seen his wife. She'd been deep in conversation with the woman they'd hired to oversee the kitchen for the evening. The food, a variety of beef and pork, besides numerous side dishes had been prepared the days before and safely stored in the ice-filled cellar beneath the hotel. The woman had already been instructed on how to re-heat the different dishes on the huge oil-burning stove, and he had no idea what more Randi needed to oversee.

He sidestepped around two servers, carrying full trays out the swinging door, and then eased his way forward to peek through the glass opening, making sure he wouldn't collide with another server.

A smile twitched at his lips. She was there, standing at the high work table, fussing with something or another. He pushed the door open and sauntered in. Too engrossed in the task at hand, Randi didn't realize he'd approached until his hands settled on her trim hips.

Startled, she gasped and turned to stare up at him. A smile instantly formed.

"Hello," she said.

He kissed her earlobe. "Hello." After another small peck, he asked, "What are you doing?"

"Oh, I noticed the trays of beef in the dining room were almost empty. I thought I'd put another one together."

"We've hired people to do that tonight." He twisted her around to face him. "We'll be filling trays and cooking meals for many years. Tonight is our chance to enjoy our guests."

She glanced around the room, where over half a dozen people hustled about.

"Someone else can refill the meat trays," he said.

"I suppose you're right," she said, picking up a towel to wipe her hands.

"You suppose?"

She nodded. "I suppose." A teasing glint settled in her eyes. "And I love you."

His heart all but burst right out of his chest. They expressed their feelings for each other all the time, but for some reason, at this moment, standing in the kitchen with employees bustling about, and with a hotel full of more guests than he could count, the admission meant more to him than life itself.

"And I love you, so very, very much," he said, lowering his face to capture her lips in a deep and loving kiss. They were both trembling when they separated. He had to lean against the table to keep his balance and felt the quakes of her shoulders as she pressed against him.

"It's turned out to be quite a success. Tonight," he said, needing a moment to gain his composure.

"Yes, it has," she agreed. "Did you have any doubts?"

"No," he said, "No doubts and no regrets."

She lifted her face, met his gaze. "No regrets," she repeated. "Never."

His legs once again promised to support his body, so he took her hand. "Come on, I don't believe you met the governors yet."

She paused.

He ran a finger down the side of her face. She was so beautiful. The slightest glance had the ability to steal his breath away. And she was his, would be forever.

"No doubts," he said, "And no regrets."

She took a deep breath and thrust her elegantly exposed shoulders back just a touch.

"Yes, I think I would like to meet the governors."

Hours later, after the food had been cleared away and men twirled women across the dance floor, Howard once again found himself searching for his wife. Her father still hadn't appeared, and the knowledge left him as edgy as a coiled rattler. He made the rounds, the kitchen, the foyer, the dining room—now cleared into a dance floor, and the wide veranda running along the front of the hotel outdoors. There hadn't been even a hint of her anywhere, so he turned around, back-tracking his path.

In the kitchen, now cleared of workers, who upon leaving the area immaculate had either gone home, joined the party, or were serving drinks from the portable bar set up on the front stoop, he ran into Jessie.

"Have you seen Randi?"

"No, I haven't. But I'm on my way up to check on the children. I'll let you know if she's upstairs."

Two of the Timmer girls had been hired to watch the children in the apartment above, giving Jessie and Lila the freedom to join the party. Howard figured between the two women and his brothers, the children had most likely been checked on every ten minutes throughout the night.

He nodded in acknowledgement, but then changed his mind. More than likely, Randi had been up to peek in on the children more than a few times as well. The tight, nagging feeling of unease tickling his shoulders had become overly strong, and he knew it wouldn't ease until he found her.

"I think I'll just come up with you. See if she's there myself."

Jessie smiled, giving him a look of understanding and turned to climb the stairs ahead of him. She started gushing, going on about the festivities, the food, the Cowboy Band, and a million other tiny details. He didn't need to respond. For one, Jessie didn't expect him too, had known him long enough to know he wasn't much for small talk, and for two, his mind was too busy all on its own.

The evening really had gone on without a hitch, besides showcasing the upscale accommodations their hotel offered to travelers and locals alike, his brothers, namely Kid and Skeeter, had been very efficient in quelling the rumors of the Quinter's being members of the Populist Party. Not only was the crowd enamored with The Majestic, the family's reputation was once again held in high regard. The knowledge was a relief to say the least, but still he couldn't help but wonder where Fulton was and when he'd show up.

Part of him really hoped it wouldn't be tonight, wouldn't put a damper on the success of the event. The other part of him wanted the man to walk through the door so he could confront him and have the deed over.

Danny J had gathered evidence on Fulton. Not only had the man rode with Quantrill after the war, but he'd been part of several criminal acts since then. Danny had the proof to have the man arrested, and Sheriff Sughrue was in-house, ready to march Fulton straight into the new jail built on the other end of town. Howard wanted it done and over with. Wanted the man sent away where he'd never bother Randi again, so they could set about living their lives, maybe even start a family. She was well suited for motherhood, the way she hovered over his nieces and nephews made the fact as clear as the Kansas summer sky.

Jessie had stopped talking. He glanced down, caught the expectant look on her face.

"The door's locked," she said.

He frowned and stuck a hand in his hip pocket to retrieve a cluster of keys.

"Has it been all night?"

"No. It wasn't locked when I was up here half an hour ago."

He inserted the skeleton key, and the nagging weight on his shoulders turned into jolts of apprehension. His mind, trying to work out who would have locked the door and why, flipped to where the children were as soon as the door swung open to reveal an empty sitting room.

Jessie hurried to the stairs leading up to the bedrooms.

"The girls must have put them to bed."

He followed, for some reason not quite believing that was true.

****

On the second floor, Randi, having just aided the governor of Colorado's wife—who'd clearly sampled too many glasses of wine—into their guest room, was just pulling the door closed when a scream vibrated from above. She froze in her steps for a moment as quivers raced her loins. A keen sense told her it was Jessie screaming. Goosebumps leaped to life on her skin.

She hoisted her skirt and ran along the hall. Guests, stopping to gape both at her and the direction from which the sound came, blocked her path every now and again.

"Excuse me, excuse me," she repeated over and over, making her way to the door leading to her and Howard's accommodations.

By the time she arrived, a crowd was forming with every Quinter family member racing into her sitting room from both doors. She ran to the far side, where Howard stood in front of the tall windows. Noise filled the air, everyone talking at once.

Howard let out a shrill whistle as she arrived at his side. When the noise settled a touch, he said, "Someone locked the children in a closet upstairs."

"What the hell?" one of the boys shouted.

"Who?" someone else wanted to know.

"Why?" Ma shouted above the rest.

"We don't know who or why," he answered, stopping the stream of questions. "But whoever it was took Winifred."

Randi's heart stopped dead in her chest, and she grabbed his arm.

"It only happened a few minutes ago, so whoever it was is still here," he continued. "Mary Timmer said it was a woman in a black dress."

A bitter blast of the coldest chills she'd ever experienced raced over her. Randi turned to Howard, praying he nor anyone else, could possibly imagine it had been her. There was no questioning in his gaze, no blame, but they were full. She'd never seen vengeance so clearly before.

Twisting, unable to view something so hard and dark coming from Howard, her gaze went out the window to where the moon cast a mellow beam upon the water fountain. Movement near the water made her squint and take a second look. A shadowy figure, racing across the yard stumbled, fell, and something landed in the pond.

"Winifred," she screamed.

Howard's arm grasped her shoulder. She twisted, trying to break his hold.

"She's in the pond! A woman just tripped and the baby fell in the pond!" she yelled.

The room exploded with movement. Randi, balling her skirt with both hands, was amongst the mass racing for the stairs. Somehow they all managed to descend the stairs, run through the kitchen and into the back yard without tripping over each other.

Kid had already arrived at the pond and stood in the center, a dripping mass of blankets in his arms. Randi stopped dead in her tracks. The look of horror on Kid's face, the unnaturally still bundle he held, and Jessie's pain-filled scream splitting the air, slapped her all at once.

A second later, as if she had wings instead of feet, Lila flew past. She landed in the pool and wrenched Winifred's little body from Kid. He moved to take back his daughter, but Skeeter, having jumped in right behind Lila, grabbed him.

"No," was all he said.

Her blood pounded like drums in her ears as Randi watched Lila rip the blankets away. They

239

floated to the water and Lila covered the baby's mouth with her own. Winifred's limp little arms and legs hung from her body, but Lila kept breathing for the infant, and every few seconds she'd press on the baby's miniscule chest.

Randi had to blink. Twice. And then cover her gasping mouth with a trembling hand, wondering if she'd seen correctly.

She had. Winifred's arms and legs had moved. Within seconds the baby started coughing, and the next thing Randi knew, Lila was handing a crying Winifred to a sobbing Jessie.

The thrill, the exhilaration, the blessing bestowed upon them, would live in their hearts forever, but at that moment, the elation was short lived, for someone, Randi wasn't sure who, yelled, "Hog, the hotel's on fire!"

Flames, blazing orange and growing, licked at the back porch. The men scrambled, and Randi, knowing she'd left a bucket near the windmill, ran as well. She was filling it at the pond when Howard, a bucket in his other hand, grabbed her arm.

"Get to Ma's tent," he shouted.

"No!" She wrenched out of his hold and hoisted her bucket out of the water.

He snatched away her bucket, handed it and his to a man beside him, and then bent to fill another.

"Yes," he shouted.

Empty handed, she stood, watching. Men had formed a long line, and buckets, one after the other, passed between their hands. Full ones going one way, empty the other. Howard was refilling them as fast as they were handed to him.

"Please, Randi, go to Ma's tent with the rest of the women."

Randi didn't answer. She wanted to tell him it was her hotel, too, it wasn't just his dream, his livelihood, it was theirs, and she needed to help. But couldn't because she was pushed out of the way. A second line of men, dressed in their fancy party clothes, had formed another line right where she'd been standing.

It was Aunt Corrine, saying, "Come on, Randi, get out of the way so the men can work," and tugging on her arm that made her move farther away from the pond.

Her gaze went to the porch, where flames ate at the wood pillars with ferocity. Standing there, watching her dreams go up in smoke, something landed in her stomach with enough gusto to make her pitch forward. Her hands clutched the area. Nothing had struck her on the outside, it was on the inside. A strong wrenching that told her there was nothing she could do.

Still clutching her waist and fighting to hold in a scream building in her throat, she twisted and ran for the tents. Her arrival garnered hugs from many, even Jessie seeing to little Winifred's needs, slowed to embrace Randi before ducking into Ma's tent. She did experience a sigh of relief and joy, when she noted all of the other Quinter children were accounted for. Ma quickly explained she, Willamina, and Eva had carried Kendra, Charles, and Joel out to the pond during the mad rush to rescue Winifred.

Ma, with a mass of gratitude and tears, thanked Randi profusely for saving her precious granddaughter.

She shook her head. "It wasn't me. It was Lila." Turning to her red-headed sister-in-law, Randi asked, "How did you know what to do?"

Lila, with Charles on one hip, kissed his curly-topped head. "I learned it in my other life."

Randi probably should have commented, but she didn't. Not only was there the fact she had no idea what Lila meant, her mind was stacked with a plethora of other concerns. Yes, there was the fire, but more than that there was the indisputable fact that she was worthless. No matter what Lila and Jessie said, she wasn't fit to be married to a Quinter.

She glanced around. Lila had saved Winifred's life. The other children would be in a burning hotel right now if Ma, Willamina, and Eva hadn't carried them out, and Jessie had probably saved them all. If she hadn't gone upstairs to check on the children, they all might have perished.

It hurt, crushed her heart like one steps on a bug, this devastating truth that she didn't belong here—with the family she'd come to know and love. She flinched at the pain that told her it was all her fault. She'd recognized the woman who'd tripped, dropping Winifred into the pond, and a sixth sense told her who started the fire. She'd caused nothing but trouble for the Quinters since she'd snuck into Hog's tent.

Lila laid a hand on her shoulder. "It's hard, isn't it?"

Randi looked up, wondering if she'd said something aloud.

"Being a woman, it's hard, isn't it?" Lila stared at the hotel. "Men," she said, never pulling her gaze off the fire, "see everything as an immediate problem that needs to be solved. They just jump in and put out the fire." She then turned, her green eyes met Randi's gaze. "But women, we contemplate it all. We look deep to find the root of the cause, for we know that's where the real problem lies."

An eerie, hair-on-the-back-of-her-neck-rising sensation thundered over Randi. She knew the root of the problem. Lila and Jessie were right, and it was time she fought for what she wanted. She was the only one who could.

A tiny seed of hope planted itself in her soul. Maybe, just maybe if she found Belinda, she'd not only find the root of the problem, but it might be enough to prove she wasn't worthless. She wasn't a Fulton, she was a Quinter.

Randi twisted, glanced to Ma's tent. Jessie had said to stand up and fight with all your might, and that's just what she would do, and knew where to find the tools to do it with.

Ma's hand came to rest on her shoulder. "Don't fret so," she said heavily. "Hog never really wanted a hotel. All he's ever wanted was to cook. That boy's been cooking since he could reach a pot to stir. It was his brother's who said he needed to turn his cooking into a business." She shook her head. "Nope, all he ever wanted was to cook."

Randi's gaze went back to the men fighting the fire, and she shivered as if a blast of cold water rained upon her.

Chapter Twenty

When he took the time to glance over his shoulder, Howard caught sight of Corrine tugging Randi away from the pond. *Thank goodness*! The last thing he needed was her to get hurt fighting the fire. He thrust another bucket into the pond. It clanked against the bottom with a solid thud. A second water brigade line had formed, and though the buckets of water now being tossed on the flames had doubled, the fire still ate away at the wooden porch. Not only that, but the pond was almost empty.

His eyes went to the bricks. If they could at least keep the flames from entering the interior, they had a chance. Bug appeared at his side, dragging a long coil.

"Kid! Skeeter!" Bug yelled. "Grab this end!"

The older brothers arrived, each grasping a handful.

"What's this?" Skeeter asked.

"It's a fire hose that Snake ordered from New York. He's hooking up the other end," Bug explained, dragging more length of the coil forward. "Hog, you and Danny grab it here in the middle. Snake says to hold on tight, he's got a pressurized tank down in the hole under the windmill and says when he turns it on water's gonna shoot out clear to the sky."

Hog tighten his hold. "Grab on men, if Snake say's it's pressurized, it's pressurized!"

All of them, Kid, Skeeter, Danny J, and himself, had just gotten their feet planted in preparation when the thick, canvas hose in their arms started to rumble. The next second the material swelled to ten-times its size and water shot out the end like buckshot out of Ma's double-barreled shotgun.

It couldn't have taken more than five minutes, but with the way the hose fought them like a huge, powerful and almost uncontrollable snake, they were all heaving when Bug shouted. "Turn it off, Snake! The fire's out!"

The great snake relaxed, fell limp in their grasps, and joyous shouts, now that the sounds of blasting water no longer filled the air, could be heard. Hog dropped the hose, and along with a crowd of others, raced to inspect the damage. Men moved aside, letting him be the first to tread upon the soaking ground and charred wood.

It was nothing shy of a miracle, he thought to himself, as he examined the structure. The porch would have to be torn down and rebuilt, but other than that, the hotel was unharmed. The porch door, leading to the kitchen had been closed. Fire had scorched the outside of the door, but between the buckets of water and Snake's New York City fire hose the flames hadn't entered the inside of the building.

He stepped off the porch and raised his hands. "It's fine! We saved it!"

"I knew that thing would work!" Snake, grinning from ear to ear stepped forward.

Hog hooked his elbow around Snake's neck. "Damn right, it worked. I'll never, ever, doubt one of your ideas again."

"Doubt one of his ideas?" Kid, soak and wet from holding the live end of the water hose, laughed. "Hell, Hog, haven't you learned by now to never doubt one of your brothers?"

"Hot damn!" Skeeter yelled and then shook his head like a wet dog, not caring that droplets from his hair splattered the crowd. "What you call that thing,

Snake?"

"A fire hose," Snake supplied.

"I gotta get me one of those!" Without missing a beat, he added, "How 'bout you, Kid? You want one. Order us two of them, Snake. And don't forget the pressurized tanks!"

The crowd, downright jubilant, spent the next several minutes, laughing and cuffing each other on the back, and inspecting every inch of damage done by the fire. After a unanimous decision the repairs could be made in less than a day, most of the men who'd help fight the fire moseyed back to the front of the hotel, where the party, now that the scare was over, was back in full swing, and the Quinter brothers, along with Danny J, made their way to the tents.

The closer he drew to the tent, the more fearful Howard became. God, he hoped little Winifred was all right. She'd appeared to be okay before the fire but had that been a figment of his imagination? Had Lila really blown life back into her little body?

He'd experienced some bad things in his life, but nothing could compare to the moment he saw that little, life-less body cradled in Kid's arms. The wrenching in his chest had almost strangled him at that moment. He had an idea as to who the woman in the black dress had been, and as soon as he saw for himself that little Winifred was fine and dandy, he'd hunt down Belinda Fulton and strangle her with his own hands.

He and Jessie had barely started to climb the bedroom stairs when they heard the pounding. They'd raced into the first room, where someone had stuck a chair below the closet doorknob. He'd tossed the chair aside to wrench open the door, and seeing all those little babies, crying their little eyes out, had been enough to make the top of his head blister. The oldest Timmer girl, Mary, had a bruise on her cheek, the shape and size of a handprint, from fighting to keep the black-dress-woman from taking Winifred. But it was the handful of hair still clutched in the other Timmer girl, Ellie's, hand that told him exactly who the culprit was.

He had no doubt when he found Belinda Fulton she'd be missing a clump of coal black hair.

Their arrival at the tents was hectic, the women asking about the hotel, the men asking about the children, especially Winifred. Howard wondered why Randi didn't rush to his arms the way the others rushed to his brothers, but figuring she was miffed 'cause he wouldn't let her fight the fire, he held up searching her out until after he took his turn to hold Winifred, seeing for himself that she was breathing.

Not only was his niece alive, but she was well. Smiling and cooing at all the men passing her from arm to arm. And even as young as she was, barely old enough to hold her little head up, she knew the moment her daddy took her. A big lump formed in Howard's chest when he handed Winifred to Kid. His older brother, the one man who would forever seem larger than life to all the brothers, had tears streaming down his face when he kissed his daughter and then snuggled her little head beneath his chin.

Howard had to blink away the tears forming in his eyes and took the moment to escape the crowd. He moved to Ma's tent, expecting that's where he'd find Randi.

It was empty. After peeking in the storage tent, now holding little more than Ma's sewing machine, he went back to the crowd.

Settling an arm around Ma, he asked, "Where's Randi?"

Ma, frowning, twisted about. "Ain't she in my tent?"

"No."

"She ain't?" Ma asked, sounding doubtful.

'No, she's not."

"Hey, Lila? You seen Randi?"

Lila peeled herself from Skeeter's chest. "She's in your tent, isn't she?"

"She was." Jessie had one arm looped around Kid while the other patted Winifred's little back as the baby snuggled with her daddy. "She found this material to wrap Winifred in," she added, pointing to the same material that decorated the tables at the hotel.

Howard, tired of everyone doubting his discovery, assured them, "Well, she's not there now. I just looked."

Ma huffed, shaking her head and moved to her tent. "You boys can't find nothin' lest it jumps at ya."

He followed "I'm telling you, Ma, she's not in there."

She looked anyway, and it was the second time she glanced about that her gaze settled on his face.

"My gun's gone. And my new rope."

"Shit!" He thrust the flap aside and exited the tent.

"You find her?" Lila asked.

"No."

Before he could say more, Ma piped in. "My gun's gone. And my new rope."

"Randi wouldn't take your gun, or rope," Jessie said. "Maybe she went to the hotel."

"I bet she did," Snake said. "I'll go look."

"We'll all go look," Bug said. "Snake you take the front yard and foyer. Kid the kitchen and restaurant. Skeeter the second floor, and Hog you check your apartment. Everyone meet back at the pond in five minutes."

Howard did pause for a split second, wondering when the youngest Quinter had become so superior he thought he could boss everyone around. But the need to find Randi outweighed any thoughts of Bug and his new found haughtiness. Besides, he was right, they did need to spread out, it would make finding her that much faster.

Fifteen minutes later, when the hotel, the grounds, and the tents had been searched several times over and there was still no sign of her, Howard's heart was once again failing to work right. With every beat dread filled his veins.

"She couldn't have gotten far," Kid said, saddling a horse.

Howard tightened the saddle cinch on Ted. "It's her father, he took her. I know he did."

"We'll find him, Hog." Snake assured, already mounting a dapple gray. "We'll find him, and we'll find Randi."

He didn't trust himself to respond. The events of the past few hours, as well as the people responsible, had left him too full of hate. Biting his lip, lest he let out a flurry of words describing exactly what he would do to Thurston Fulton when he found him, Howard stuck a foot in the stirrup and hoisted himself onto Ted.

****

Randi settled the heavy weight of Ma's shotgun against her shoulder. She'd fired a gun before, many times. It had been her responsibility to see her mother ate every day. Her fingers trembled as one settled on the trigger. But this was the first time her sites had been aimed at a human.

She squeezed her eyes shut, took a fortifying breath, and reopened them to line the sights up. The shoulder would work. She didn't want to kill him, not because he claimed to be her father, but because if she resorted to murder she'd be no better than him.

"You've really messed it up this time." Belinda paced beside the fire.

"Me?" Thurston half sat against a large boulder. "What are you talking about? A fire is perfect. We should be able to see the smoke over the trees any minute. I can already smell it." He crossed one leg over the other at the ankles. "Sit down. You're making me nervous."

"Nervous?" Belinda screeched.

A protruding branch from the cluster of buck brush separating her from the camp interfered with the sights. Randi eased the barrel just a touch to the left.

"Yes, nervous. And quit yelling. Christ, they can probably hear you in Dodge. You want to blow our cover?"

Belinda plopped on the ground. "I wanted to go to that party tonight."

He let out a long sigh. "I already told you that's impossible. We can't be seen anywhere near that party tonight." He twisted to glare at Belinda. "You didn't go down there while I was gone, did you?"

She shook her head.

"Good. Tomorrow, while the hotel is nothing more than a smoldering heap of ashes, we'll make our arrival. And of course, I'll have to tell Hog Quinter how my daughter is a terrible firebug."

"He won't believe you. Randi has him tied around her little finger," Belinda huffed.

"You forget. I'm the one with proof that she started that fire under his back porch. You see the little candle she lit and slipped under the steps was in a metal box, engraved with her name. I'll tell him it was a gift from her mother and me. The box was lined with just enough gun powder so when the candle melted and the wick, moments before it fluttered out, went... Poof!" He thrust both hands in the air. "The powder then caught fire with enough dancing sparks to set the carefully placed straw around it on fire. The rest was sequential of course.

The straw caught the stairs on fire, the stairs the porch, the porch the kitchen...Well, you know." He folded both arms behind his head. "The engraved, metal box is one of the few things to survive. It's a fail-proof plan. And everyone will believe she did it."

Randi had heard enough. Fear, anger, hatred, as well as a slew of other hot and torturing emotions made the want to scream almost uncontrollable. She squeezed the trigger, and as the blast sliced the air, so did her scream. But it was a yell of marksmanship, that prideful exclamation one makes when they hit the target dead center.

Not that she'd hit him dead, or center, but exactly where she'd been aiming. With his arms raised, Thurston Fulton had taken the full blast of buckshot into his right armpit.

Squealing like a stuck pig, he rolled onto his side. "I've been shot. I've been shot," he moaned over and over again, as if he didn't believe the words.

Belinda stood near the fire, screaming at the top of her lungs.

Randi stepped out from behind the brush. "Shut up, Belinda. I got one more barrel full and won't mind using it on you."

Belinda swirled around, her black dress and hair flaying in a quick twirl.

"Randilynn Fulton, don't you dare speak to me like that."

Randi leveled the gun. "I said shut up."

When Belinda, lips pursed, but silent, remained that way for several seconds, Randi un-looped the coil of rope hanging over one shoulder and threw it. Still wound, it landed at Belinda's feet.

"Tie him up," Randi ordered.

"She will not!" Thurston said, still flapping on the ground like a fish out of water.

Randi, catching site of the pistol he was squirming to acquire, leaped sideways and snatched it seconds before he did. She threw it off to the side and was pleased at the splash it made.

They were camped no more than two miles from the hotel. Instinct had told her, after she swiped Ma's gun and rope, to follow the river and she'd find them. At this moment she knew without hesitation her 'instinct' was her mother's spirit.

"Tie him up," she repeated.

Belinda hefted the rope and stomped toward Thurston. Randi used the gun to nudge his side.

"Sit up."

"I can't!" he proclaimed.

She poked harder. "Sit up or I kill you."

"You won't—" he started.

"Oh, yes, I will," she interrupted. "You have no idea how much I hate you right now." Her glare went to Belinda for a moment. "How much I've always hated both of you for the way you treated my mother." Tears stung her eyes, but she held strong, refused to let them spring into life. "For all the nasty, awful things you've done."

Thurston scrambled onto his hind end. "Randi, you're my daughter."

"Shut up," she said, not wanting to hear anymore. "Put your arms down."

"I can't put my arm down," he shouted. "You shot my armpit. It's on fire." He huffed in a breath as she'd heard him do countless times while gaining control of his anger. A second later and more calmly, he continued, "Randi, as your father—"

"You're no more her father than I'm her mother," Belinda snapped.

"Belinda!" he barked, warningly.

An unimaginable sense of relief washed over Randi. She turned it into determination and shoved Belinda aside with the gun barrel.

"Give me that rope." Belinda released it, and Randi gestured with the gun. "Get over by that rock and don't move."

Quick and efficiently, she flopped the end lasso over Thurston and once it settled on his chest, pulled the slack tight. He fought, thrashing about, making it impossible for her to loop the rope around him again.

After several tries, she'd had enough. Without any real regret, she lifted the gun and smacked the butt end to his temple. He collapsed into a silent heap, and Belinda, eyes agog, screamed again.

Randi had him trussed tighter than Aunt Corrine's corset in no time and wielding the gun, moved on Belinda.

"I," Belinda started, "had nothing to do with that fire."

"You kidnapped Winifred."

"I did not! Do you see a baby here?"

"You threw her in the pond."

Belinda's eyes grew wild, like a beast who was about to be trapped.

"No, I didn't," she challenged.

"I saw you," Randi sneered.

Belinda dove. The movement was too fast for Randi to get off the shot. Her legs were ripped out from beneath her as Belinda's head-first attack drove her to the ground.

Scratching, biting, kicking, and slapping they rolled over the ground. Belinda's teeth painfully sunk into one of Randi's shoulders, and one of her hands held a handful of hair so tight Randi thought her scalp was separating from her skull. The pains ripping her body were strong enough to make rational thinking close to impossible.

Then for some reason, Lila's words re-entered Randi's mind. *Men jump in to fight the fire, women go to the root.* With a thrust of newfound power, Randi arched her back, planting both feet on the ground. There were two things she knew—one,

Belinda couldn't swim, and two, Randi could swim like a fish.

Thrusting with every muscle in her legs, she flung her body upwards, and twisting while they were both in the air, she heaved them both over the riverbank. Still clinging onto one another they flew through the air.

The water was shallow, little more than a couple of feet deep, not nearly enough to cushion the landing of their entwined bodies. Jointly, they slammed into the riverbed. The shock was enough to separate them, and Belinda flew into full panic mode.

Splashing, splaying, and gasping for air like she was caught in raging rapids, Belinda cried, "I'm drowning! Save me! Someone please save me!"

Randi stood, the water barely covering her knees, and stretched out a hand to grasp a full handful of Belinda's hair. She overrode the want of thrusting the women's head below the surface, telling herself, *no, not just once even.*

After dragging Belinda, still pathetically weeping, up the short bank, she tied her with the other end of the rope circling Thurston Fulton. She'd never, ever consider him her father again.

It took two coffeepots full of water dowsed across his face before Thurston regained consciousness. While he moaned and Belinda sobbed, Randi hitched the single horse tethered near the river to the rented buggy and stomped out the camp fire.

Whether the two were too beset with their injuries or had finally decided not to struggle with her any longer, she didn't take time to contemplate. Meekly, and somewhat comically, trying to balance tied together as they were, Belinda and Thurston Fulton climbed aboard the springy seat. Gathering the reins with one hand and hoisting Ma's gun over her other shoulder, Randi set about leading the horse, buggy, and outlaws back to Dodge.

They hadn't gone far, no more than a quarter mile, when a group of riders formed in the pale moonlight. Randi lowered the gun, and for a split second, wished she hadn't thrown Thurston's pistol into the river. But then, the lead rider charging across the ground grew familiar.

Ted skidded to a halt, and Howard didn't even take the time to leap from his back. Instead, he leaned down, grabbed his wife, and hoisted her onto his lap where he could kiss the hell out of her.

Once that was complete, and his hands had inspected her for injuries, he drew back his head. Upon seeing the big brown eyes, gazing up at him as if he were an angel cast down from the heavens, his mind went blank. Completely vacant of any of the questions he'd formed while searching for her.

Kid, his horse prancing about, said, "Got yourself a couple criminals, there, Randi?"

She turned, and Howard could have sworn he saw a smile form as she said, "Yeah, I do, Kid."

Kid glanced over his shoulder, to the posse of men still riding across the way. "The Sheriff's on his way."

"Thanks," she said, turning her head back.

Howard had to tighten the muscles in his chin to keep his mouth from falling open. There was a smile on her face, the biggest, brightest one he'd ever seen. All night, even before Winifred was taken and the fire, he'd been trying to figure out how he was going to tell her her father was a criminal. And not just any criminal, but one of Quantrill's raiders.

As if she read his mind, she reached up, cupped his jaw with a warm and tender palm. Her fingers, soft and gentle massaged his cheek.

"He's not my father."

Howard felt as if he was just snapped out of some kind of hazy dream. "What?"

"Thurston Fulton is not my father."

The sheriff arrived, but before the man could question Randi, Kid thrust the reins of the buggy in the man's hands.

"You can talk to her tomorrow," he said.

Surrounding the buggy carrying Thurston and Belinda Fulton, the sheriff, along with the posse of family, friends, and even a few strangers, rode away.

"He's not?" Howard asked, once they were alone, not really knowing why.

"Nope," she said, as confident as the sun in July.

"Then who is?" The instant the words left his mouth he wished he could pull them back in.

She shrugged. "I don't know."

He shifted in the saddle, made a bit more room for her to settle onto his lap. "And it really doesn't matter, does it?" he asked.

Without hesitation, she said, "I hope not. I-ah," she paused, and it reminded him of that first morning, when he'd found her in his bed, this little, unsure woman on his lap. "I'm hoping the Quinters are all the family I'll ever need."

His eyes never left her. "I hope so, too." A frog had inhabited his throat. He cleared it away. "You and me and the babies we'll make." He smiled, a full-blown, all out, from head to toe smile. "I promise, as a Quinter, you have all the family you'll ever need."

Her eyes glimmered in the moonlight, or maybe it was an inner light shining somewhere inside her. "Once a Quinter, always a Quinter," she said.

Heart bursting with pride, he nodded. "I like that."

"So do I," she said.

It was during that next kiss, while his hands roamed where they may, he realized her dress was wet. Regretfully, the knowledge made him end the kiss.

"How did you get wet?"

"Oh, I had to take a little swim," she said, as if it was of no importance whatsoever. The tiny kisses she plastered over his neck stopped, and she lifted her face.

"The hotel?" she asked, "How bad is it?"

"Not bad at all," he said. "We only have to replace the back porch. Matter of fact the party was still going strong when I left."

"Really?"

He nodded. "Snake's fire hose put the fire out before it could do much damage. It seemed the event just added cause for people to celebrate a bit longer."

She nodded, and bit her lips together, as if holding something in.

"What?" he asked, "What else is wrong?"

"I promise, from this moment forward, I'll stay out of the kitchen."

"Why? What are you talking about?"

"Ma said all you ever wanted to do was cook. Yet, since you started building the hotel, it's the one thing you haven't had time to do. So from now on, I'll take care of everything else so you can cook."

He let out a hearty laugh. One that felt good all over. "You," he said, touching the tip of her nose, "Am a much better cook than I. So you will not stay out of the kitchen." A hint of seriousness took over. "Don't you know by now that I'd give up everything for you? The hotel, cooking, everything. I want you more than anything else in the world. I *need* you more than anything else in the world."

"Really?" she whispered.

"Really," he answered, covering her mouth with a kiss that should drowned any lingering doubt she may have.

When they separated, her gaze locked with his. "I do know that. Maybe I just had to prove it to myself."

"No doubts," he said, "ever."

She nodded. "Never-ever."

"Remember that."

"I shall," she whispered, kissing him.

He held her tight, thanking the heavens above for all he had. When the stinging in his eyes eased, he said, "I suppose we should head back."

"I suppose," she laughed and plucked at the material of her gown. "I'm afraid I'll have to take a bath before I can rejoin the festivities at our hotel."

He nuzzled her neck, kissed her ear lobe. "Want some company?"

Both of her arms encircled his neck, and she arched her back, bringing them as close together as possible while sitting on Ted. "Always," she said.

Howard lifted her hips and swung her around, pushing her wet dress aside so she straddled his lap. "Come here, my Boot Hill bride, you're bath is going to have to wait a bit longer," he said, kissing her face from top to bottom.

She giggled an enticing little sound that was more welcoming than a soft spring rain. "I love you, Hog Quinter."

He laughed, loving his nickname for the first time in his life. "And I love you, Randilynn Quinter. Have since the first moment I laid eyes on you and always will."

A word from the author...

As a young girl I remember spending warm summer days and long winter nights with Nancy Drew and Laura Ingalls-Wilder. As the years slipped by the books evolved into romance novels by Kathleen Woodiwiss, LaVyrle Spencer and a host of others.

In 2000 when my husband said I should write one, I took the challenge, and have loved every moment of the journey. To create characters from once upon a time and lead them through a life that ends in happily ever after is a joy. Of course, you have to torture them a little bit along the way, and just like real-life children you often have to clean up after them. But, just like real children, they are worth it.

My husband and I live in Minnesota, have three grown sons, two precious granddaughters and two handsome step-grandsons. I'm a life-long Elvis fan (yes, I've been to Graceland) and love spending Sunday afternoons watching NASCAR with family and friends.

Visit Lauri at www.laurirobinson.blogspot.com

Thank you for purchasing
this Wild Rose Press publication.
For other wonderful stories of romance,
please visit our on-line bookstore at
www.thewildrosepress.com

For questions or more information,
contact us at
info@thewildrosepress.com

The Wild Rose Press
www.TheWildRosePress.com

Breinigsville, PA USA
04 April 2011
259102BV00002B/6/P

9 781601 547385